The Loversall Novellas

Books by Maggie MacKeever

The Purloined Heart
Quin
Point Non Plus
The Tyburn Waltz
Vampire, Bespelled
Waltz With A Vampire
An Extraordinary Flirtation
Lover's Knot
Love Match
Cupid's Dart
Lady Sherry and the Highwayman
French Leave
Our Tabby
Sweet Vixen
An Eligible Connection
Strange Bedfellows
Lady Sweetbriar
A Notorious Lady
Fair Fatality
The Misses Millikin
Jessabelle
Lady Bliss
A Banbury Tale
Lady in the Straw
Lord Fairchild's Daughter
El Dorado
Outlaw Love
Caprice

The Loversall Novellas

Maggie MacKeever

Vintage Ink Press

This is a work of fiction. All of the characters, organizations and events portrayed in this novel are either products of the author's imagination or used fictionally.

Copyright © 2013 by Gail Clark Burch
All rights reserved.

No part of this book may be reproduced, scanned, or distributed in any printed or electronic form by any means without the prior written consent of the Publisher, excepting brief quotes used in reviews.

ISBN: 978-0-9889799-3-2
Point Non Plus ISBN: 978-0-9826239-9-2
Quin ISBN: 978-0-9826239-8-5
A Biddable Female: 978-0-9889799-2-5

This book is an original publication of Vintage Ink Press.

Printed in the United States of America.

Point Non Plus

A situation with no options.
A state of utter perplexity.

Chapter One

Claret and champagne, thought Mina. *And oh! The price of peas.* The expense of maintaining a gambling house was enormous, even though that house was not in Piccadilly but rather the raffish Haymarket, alongside hotels and cafes and taverns, the King's Theater for Italian Opera and the Theater Royal, vying for attention with popular entertainments from human curiosities to animal prodigies, her own favorite to date being a half-dozen turkeys executing a country dance.

She was the proprietress of a Pandemonium. Mina marveled at herself. Since said Pandemonium was in the Haymarket, did that make her Haymarket ware?

The hour was late, the gaming rooms in full swing. Those rooms were as fine as their more fashionable rivals, furnished with thick carpets and marble fireplaces, rich woods and comfortable sofas and chairs. Moxley, admitted Mina, had known what he was about. Moxley had known what he was about in regard to many matters; had possessed a certain exuberance, a *joie de vivre*. But Moxley was water well run under the bridge and there was no use sniffling over milk that had been spilt.

Moxley House stood on the west side of the street, at the northern end; two residences combined, with basement, three stories and a garret, four chambers to each floor.

The first floor was given over to gaming. Mina entered the front room. On each side of the rouge et noir table — marked with two red and black diamond-shaped spots on which the players placed their stakes — a croupier waited with rake in hand, her task to watch the cards and gather in the money for the bank. Moxley's employed more females than any other

London hell, all of them dressed in gowns as expensive as any worn in fashionable drawing-rooms, if with even more bosom put on display.

The dealer laid out two rows of cards, one designated as rouge and the other as noir; the players bet on which row would have a count nearer thirty-one, on whether the first card of the winning row would be of the color for that row, or whether it would not. Mina noted the pile of markers, none less than a half-crown. A buffet laden with various alcoholic beverages stood against the far wall.

The next room was dominated by a long table covered with green cloth and divided by tightly stretched pieces of string. These croupiers were equipped with hooked sticks instead of the usual rakes.

The game here was hazard. Intent players crowded around, most of the masculine persuasion, clean-shaven or whiskered or mustachioed, hair pomaded or dressed with fragrant oil; clad in evening coats of blue and brown, pantaloons or trousers, square toed shoes or Hessian boots, bulky neck cloths and waistcoats of every imaginable hue. Mina recognized several familiar figures, among them a slender, fair-haired young man leaning on the back of a chair. Abercorn was a reckless plunger, who would lay odds on anything from the turn of a card to a race between flies crawling up a windowpane.

A smile here, a quick word there, a raised eyebrow answered with a nod or a slight frown— Mina glanced into one of the private alcoves where whist was being played for stakes that would have satisfied the legendary Charles James Fox. The atmosphere was hushed, the shutters closed, the thick curtains drawn.

In the third large chamber, a statuesque brunette presided over the faro table. Faro was a complicated game, involving a banker and an unlimited number of players who staked their bets against the dealer over certain combinations of cards. The odds in favor of the banker were second only to those in roulette. The majority of the players were paying as much attention to the dealer's neckline as to the cards she dealt.

Moxley had definitely known what he was about.

The E.O. table was being set in motion by a russet-haired young woman. Mina appreciated humankind's fascination with gambling on the revolution of a circular device. Romans had upended chariots and spun the wheels. The ancients twirled shields balanced on the points of swords.

The Loversall Novellas

Mina suspected that was how cavemen came to invent the wheel.

The quiet was broken by the rattle of the dice, the clatter of the ball, the low murmurs of the players, the soft voices of the dealers as they announced the result of the last gamble, or requested the players to make their game anew.

Wagers, gentlemen. There was the cost of wax candles and champagne to offset.

Intent as they were upon their various games, on the dice, or cards, or ball, not one of the gamblers failed to notice their hostess pass by. Wilhelmina Moxley belonged to a family famous (or infamous) for their amorous adventures, the gentlemen renowned for the number and quality of their mistresses, the women for their inclination to give their hearts unwisely and too well. Had the Loversalls a motto, it would be: *Love fully, with complete abandon, and always with great style.*

This Loversall remained a Nonpareil at forty, a deep-chested woman with red-gold hair drawn up in an Apollo knot, stunningly sensual features and dark-fringed sapphire eyes. She wore a scarlet gown with frills around the hem, the fitted bodice cut low to display her enviable décolletage, the puffed sleeves threatening to slip off her shapely shoulders with the slightest shrug. The widow's refusal to wear mourning shocked some and titillated all. Odds were being laid as to whom she'd bed and bury next.

Mina pretended to be amused.

The last of the public chambers had been made into a supper room. Crystal chandeliers illuminated small tables laid with silver and fine china upon pristine linen cloths.

Several patrons were enjoying a substantial supper. A number of spirited conversations were underway. Mina paused to speak with a wealthy silk merchant, ordered a glass of wine, selected an apple tart.

Her gaze fell upon a gentleman seated alone at one of the small tables. He was perhaps thirty years of age, with grey eyes and close-cropped brown hair; a successful solicitor with offices located near the Royal Courts of Justice, in the vicinity of the Temple Church.

Mr. Eames seemed somber. Mina hoped he hadn't wagered more than he could afford to lose.

She moved toward his table. "Why so morose, my friend? Has Dame

Fortune not smiled on you this eve?"

He got to his feet. "I've gone down more heavily than I like, but I'm not yet lurched. May I have the pleasure of your company?"

Mina seated herself. Mr. Eames sank back into his chair. She picked up her fork and took a bite of apple tart. He raised his wineglass, swallowed, tried not to grimace, didn't succeed.

Mina raised her brows. "Is the quality of my claret so inferior?"

"It is I who am inferior, or so Sir Ian informs me," he replied gloomily. "And Lady Anne will do nothing of which her father disapproves."

Mina marveled, not for the first time, at the astonishing perversity of the human heart. "Have you considered Gretna Green?"

"I would not dishonor the lady with an elopement." Mr. Eames set down his glass. "Or if I would, she wouldn't, so there's an end to it."

"You will think of something."

"I have thought of numerous things, each one frowned on by the law."

Mina wondered how many things she had done — was doing at that moment — that were frowned on by the law. She took another bite of apple tart.

A man entered the room. His head was shaved, his eyes cold, his nose as flattened as his ears. He looked every inch the bruiser he had been before Moxley hired him to oversee the hell. Samson knew all the ways of cheating, with cards and dice, by means of handkerchief or snuffbox or rubbing the eye; recognized at first glimpse a Greek or Captain Sharp or law officer's spy. Conversation faltered, then more quietly resumed.

What now? Mina pushed back her chair. Samson threaded his way among the tables, bent and murmured in her ear. A woman claiming to be 'Cousin Ianthe' had invaded the premises at pistol-point, he said, and was demanding to speak with the proprietor. "That one's no more Miss Ianthe than I'm David's sow, and so I told her, upon which she threatened to shoot off my cullions if I didn't fetch you to her straightaway."

Ianthe, here? Impossible. Ianthe was traipsing around Russia with a pair of German princelings. Furthermore, Ianthe disliked bloodletting and was unlikely to be brandishing a firearm, unless she had gone out of her head.

Loversalls not infrequently went out of their heads.

Mina glanced at Mr. Eames, who had withdrawn into his own unhappy musings. "You put her in the morning room?"

"Aye, and locked the door."

Leaving Samson to keep an eye on the gaming suite, Mina made her way to the private portion of the house. With a feeling of foreboding, she unlocked the morning room door.

In front of the fireplace stood a small figure wrapped in a voluminous dark cloak. On her nose perched a pair of dark spectacles, on her head a mass of mud-brown hair so ugly it could only be a wig. In her right hand she held a double barreled, double triggered handgun with brass fittings, an engraved ivory grip, and a relief carved wooden stock. The pistol was pointed not at Mina's cullions, since Mina had none, but instead at her heart.

"You asked to speak with me?" Mina inquired, more politely than she felt. "I might be more amenable if you aimed that gun elsewhere."

The pistol lowered, fractionally. "*Buonsera,* Cousin Wilhelmina. *I* might be more agreeable if I had not been made to wait! I do not *wish* to shoot you, no or anybody else, except maybe Paolo, but I am tired and hungry and have travelled a great distance, and your man tried to turn me away."

Cousin? Mina had numerous cousins, Loversalls being prone to rather indiscriminately procreate. Ianthe was otherwise occupied in Russia. Cara was busy procreating with her spouse. Whereas Beau—

Mina experienced a sinking sensation, as if the apple tart she'd recently consumed had bypassed her stomach altogether to take up residence in her toes. *Bloody hell*, she thought but said, "Oh, mercy! Zoe."

Chapter Two

"Well you may say 'Oh, mercy!" cried Zoe. "I mean, look at me. Have you ever seen such a fright?"

Mina sank down on a sofa. At seventeen, Zoe had been a beautiful spoiled minx with a host of admirers and a willful nature that earned her such sobriquets as 'limb of Satan', and an excited expectation that she would be swept off her feet at any moment by her own true love. Now, ten years later, she was unrecognizable in an unflattering gown of a singularly ugly grey. The wig — those spectacles — her mottled complexion must be due to a copious application of theatrical paint.

Did Mina want to discover why Zoe wore a disguise? Most definitely she did not. "You are not at your best, I think," she murmured, diplomatically. "I am of course delighted to see you, but what brings you here?"

Zoe clasped her hands to her bosom. "Oh, Cousin Wilhelmina! I am quite undone." She still clutched the pistol. Mina experienced a brief fear — or hope — that the firearm might discharge.

The firearm did not. "Are you mad?" Mina inquired. "Give me that at once! Waving guns around – you could have killed someone!"

"Did you think I meant to shoot you?" Barrel first, Zoe handed her the weapon. "How absurd! If I was going to shoot anyone it would be Paolo, and I'm not certain I won't yet."

Mina grasped the pistol gingerly. Where to put the blasted thing? She tucked it behind a sofa cushion. Time enough later to decide where the handgun was best hid.

"I have been betrayed!" Zoe dropped gracelessly into a chair. "You look shocked, and so you should be. I shall tell you all — but first, may I have something to eat? I have not eaten for a prodigious long time."

Mina rang a bell. The summons was answered by a footman. Mina issued orders. The footman bowed himself out of the room.

Zoe took off her dark spectacles, revealing bright blue eyes. "So you inherited a gaming hell. How *bold* you are to manage it yourself."

"Hardly," said Mina drily. "I require some means of support, jointures and widow's portions not being something with which, in the excitement of the moment, I concerned myself."

"We have all done absurd things," sighed Zoe. "It comes from being a Loversall."

The footman returned, placed his tray on a table, then silently departed. Zoe fell upon the food as if she hadn't eaten in days.

"It is astonishing," said she, whilst nibbling on a chicken leg, "how *quickly* one can come down in the world. A mere fortnight ago I had never ridden — under a load of cabbages, mind you – in a farmer's cart; nor crossed the Channel in a sea so rough that I cast up my accounts over the side of the packet boat; nor travelled on a common stage. It was a horridly dirty stage, and as a result I am none too clean myself, which is something else I am not accustomed to, and everything is Paolo's fault." She discarded the remnants of the chicken leg, licked her fingers, and picked up a wing. "I didn't believe Beau when he said I was too young to wed. I realize now he may have been correct. Paolo was so bold and brave and dashing. I was overset with passion. My heart overcame my head."

She had not been alone in that reaction. The extravagantly handsome young Conte de Borghini had sent all the damsels into a romantic twitter and their mamas to devising diabolical matrimonial snares. "You fled your husband?" inquired Mina. "All the way from Milan?"

"It was not Milan but Paris," said Zoe. Cousin Wilhelmina gave much less the appearance of a lady smote by sympathy than one wishing her unexpected guest to Hades, but surely that couldn't be the case. "And I did not 'flee', I *left*."

From beneath the sofa crept a plump grey feline with white chest and paws and whiskers. Mina lifted the cat into her lap. It curled up with its nose beneath its tail and promptly went to sleep. "Grace is growing old," Zoe ungenerously observed.

Grace wasn't the only one. Mina felt herself growing more decrepit with each moment passed in Zoe's company.

Zoe pushed away her plate and chair, rose and began to pace. "If I learned anything from my father, it is that before one purchases a new pair of shoes, one should first try them on to make sure they *fit*. But I paid no heed. And I am well served for it, because my true love has turned out to be a toad."

Mina was taken aback by this comparison of paramours with footwear. "The path of true love is often set with difficulties," she soothed.

"Platitudes, from a woman who has put five husbands in the ground thus far? You should know!" snapped Zoe.

"What I know," retorted Mina stiffly, "is that hearts do not truly break, and one does not die of the dumps. You have fled to London. Now what do you mean to do?"

Zoe paused to grimace at her image in the gilt-framed looking-glass. "I shall go to the Opera, and have an ice at Gunther's, and ride in the Park."

"Oh?" Mina felt her right eyelid twitch. "I assumed from your disguise that you didn't want your husband to know you are in Town."

Zoe swung away from her reflection. "I don't! By the time Paolo realizes I have left him I shall be safely hid away. Like Grandmother Sophie after she got caught with that foreign dignitary lacing up her stays."

"In a nunnery? You can't be serious." Mina's own stays, alas, were being unlaced by no one but her maid.

"Why not? Paolo will never think to search for me there."

Pity the poor nuns. "You haven't explained why you came to me."

"You might be more sympathetic!" cried Zoe. "My heart has been broke. I can't go to Beau, because Paolo will expect me to do just that. He'd never expect me to take up residence in a gaming hell. And if he *should* discover I have taken up residence in a gaming hell, he won't like it above half."

Mina's own heart had been first bruised by a fickle Frenchman. Many years had passed since she recalled the perfidious Pierre. Since she was recalling him now, it took a moment for her companion's words to sink in.

Zoe, here at Moxley House? Heaven forfend! "What about the nunnery? I thought—"

"You *haven't* thought!" Zoe said sternly. "Or you wouldn't expect me to turn my back on the world without first understanding what I'm giving up. You may find this difficult to believe, but I haven't had a single *affaire de coeur*."

Mina's eyelid twitch was fast developing into a throb. "You had Paolo."

"I was married to Paolo! Paolo doesn't count."

"You can't remain here!" Mina protested. "Your reputation would be ruined. The polite world considers it scandalous that I run a gaming house."

"The polite world considers you scandalous altogether." It occurred to Zoe that she might be a bit more conciliatory toward the lady beneath whose roof she wished to dwell. "They would consider you scandalous whatever you did, because you are a Loversall. I will be even further beyond the pale than you, once I am divorced."

Divorced? Despite their various misadventures, no Loversall had ever been divorced. "Was your marriage so bad?"

"It was worse than bad." Zoe plucked at the fabric of her gown. "I am no more to Paolo than a pretty trinket who is supposed to provide him heirs. Well, there are no heirs, and it serves him right! I spent ten miserable years being chaste — and as you are well aware, Loversalls are not noted for being chaste — and I'm sure I needn't have been, because men flock to me like bees to the honeypot. Paolo was not equally devoted. He was not even discrete! I cannot count the hours I passed tormenting myself with visions of what he might be doing, and who it might be doing it with."

Inside all this drama was — surely — a kernel of genuine distress. "One doesn't expect a husband to be faithful," Mina pointed out.

"*I* did! And you needn't say I should have known better, because of course I should. I daresay your husbands weren't faithful, either. And you had five of them, poor thing!" Zoe dropped to her knees in front of the sofa. "Do say I may stay. I can help you in the gaming rooms."

Mina gazed down into the vivid little face turned so pleadingly up to hers. It was an enchantingly heart-shaped face, with big blue eyes and a perfect little nose, lush lips, and a dimple in each cheek. "You are obviously a Loversall, even wearing that horrid wig."

Zoe pulled off the wig and flung it over her shoulder, revealing a matted mop of red-gold curls. "We can say I am a distant relative. I will call myself Prudence, since prudent is what I have been. Oh, Mina! You cannot be so cruel as to turn me away."

Alas, Mina could not. "Very well. But there is to be no flirting with the customers."

Zoe enveloped Mina's knees in a bone-crushing hug. "*Best* of all my cousins! I promise I shan't cause you a moment's unease."

Mina laid a wager with herself as to how long this resolution would last. Grace took exception to the interruption of her slumbers, and batted at the interloper's cheek.

"Ouch!" cried Zoe, springing to her feet.

Mina stroked a soothing hand over Grace's soft fur. "You have not told me what the conte did that was so bad. Perhaps this is merely a misunderstanding and—"

"*Col cazzo!*" interrupted Zoe, cheeks flushed with temper. "Paolo wagered me at play."

Chapter Three

"*Wagered* you?" Beau stared at his daughter, whose appearance had been greatly improved by a bath and a good night's sleep. "I've never heard of such a thing."

"Yes you have," said Devon Kincaid. "There was that high-flyer Montcrief had in his keeping not so long ago."

Beau turned an irate eye on his friend. "I'll thank you not to be so busy about my affairs."

"The point is, I think, that it *was* your affair," remarked Mina. "Dev, come sit by me."

Mr. Kincaid left the window where he'd been lounging. He was tall, with hazel eyes and sun-darkened skin and thick auburn hair, a rebellious lock of which had tumbled forward on his brow; an athletic physique that showed to advantage in excellently fitting unmentionables and bottle green coat; and the easy assurance of a man who had charmed his way into — and out of — more boudoirs than he could count.

Zoe watched as he joined Mina on the sofa. If one was going to explore one's baser nature, there would be no better guide than a notorious rakehell.

Currently she was more concerned with the rakehell who had sired her, who was looking as appalled as it was possible for a profligate to be. Beau possessed the unmistakable Loversall features, the red-gold curls and sapphire eyes. His hair was tousled, as if he'd but recently risen from his – or someone's – bed, which was no doubt the case: it had taken Cousin Wilhelmina's footman half the day to track him down. "*Did* you wager a high-flyer, Beau?"

"I didn't wager her, I won her," Beau protested.

Mina turned to Devon. "And to think I was recently feeling so dull I almost walked across the street to inspect the mechanical figures at Week's Museum."

He smiled his careless smile. "Come to me the next time you feel dull. I can recommend a great many more interesting activities."

She narrowed her eyes at him. "Do those activities involve you?"

"They do."

A dalliance with Dev, mused Mina; unthinkable, but still a pleasant thought. Mr. Kincaid must by this time be an expert in the amatory arts. He was an easy, entertaining companion, and possessed a comfortable inheritance that allowed him to do as he pleased.

He was also a long-time friend of Beau's, and cut from the same faithless cloth.

Grace was curled up on Mina's lap. Devon reached out to tickle her chin. The cat opened one eye, contemplated him, then rolled over on her back.

He rubbed her belly. Grace curled around his hand and nipped his wrist, as if to say 'more'. "Hussy," Mina remarked.

Devon raised an eyebrow. "I assume you refer to the cat."

She smiled. "Ah no, I shan't rise to that bait."

"Is there bait you *will* rise to?" inquired Mr. Kincaid. "Shall I try and find out what it is?"

Mina laughed.

Beau glanced at the sofa, where Mina and Dev were having a pleasant coze. *He* had been having a pleasant coze — or, more specifically, a tryst — when interrupted by a footman who insisted his presence was required posthaste. Beau had been unable to imagine what might be so urgent, but was fond of Mina, and so had obliged. Now he wished he'd stayed in bed.

He adored his daughter; she was the apple of his eye; but life had been more peaceful when she dwelt a couple continents away. Or as peaceful as life could be for a man with as many mistresses as Beau.

Zoe hadn't fallen silent. "You are as bad as Paolo. I was prepared to give my all for love. I was *not* prepared for my love to give me away as if I were of no more importance than an old boot. Although I *should* have been prepared, now that I think on our wedding night. Don't look so disapproving! No daughter of yours could go to her marriage bed without an excellent notion of what to expect there."

"How glad I am that I encountered Beau in St. James's," murmured Devon. "When did she arrive?"

"Last night," confided Mina, in equally low tones. "She hasn't stopped complaining yet. Zoe has realized she married not the figure of her fantasies but a young gentleman as spoiled as she, and it has put her out of sorts. It makes *me* think of divine justice and the Hand of Fate."

Beau studied his daughter. "You swore de Borghini was your true love."

"One's true love doesn't put one up as stakes at chemin de fer," retorted Zoe. "Especially when he has no luck with the cards."

Devon left off rubbing Grace's belly to instead tickle her chin. "Speaking of ill-luck, is it true young Abercorn went down last night to the tune of five thousand pounds?"

Mina was intent on the drama playing out before her. "Hush!"

Beau wore an expression of extreme discomfort. "You didn't— That is, ah!"

Zoe's pretty features puckered. "I most definitely did not! Oh, how can you be so *heartless*?" She flung herself, weeping, at her papa.

"Good God!" muttered Dev.

Mina regarded Grace, sprawled now across Devon's lap. "We are to call her Prudence. She is posing as a distant relative. I'm told Mme. Villiers induced you to drink champagne from her slipper. She probably thinks she's brought you to heel, poor thing."

"You of all people should know better than to believe all you hear." Devon leaned closer and added, "It wasn't her slipper — but it was indeed champagne."

Mina wondered from what article — or orifice — Mr. Kincaid had sipped the beverage. She flushed. He grinned.

"As Paolo's wife, you are his property. He can do anything he wishes with and to you." Beau grasped Zoe's shoulders and gave her a little shake. In Italy, where divorce was impossible, murder was a time-honored way of ridding oneself of an unwanted spouse. Not that shedding a spouse was much easier in England, where an act of Parliament was required. "Mark my words, this will turn out to be a tempest in a teapot. Your toad will come to fetch you home."

"Not right away he won't. I have laid a false trail." A perfect tear trickled down Zoe's cheek. "And though I may call the rat a toad, *you* may not!"

"Then I shan't." Beau offered her his handkerchief. "What a clever puss you are.'"

"Aren't I just?" Zoe snatched the handkerchief from him, and briskly blew her nose.

Mr. Kincaid looked revolted. Mina said, "I had thought five-and-forty a good age for a man: you are no longer wet behind the ears, but don't yet have one foot in the grave. Now I begin to wonder. You do not seem to admire our Zoe."

Devon eyed her lazily. "I prefer a female I can embrace without worrying about breaking her bones."

"Piqued and repiqued," acknowledged Mina, who was no longer as slender as once she had been.

Zoe wadded up the handkerchief. "By the time Paolo locates me, I shall have determined how to secure my revenge. Shooting him doesn't seem a viable solution, tempting as it is. I would prefer not to hang."

Beau also preferred that his daughter didn't hang. Cautiously, he suggested Zoe stay out of sight. In response, she flopped into a nearby chair.

The door opened, admitting Samson, who brought Mina a note. She broke the wafer and scanned the crossed and re-crossed lines. The recent loser of five thousand pounds regretted to inform her that he had unexpectedly been called from town. Additionally, to his regret, his hitherto-indulgent father refused to pay his debt. Mr. Abercorn promised to redeem his vowels immediately he returned, and in the interim was leaving his most precious possession in her care.

"His 'most precious possession'," said Mr. Kincaid, reading over Mina's shoulder. "The words have an oddly familiar ring."

Mina folded the letter. She had, since Moxley's came into her possession, allowed more than one unlucky gambler to turn her up sweet. As a result, in lieu of monies owed, she was in temporary possession of watches and rings; a fine umbrella, little used; and a goat named Romeo who was busily eating his way through the kitchen garden while the cook threatened to turn him into a stew. "I may be too softhearted for this business, as my late spouse more than once pointed out, but no gamester will depart Moxley's and put a bullet in his brain."

The Loversall Novellas

"No, but you may put a bullet in yours," said Samson. "Figg!"

The footman approached. By one hand, he led a fair-haired urchin. The child looked around, opened her mouth, and let out a horrific howl.

Chapter Four

Mina blanched. Grace scrambled off her lap and dove under a chair. Beau eyed the window as if in hope of a similar escape.

Mr. Kincaid rose from the sofa. "Poor poppet," he said, as he went down on one knee. "Are you afraid we'll eat you? But you are the merest morsel and hence beneath our interest. We are people who enjoy a hearty meal."

The child ceased her wailing. "Poppet," she repeated, and thrust her thumb into her mouth.

"That's the ticket!" He scooped her up into his arms. "You are a very good girl."

Mina squinted at the note. "Her name is Eleanor."

"Eleanor is much too large a name for so wee a mite." Devon reclaimed his spot on the sofa. "I shall call her Nell. Jelly belly Nellie." The child chortled, removed her thumb from her mouth, and stuck it in his ear.

"Astonishing," observed Mina, and dropped the missive on a table. "No female of any age is immune to you. What *am* I to do with her?"

"You give me too much credit," countered Devon. "I have several sisters, and more nieces and nephews than I can count, and have in the interest of self-preservation learned to deal with them to the best effect. You might inquire whether any of your staff has experience with small people of this sort." Mina nodded to Samson, who departed with unseemly haste, Figg hard on his heels.

Zoe wandered closer, curious about the diversion that had drawn all eyes. She disliked not having attention focused on herself. Nor had she a fondness for children, a circumstance Paolo should have understood, instead of demanding she produce one. "You can't mean to keep it!" she protested.

Mina sat down beside Devon. "Nell is not an 'it'. You would have me hand her to the rag-collector, I suppose?"

If Cousin Wilhelmina moved any closer to Mr. Kincaid, thought Zoe, she would be on his lap. It was unbecoming conduct for a woman her age. "Not the rag-collector, goose. There are foundling hospitals and—" Zoe floundered, previously having had little occasion to exercise her mind about such things.

"She is hardly a foundling," Mina objected. "Her father has entrusted me with her safety."

Zoe regarded Nell, who possessed the usual assortment of features, including a rosebud mouth and button nose. Whereas cornflower blue eyes could never compare with sapphire, or cornsilk hair with red-gold, the brat might well grow into a beauty, a realization that made Zoe cross. "She must have a family. Perhaps they would like her back. "

Mina regarded this member of her own family. "And perhaps they would not."

Before Zoe could respond, a gentleman entered the room. An attractive gentleman, Zoe noticed — she made it her habit to notice gentlemen — with regular features and nice grey eyes and close-cropped brown hair.

George Eames gazed at his surroundings. He had never before been admitted to this portion of Moxley House. The morning room was a pleasantly proportioned chamber with green and white foliate striped wallpaper and a plaster ceiling enriched by simple low relief ribs. Green linen draperies softened the sash windows. The floor was polished oak, the furnishings rosewood. The occupants of the room were arranged in various attitudes around and upon the sofa, where a fair-haired waif perched on Devon Kincaid's lap.

"My apologies for interrupting, Mrs. Moxley. Your man seemed to think my presence was required. Is that Abercorn's by— ah, daughter? Why is she here?"

Mina beckoned him toward the sofa. "Abercorn left Eleanor with us. I hope he may retrieve her soon."

George frowned down at the subject of this conversation. "What was Abercorn thinking, to leave his child in a gaming hell?"

The Loversall Novellas

Nell thrust out her lower lip. Her eyes filled with tears. "There, there, princess," Devon soothed. "Your papa will be back in the twinkling of an eye. In the meantime your Uncle Beau will tell you the story of the enchanted pig."

Beau rose manfully to the occasion. Explained Mina, "Abercorn was probably thinking he owes me five thousand pounds."

"Five thousand pounds!" echoed George.

Zoe was growing cross. Everybody seemed to have forgotten she was in the room.

She undulated toward the sofa. "Hello! Since no one has seen fit to make us known to one another, I shall introduce myself. I am the Contessa— That is, Prudence Loversall."

"And I am rag-mannered," acknowledged Mina. "Zoe— Prudence! Allow me to present Mr. George Eames."

Mr. Eames wore an odd expression. Bedazzlement, Zoe supposed. "Dear sir, you cannot help but be stricken by the plight of this poor, poor mite! *My* heart quite goes out to her for I realize — none better! — what it is like to be wagered at play." Nell grinned toothsomely first at Beau, who was leaning over the back of the sofa, and then at Devon, demonstrating a marked preference for rakehells.

"This little miss wasn't precisely wagered," Beau pointed out. Nell chortled as he tickled her ribs.

Zoe spun on her heel. How very disappointing that her papa should be so undiscerning as to favor Mistress Nell. On the other hand, she *was* his daughter and therefore it would be shocking if he favored her — but he hardly favored Nell in *that* manner, and if he did, he was a worse reprobate than she had previously realized.

Zoe abandoned this somewhat muddled train of thought and again approached the sofa. "Ah, bah! Nell is here, as am I. Both victims of the whims of Fortune. Tossed about by the winds of Fate. Callously abandoned by those who should hold us most dear."

"Bah!" echoed Nell. "Bah bah bah bah bah!"

Beau winced and said, unwisely, "Cut line, Zoe."

Zoe pressed one hand to her forehead. "This exceeds all belief! How can you tell me to cut line when I have just discovered my true love has feet of clay? I *should* have shot him. Even if he wagered me only for a night, I don't like Cesare."

Beau stared at her. "Who the devil is Cesare?"

Mina spoke apologetically to Mr. Eames, who was regarding Zoe as he might a human curiosity strayed from a neighborhood freak-show. "We Loversalls place considerable importance on true love," she explained.

Devon glanced from Nell to Mina. "Did you find *your* true love? I have been meaning to ask."

"I thought I had," Mina replied. "Several times,"

Most unbecoming conduct, Zoe reflected sullenly, as she took another turn around the room.

Beau kept a cautious eye on his daughter's perambulations. "How do you know about Abercorn's by-blow, Eames?"

George was uncomfortable speaking of by-blows in front of ladies. He reminded himself that the ladies were Loversalls. "Abercorn came to me for advice."

"Why should he do that?" demanded Zoe, distracted from her sulks.

"Because I am a solicitor." George awarded her the merest glance. "Eleanor is the result of a youthful indiscretion. Her mother died in childbirth. The elder Abercorn washed his hands of the business. Abercorn the younger placed the child with a foster family here in Town. I can make further inquiries if you like."

"I am beginning to develop a strong dislike for the elder Abercorn," remarked Mina. "First he refuses to stand the reckoning and now he dumps his son's bastard in my lap."

"She isn't in your lap but mine," Mr. Kincaid pointed out. "And Abercorn the younger is responsible for that. You can hardly blame the old man for encouraging his pup to grow up. Five thousand pounds is a significant sum."

"I can blame him for not encouraging his pup to grow up sooner," Mina retorted. "Preferably before he ever darkened my door."

A distraction was due, decided Zoe, before her cousin took to ruminating further upon darkened doorways. She edged closer to the chair beneath which Grace was hiding, and stepped on the cat's tail.

Grace shot out into the room, drawing everyone's attention. "Kitty!" cried Nell. She squirmed mightily in an attempt to descend from Devon's lap.

"Kitty it is," agreed that gentleman, attempting to maintain his grip. "Why doesn't Uncle Dev tell you the story of—"

"No!" howled Nell, and kicked him. "Want Kitty!"

"That may be," interjected Mina, "but the kitty doesn't want you. She is growing old, you see—"

Nell saw that these strangers meant to thwart her. "Kitty!" she shrieked. "Kitty, kitty, kitty! Now!"

Zoe clapped her hands over her ears. Really, the child might be even more spoilt than she was herself.

The door opened. Samson entered. Trailing close behind him was a young girl wearing a plain dark-colored dress. She was thin and carroty-haired and freckled, and her brown eyes were saucer-wide.

"Meg has ten brothers and sisters, all younger," said Samson. "She allows as she wouldn't mind temporarily exchanging the scullery for the nursery. Make your curtsey, girl."

Meg curtsied, awkwardly. She appeared terrified half out of her wits, perhaps because her prospective charge was shrieking loud enough to summon Beelzebub from hell. Mina said, "We are grateful to you, Meg. Come meet Nell."

Meg bobbed another curtsey, and edged closer. "Yes, mum."

Nell broke off howling to glare at this new person. Meg held out a sugarplum. Nell grabbed the sweet and popped it into her mouth.

Chapter Five

It was a quiet night at Moxley's, save for the brief excitement when a brace of bosky young lordlings demanded entrance under the erroneous impression that within lay a house of civil reception where ladybirds eagerly awaited partners for the buttock ball; and the additional to-do when a luckless gamester attempted to cut off an ear and throw it on the table in lieu of funds.

The rouge et noir table was doing a lackluster business, the pile of markers alarmingly small. Mina inspected the liquor buffet to insure it was well-stocked. Moxley's functioned under the assumption that men played most recklessly when in their altitudes.

Before they could play recklessly, they must first be present. Mina reminded herself that it was mid-week. Moxley's was seldom busy in the middle of the week.

She found Zoe at the E.O. table, surrounded by gentlemen, one of whom was attempting to explain the game. It was not, he said, difficult to understand. The circular table spun; the ball came to rest in a niche marked either E or O, or alternately in one of two bar holes, in which case the house won all the bets played on the opposite letter, and didn't pay to that which it fell. The player had nineteen chances of winning, and one chance to break even on a bar, which was disregarded in figuring percentages.

Zoe, who had stopped listening at 'bar hole', said, "Gracious! How interesting."

Mina grasped Zoe's arm and drew her away, thereby disappointing the wolves who had been paying less attention to the cards than to the lamb in their midst. "You may also be interested to know that the player's chances are nineteen in thirty-nine. It is the way of E.O. banks to frequently win. Macao more effectively relieves reckless gamesters of their fortunes than either whist or loo. To hazard goes the honors for the greatest amount won or lost in the shortest space of time."

Zoe tried to wriggle free. Mina gripped her harder. Zoe demanded, "Let me go!"

They were the cynosure of all eyes, two Loversall females in one room together rousing more interest even than the low-cut necklines of the croupiers' gowns, so much female magnificence being almost more than the senses could withstand. One Loversall was short, the other tall; the younger resembling an angel descended to earth and dressed in ivory silk moire with a tight bodice and elevated waist, small sleeves and froth of frills at the hem, courtesy (though the observers could not know it) of her notoriously nipfarthing father, who had been persuaded that a contessa should not appear in inferior garments, even *incognita,* the elder every bit as lovely but with something in her demeanor that suggested she might be deliciously flawed.

The ladies were moreover at odds, thereby presenting an excellent opportunity to lay wagers as to whether they would descend to fisticuffs and if so, which would win.

Zoe dimpled at the nearest gentleman. Mina propelled her into the chamber where a voluptuous dark-eyed brunette presided over Moxley's faro bank.

The players looked up from the table. Zoe lowered her lashes and allowed a becoming flush to delicately tinge her cheeks. The gentlemen were all so friendly, and eager to explain things to her, and if she had little interest in combinations and sequences, and even less understanding of the doctrine of probabilities as used in calculating odds, it did not prevent Zoe hanging on their lips.

She didn't understand why Cousin Wilhelmina must grip her elbow in so odious a manner, as if she hoped to prevent something shocking taking place. Zoe had done nothing shocking in a very long time, save to run away from Paolo, and that didn't count because she'd been sorely provoked.

"Are you afraid I'll develop a taste for play? All I have to wager is myself, and Paolo has already done that." Zoe eyed Mina's gown of cotton muslin with its woven stripe pattern in graduated shades of yellow to brown. "You should have let me persuade my father to dress you also. I don't mean Beau should *dress* you precisely — or undress you, either, unless he has already? I didn't think he had; you *are* related, not that it would signify — but he would never suggest a gown so practical as to have detachable lower sleeves for day wear. Not that I mean to criticize! I daresay in your position you must consider such stuff."

Mina in that moment was considering strangling Zoe with her detached lower sleeves.

She glimpsed George Eames, coming toward them. He was dressed for evening in black kerseymere trousers, white waistcoat, and a coat of superfine. Mina released Zoe's elbow. "Have you brought us news?"

Mr. Eames shook his head. "I have learned very little. Abercorn the elder has also left town. I did locate the woman who had the care of Nell. She isn't especially eager to have the child returned."

Mina sympathized. Nell's disruptive abilities rivaled those of Romeo the goat, who was almost as terrified of her as was Grace the cat.

"If you will excuse me, I have a previous engagement," continued Mr. Eames. "I merely wanted to acquaint you with what I have — or haven't — learned."

"You will continue to make inquiries?" asked Mina.

"If you wish."

Mina watched him leave the room, reflecting unhappily on her five thousand pounds.

Zoe watched him also. She wondered where Mr. Eames was going, and where he had been. Perhaps he had attended the theater. Perhaps he would now present himself at a ball, or a soiree.

Why did Mr. Eames dislike her? Gentlemen did not generally dislike her on first sight. Were they previously acquainted? Could he have been among the legion of admirers once known as Zoe's Zoo?

Zoe had allowed each of her admirers to think she might misbehave a little bit with him, when in truth she hadn't meant to misbehave at all, or at least not very much, for she had been saving the exploration of her baser nature for her own true love.

If Mr. Eames had numbered among those misguided swains, Zoe supposed he might still be a little cross.

She wondered idly if he might be persuaded to admire her again.

Zoe nudged Mina. "Has Mr. Eames a wife?"

Mina linked arms and steered her cousin on another perambulation of the gaming rooms. "He does not. But you must not annoy— That is, seek to engage Mr. Eames. He is enamored of a lady whose papa discounts his standing in the world. Sir Ian is excessively high in the instep. Lady Anne isn't so top-lofty, but she is shy."

Lady Anne sounded dull as ditch-water, decided Zoe. To flirt with Mr. Eames would be to perform a public service, like the Good Samaritan assisting the poor traveller who had been left beaten, robbed, and half dead beside the road.

And if Paolo learned of her flirtation, he would be very cross, which was no more than he deserved.

She had been too long silent. Mina might be arriving at conclusions Zoe would rather she did not. "I have been wondering how I may best further my knowledge of the world. Or not my knowledge — Loversalls are born knowing — but the practical application thereof. It will require the assistance of a gentleman with vast experience. Such as Mr. Kincaid."

The minx meant to set her cap at Devon? Mina said, "Have you gone mad?"

"Oho! You want him yourself."

"Don't be absurd."

Zoe recognized a clanker when she heard one, and she believed she heard one now. "If you want Mr. Kincaid, why act like you do not?"

Mina felt a now-familiar throbbing behind her right eyelid. "Devon Kincaid is a rakehell. A wise woman avoids rakehells. You of all people should know that."

Zoe did not dignify this comment with response. Naturally she knew about rakehells — how could she not when her own papa had been involved in various escapades and scandals since the moment she was born? Hitherto she *had* avoided rakehells, but now she thought: with whom better to have a grand affaire?

If Paolo was made cross by a flirtation, a grand affaire would surely drive him to an apoplexy, oh lovely thought.

Zoe did not share these ruminations. It was a foolish female who informed another of her romantical ambitions, consequently sparking competition where there hitherto was none.

Mina had fallen silent, marshaling further arguments. Zoe, facing the door, was first to see the man dressed in black. He was of above average stature, lean and devastatingly handsome in a deliciously wicked way, with wavy black hair worn unfashionably long and eyes as dark as sin, austere features upon which dissipation had left its paradoxical stamp.

He strolled into the room.

"*Santo cielo!*" breathed Zoe.

Chapter Six

Lord Quinton was a man of regular habits: he habitually drank and gamed and whored all night, then retired at dawn to sleep through the day until time to embark upon another bacchanal. He was a man of libertine propensities, a gambler and a wastrel who lived on his wits, who had corrupted countless women and thrice killed his man in a duel; a buck of the first head who had sampled every vice not once but many times, in every variation possible, and with such utter boredom as to make his fellow reprobates appear rank amateurs.

Heads swiveled in his direction. People whispered as he passed. It amused Quin — as much as anything amused him — to be universally despaired of, envied and disliked. All this at a mere four-and-thirty. Just think how much he might accomplish before he stuck his spoon in the wall.

Moxley's wasn't the sort of establishment Lord Quinton normally frequented. He was accustomed to more raffish company. However, Moxley's was rapidly gaining a reputation as a place where one could lose a large amount of money in a short space of time. In the furtherance of his ambition to gamble away the entirety of his vast fortune, Quin meant to leave no stone unturned. The female employees were a nice touch.

Too, he was curious about Mrs. Moxley, who was almost as beloved of the gossipmongers as he was himself. He spied her immediately he entered the supper room.

He had forgotten how tall she was. Tall and lush and goddess-like with a bosom that beggared description; red-gold hair that, unbound, would tumble to her waist; sapphire eyes so unfathomable that one or another (or several) of her husbands had declared a desire to drown in their depths.

She was in animated conversation with a younger woman who could only be a relative. Loversall women drew the gaze and held it, possessing an innate sensuality that made the beholders' blood run warm.

Most beholders' blood, at any rate. Quin was exempt.

He moved further into the room. Mrs. Moxley glanced up, saw him, and looked as shocked as if she had set eyes upon a ghost. She'd changed, he thought. Once she hadn't worn dignity wrapped around her like a shroud.

Would he now become the subject of her conversation? Lord Quinton was the sort of man mamas warned damsels against, it being generally agreed he was the greatest blackguard alive. There were additionally rumors he was pox'd.

The latter was untrue. The former might well be correct. Quin approached the drink table. As he recalled the occasion, which wasn't all that clearly, Mina had emptied a chamber pot over his head the last time they met.

What was her last name then? Chickester? Ward? Memory eluded him, as memory frequently did, a circumstance for which Quin was more often grateful than not. He turned away from the table, a glass of burgundy in his hand, only to draw up sharply before he walked smack into the woman who stepped into his path.

The woman who mere moments ago had been speaking with Mina. The top of her head reached barely to his chin.

She dimpled at him. "Hello. I'm the Contessa— Ah, Prudence Loversall. That is, I am calling myself Prudence because I spent ten miserable years being prudent and chaste. Cousin Wilhelmina says if I have the sense of a gnat I'll avoid you like the plague."

"You should listen to your cousin," Quin replied.

"Just because a person is older — and Cousin Wilhelmina is *much* older! — doesn't mean she has a better understanding." Boldly, Prudence — or, not-Prudence — clutched his arm. Though normally he would have, Quin did not shake her off, his responses rendered sluggish by ingestion of a large amount of that beverage commonly known as Strip-Me-Naked or Blue Ruin. Too, he was bemused by the notion of a prudent, chaste

The Loversall Novellas

Loversall.

He was additionally distracted by the notion of Mina Loversall grown old.

"So you are the Black Baron!" his captor continued. "It is Fate that I should meet you now, when I have decided I must broaden my understanding of the world. I am seven-and-twenty, you see, and have not yet done anything depraved."

Quin raised his glass, and drank. Females frequently vied for his favors. He was amazed (if he could still be amazed) that so many were as bent on their destruction as he was himself.

This female was still talking. "I am a married woman, so I am not entirely without experience. Such as it was! A wife is not supposed to have *cravings,* I credit. I was vastly disappointed — but that is beside the point. You are a man who understands *affaires de coeur,* and grand passions, and worlds well lost for love."

If Mina Moxley was banked fires, her cousin was a pile of kindling in search of a match. Lord Quinton had no desire to burn his fingers. "No," he said.

She tilted her head. "Whyever not?"

Quin was getting a headache. He really should refrain from combining burgundy with gin. "I prefer rigidly virtuous young women who are ripe to be debauched."

Her blue eyes widened. "Are you truly so wicked?"

Quin reflected upon the orgies he'd attended. The whores he'd tumbled. The virgins he'd defiled.

The men he'd killed.

The young married woman he had seduced on a wager, who rather than face her cuckolded husband had hanged herself.

He had won that wager. Others, he had lost. They all ran together in a blur of endless days and nights fuelled by opium and alcohol.

He said, with rare sincerity, "I am."

"Excellent!" She dimpled at him and resumed her attack. "And *I* am rigidly virtuous. Or I was. If I am to go into a nunnery — or even if I'm not — I must first be despoiled. And if I am to be despoiled, I wish it to be by my own hand, or by a hand of my own choosing, and not by someone else."

Quin had no little experience with nunneries, but doubted those were the sort of establishment his accoster had in mind. There had been a certain abbess—

He couldn't recall which flesh-pot she had presided over. Lady, ladybird or laced mutton, he mused, it all came down to the same thing in the end. Across the room, Mina was speaking with a young dandy in salmon-colored moleskin trousers and a coat with collar raised so high behind it would have better become a horse.

His companion cleared her throat. "I don't think you perfectly grasp the situation. Loversall women cannot resist the call of passion. We give our all for love. Oh, pray don't be difficult! I haven't much time. It is most important that before Paolo finds me I am ruined."

A brief spark of curiosity flared in the alcohol-soaked recesses of Quin's brain. "Paolo?"

Not-Prudence leaned closer. "Never mind. Under the circumstances, perhaps you should call me Zoe."

She paused, expectantly. The woman sounded quite mad.

Loversalls, in Quin's experience, were all a little bit mad.

The madwoman wanted him to rid her of her virtue. He could not count how many times he had been confronted by females hoping he would rid them of their virtue.

No wonder he was bored.

Quin detached himself. "I believe that I should not."

She pouted. "Oh, but why?"

Quin smoothed away the creases left by her fingers on his sleeve. "Because, my dear, you are neither rigidly virtuous nor young." Leaving the lady with her mouth hanging unflatteringly agape, he walked away.

Chapter Seven

Sunlight streamed through the linen-draped windows of the morning room, which was in disarray, not unlike its owner, who was wearing scuffed slippers and a dove-grey morning dress, her curls escaping already from an untidy chignon. The window hangings dangled askew, and the furnishings were disarranged.

Grace the cat had taken refuge under the sofa upon which Mrs. Moxley sat, with Nell on her lap, and jam on her nose. The merest tip of the cat's tail protruded. Periodically, it twitched.

"Sit still!" said Mina, as she tried once more to connect the slice of bread and jam she held with Nell's open mouth. "You said you were hungry. You specifically asked for jam."

"Bah!" retorted Nell, who at her tender age had already discovered the peculiarly feminine pleasure of changing her mind. "Bah bah bah bah bah!"

"There is my good girl," said Mr. Kincaid, as he strolled into the room. "Shall I tell you about the ogress, the prince, and the pot of peas?"

"Peas!" echoed Nell.

"Very well." Devon leaned over the sofa. "Since you said please."

She chortled. "Peas!"

Nell held up her arms. Devon lifted the child. Mina took a bite of bread and jam. Nell shrieked indignantly.

Some few moments passed before order was restored, at which point jam adorned not only Mrs. Moxley's nose and Mr. Kincaid's shoulder but also the sofa and the oil painting — Bacchanalian children playing with apples and grapes, fruit and flowers and some drunken-looking bees —

that hung on one striped wall.

Zoe wafted through the doorway, wearing a long-sleeved high-necked morning dress of white French lawn. "Good gracious, what a rumpus! Oh I see, it's Nell. She is monstrous grubby. Is that jam in her hair?" She beamed at Devon. "I am going to have an amour."

"How nice for you," responded Mr. Kincaid. Grace retreated further beneath the sofa. Nell thrust out her lower lip.

Zoe dimpled. "I haven't decided with whom. It will not pose a difficulty, because I am a Loversall. Love is our obsession and our downfall. We gamble with our hearts as freely as others gamble with their money. Just one more romance, one more throw of the dice."

"Speak for yourself," said Mina. "I no longer gamble with my heart."

Devon smiled at her. "One hopes you will relent, my pet."

Mina regarded him with exasperation. "I am not your pet."

He sat beside her on the sofa. "No, Nellie is my pet, aren't you, poppet? Would you like to hear about the donkey cabbages?"

"Fustian, Cousin Wilhelmina!" Zoe had been watching this byplay. "How can you say you don't gamble with your heart, after all those husbands you have had? But maybe it is for the best that you don't do it any more, since they invariably seem to die."

"'Men have died from time to time, and worms have eaten them, but not for love'," quoth Devon. "*As You Like It*, Act IV, Scene I."

"If you have not wished to die for love, it is because you have not met the right woman." Demurely, Zoe lowered her lashes. "Or do not *realize* you have met her. I have noticed before that gentlemen frequently do not see what is right under their noses."

What was right under Devon's nose was Zoe. Mina perfectly understood the Conte de Borghini's willingness to wager his wife. "Considering the vast number of women Devon has tumbled, he may have good reason to be skeptical," she remarked.

"Don't fret, poppet," Devon said to Nell, who had begun to fuss. "I don't mind if the pretty lady insults me. We are old friends." Zoe decided Mr. Kincaid's eyesight must be deficient, because if anyone in the room should be called 'pretty', it was she. Mina rang for a footman, requested tea and a damp cloth and Meg.

Nell was squirming. Devon set her down. She made a bee-line for

Grace's twitching tail. The cat took refuge atop the writing desk — fitted with beaded drawers, tapering square legs, and a tooled leather writing surface upon which sat two silver candlesticks and an inkwell — that sat in a far corner. In her efforts to reach the cat, Nell overturned both the candlestick and the inkwell. Grace escaped to the opposite corner of the room, and clawed her way up the long case clock. There she settled, and refused to come down. Nell flung herself, shrieking on the floor. At this point, the footman returned, bringing with him tea, warm water, cloth and Meg, who wished nothing more than to return to her duties in the scullery and had additionally decided to forego offspring.

"Gracious!" exclaimed Zoe. "What an ill-behaved child." The footman, she realized, was not unhandsome. She awarded him a smile.

Nell glimpsed Meg and shrieked louder. Meg held out a piece of toffee. Nell ceased screaming long enough to pop the candy into her mouth. While the child was preoccupied with chewing, Meg removed her from the room. The footman removed himself soon thereafter. Zoe followed. Mina sank back on the sofa with a heartfelt groan.

Devon sat down beside her. "You have the look of a slightly demented Madonna. It suits you." Mina sighed, savoring the simple pleasure of being near an attractive rogue.

The rogue was considerably less dapper than when he first arrived. She dipped the washcloth in water, wrung it out, and dabbed at his sticky sleeve. "I fear this coat is ruined. You must send me your tailor bill."

"Better I should send it to Abercorn." Devon took the cloth and removed the jam from Mina's nose. "Have you slept at all?"

"I have not, and thank you for remarking on it. Next you will tell me I am grown quite hagged. *You* would not sleep either, if you had Zoe and Nell—" Mina paused, struck by his expression. "Oh. I've kept you from your bed."

Devon contemplated his bed, and his companion, and wondered if he would ever succeed in wedding the two. "I am unaccustomed to trysting at such an early hour. However, I am prepared to make an exception in your case."

Mina, tired and jam-smeared and bedeviled, was in no mood for teasing. "Do be serious!" she snapped.

"Rather surprisingly, I *am* serious," said Devon. "But since that is not the service you require of me, what may I do for you?"

Ah, what he might do for her. Mina wrenched her mind away from tangled sheets and sweat-dampened bodies and shuddering sighs. "I don't know where to begin."

Devon stretched out his long legs, noted the ink stain on one boot. "In my experience, which as you have observed is not inconsiderable, there are only two things that prompt a female to summon me at so ungodly an hour. You have ruled out assignation, have you not? Yes, I thought you had. Then I must conclude some new catastrophe has taken place."

Mina hesitated. She knew what she must do, could think of nothing else *to* do, but was reluctant to say the words. "I had hoped to speak with you while Zoe was abed."

"Am I to conclude that the new catastrophe involves Zoe?"

The new catastrophe *was* Zoe. Mina watched as Grace climbed down the clock, padded across the room, hopped gingerly onto the sofa and stretched out across Devon's thighs. He threaded his fingers through her fur.

Things had come to a sorry pass, reflected Mina, when she was jealous of a cat. "I want you to engage Zoe."

Devon raised an eyebrow. "By 'engage', I hope you don't mean what I think you mean, because if you do mean it, the answer is a resounding no."

Mina touched his arm. "Pray hear me out. Zoe needs to be taught a lesson — no, not *that* sort of lesson! — and at the same time you may prevent someone less principled from doing her real harm."

Devon didn't immediately answer, but regarded her with an unreadable expression. "What are you thinking?" Mina asked.

"I am deciding whether I should be insulted."

"By my request that you distract my cousin?"

"By your suggestion that I have principles. What has inspired this bizarre request?"

Mina drew back her hand. "Zoe has set her sights on Quin."

Chapter Eight

Zoe peered around the corner. Mina was consoling a gentleman who had lost two thousand pounds at whist by forgetting that the seven of hearts was in, her back turned to the door. Zoe scooted past the private parlor and hurried through the chamber where hazard reigned supreme. Some of the more serious gamblers had turned their coats inside-out for luck. Others wore eyeshades and leather guards around their cuffs. Few gentlemen with money in their pocket, it appeared, could resist temptation when seeing other gamesters dicing with Dame Fortune. They set their wits aside and entered into a state of trance. When winning, they didn't want to stop; when losing, they continued to play in an attempt to recoup their loss.

Zoe derived some satisfaction from the knowledge she'd left Paolo with a debt of honor he was unable to pay.

She attracted no small notice as she passed through the rooms. Miss Loversall (as the patrons thought of her) was wearing the most demure of her gowns in an attempt to appear virginal, in startling contrast with the other females present, who put their assets on public display.

Zoe slipped into the first room of the gaming suite. Mindful of her promise, she didn't flirt — or if she did, it was just a little bit — what harm in the flutter of an eyelash, a maidenly blush? And if she caused unease when she had said she wouldn't, the person to whom that promise had been made was being positively dog in the mangerish, and so it didn't count. Cousin Wilhelmina had no flair for flirtation, as proven by her response when someone tried to flirt with her — though why that someone should try and flirt with Mina when younger prettier females were in the room, Zoe couldn't say. She positioned herself in a chair that provided her a clear view of both the rouge et noir table and the entrance door.

As a result, when George Eames arrived at Moxley's, the first thing he saw was Zoe. Though she was giving her best impression of an angel in a gaming hell, he was not deceived. As a solicitor, Mr. Eames had learned to peer below the surface and therefore recognized an imp from the nether realms.

Propriety demanded he acknowledge her, no matter that he doubted she understood the meaning of the word; she had risen from her chair to brazenly intercept his progress. "Good evening, Miss Loversall," he said coolly, hoping she would understand he didn't care to speak with her.

Zoe, however, couldn't conceive that any gentleman might not care to speak with her. "It *is* a good evening, now you are here! Cousin Wilhelmina told me about Lady Anne. You should try and make her jealous. I will assist you."

George blanched at the thought of his ladylove — who was most correct in her conduct, a model of good breeding, distinguished for her elegance and accomplishments and well-regulated mind — in conversation with this coquettish cabbagehead. "Don't trouble yourself."

"Nonsense! It is no trouble. Lady Anne's papa must be wonderfully stiff-necked. Although I have discovered there is no explaining what some people think. My own husband—" Zoe's bright smile dimmed. "I shan't speak of that! Save to say it is his fault that I ran away."

Mr. Eames was, despite his association with the Loversalls, a conventional gentleman. He said, with disapproval, "A wife's rightful place is at her husband's side."

Oh?" Zoe's fine eyes flashed. "Even if her husband wagers her at play?"

"Even then." George took a step backward. "You shouldn't tell me more. I am sworn to uphold the law."

Zoe might have sworn also, and at him, had her attention not been distracted by another newcomer. She turned away from Mr. Eames. He hastened on his way.

So might Lord Quinton have hastened, had he realized what awaited him, but Lord Quinton's memory of his previous visit to Moxley's was as vague as were his reasons for returning there. He stepped into the room and gazed around him with a vaguely puzzled air.

The Loversall Novellas

A delicious heat sizzled through Zoe. Those cynical eyes, that sinful smile — she assumed his smile was sinful; she hadn't glimpsed it yet — how delicious, this anticipation of ravishment by a rakehell.

So what if he'd said she wasn't young? Or rigidly virtuous? He had called her 'my dear' and that must count for something. "Good evening, Lord Quinton!" she said, as she neatly barred his way.

Lord Quinton's gaze fell upon the golden-haired vision who'd popped up in front of him. Had he died of barrel fever, then? Granted, Quin had indulged generously in various alcoholic beverages, but he didn't think he'd drunk *that* much.

Nor did he think celestial beings would usher him into his afterlife.

On second glance, that lovely face was vaguely familiar. He inquired, "Have we met?"

Zoe blinked. How could he have forgot her? But since he had—

She stepped closer. "My name is Zoe. I asked you to despoil me, and you said you would. My husband is a toad, you see. I should be grateful Paolo didn't touch me more often, else I might have warts."

Ah, the madwoman. Quin recognized her now. He supposed her astonishing beauty made most men willing to overlook what might in a less bedazzling creature have been extremely annoying quirks.

Quin was not most men. "I have no interest in intimate acquaintance with married women anxious to sully their reputations. As I told you before, only a virtuous female will do for me."

Zoe was not susceptible to set-downs. In a manner that caught the attention of every male in her vicinity, she nibbled at her lip. "If I'm not a virgin, I'm the next best thing."

Quin appreciated the novelty of a female trying to assure him of her virtue. Usually it was the reverse. "Virtue doesn't necessarily have to do with virginity," he idly remarked.

"Cousin Wilhelmina has told me the most amazing stories," said Zoe, reclaiming his wandering attention. "You kidnapped Norwich's betrothed and rode off with her to Gretna Green."

Cousin Wilhelmina, reflected Quin, was hardly one to talk. Were gossip to be believed, which generally it wasn't, she had done worse herself.

Mina would not care to see her cousin in conversation with the Black Baron? Then the Black Baron would converse. "We didn't make it all the way to Gretna Green. The lady and I parted company in Penrith."

"You *left* her there? Why?"

"She was no longer a virgin by that time." Zoe's eyes widened. Quin added, "You cannot be so naïve as to think I was love-struck."

"Then why did you run off with her?" inquired Zoe, less shocked than intrigued.

Try as he might, which wasn't very hard, Quin couldn't recall.

"You ruined her reputation," Zoe chided him. "Norwich married her anyway. *He* loved her, at least."

Norwich loved the fortune the lady brought with her, Quin thought cynically. Zoe was still talking. She considered Norwich a coward because he failed to challenge Lord Quinton to a duel.

"He dared not." Quin explained.

"Why?"

"Everyone wanted to avoid a public scandal. Too, I am a much better shot."

"In my opinion," Zoe announced, "the lady involved should have had more sense. You are the Black Baron, after all."

Cup-shot though he might be, Quin was far too wise to the ways of females to rise to this lure. Zoe Loversall had as queer a kick in her gallop as any other member of her family.

She had pursed her lips and widened her eyes, putting him in mind of a carp. Quin told her so. As she was still sputtering, he strolled away in search of his next drink.

Zoe stared after him, hands on her slim hips. First Mr. Eames did not admire her, and now Lord Quinton. How could they fail to admire her? Had everyone gone mad?

People were watching her, she realized. They had witnessed the conversation between the wicked Black Baron and her heavenly self, and were speculating about that conversation's content.

Among those spectators, she saw Devon Kincaid. Zoe waved. Mr. Kincaid looked as if he was not glad to see her, but of course that could not be.

One rakehell was much like another. Devon Kincaid was a friend of Beau's. Embarking upon a liaison with him would be deliciously perverse.

And if Mina had a tendre, Mina should have said so. Zoe made her way to his side. "You are just the person I wished to speak with. Pray enlighten me. I have begun to wonder if gentlemen are capable of the finer feelings. Certainly my husband was not."

In spite of his reputation, Devon Kincaid didn't set out to break hearts. He stated clearly at the onset of each alliance that permanence was no part of the proposition, but nonetheless his paramours invariably tried to dissuade him from his bachelor status. He could only conclude he had a predilection for pea-geese.

The pea-goose who had for some time held his erratic attention, not that she seemed to consider it an honor, if she was even aware, had requested that he engage the affections of this ninnyhammer. Devon steeled himself. "I cannot speak for your husband," he replied without enthusiasm, "but I am no gentleman. Neither is Lord Quinton. You should have nothing more to do with either one of us."

Zoe dimpled as she tucked her arm through his. "You cannot mean that."

Her father entered the room, then. "What the *devil?*" inquired Beau.

Chapter Nine

Weak morning sunlight filtered through leafy branches to illuminate the private walled garden behind Moxley House – or those leafy branches that lay beyond the reach of Romeo the goat, who had a taste for woody items (not to mention the occasional broad-leafed plant) and also an amazing ability to climb trees and any other impediment placed in his path.

At the moment Romeo was happily stripping foliage from a honeysuckle bush. He had already ingested morning glories and camellias and various shrubs; had consumed rambling roses and wisteria with equal enthusiasm, despite the presence of thorns; had knocked down a wooden fence to devour the contents of the vegetable patch, during which endeavor he displayed a marked fondness for runner beans.

Mina had not realized there were so many things that could be sniffed and nibbled and munched, including on one memorable occasion Cook's wooden shoes.

Romeo was not her primary concern at the moment, however, though to turn one's back on the goat was to invite being butted at the worst, and at the best having one's hair chewed. Mina's attention was all for Samson, who had just informed her that one of the customers had pocketed a two hundred pound banknote from the hazard table. "What did you do?"

Samson shrugged. "Invited him to leave. Told him I'd give him his bastings if he showed his face here again."

Mina sank down on a shell-shaped bench. The thief would have been permitted to keep his pilfered note as a gesture of good will, disgruntled patrons being all-too-easily persuaded to lay information against the proprietor of a gambling house.

Maggie MacKeever

Moxley had spent a few hundred pounds, maybe even a few thousand, to smother actions and prosecutions, which was how Mina had met Mr. Eames, who had in his employ a lawyer who alternately prosecuted and defended keepers of gaming hells.

If an information was laid, and Mina prosecuted and fined, the cost would be less than Moxley's could bring in during a good night.

Unfortunately, all nights weren't good. A large staff was required to keep the rooms operating smoothly: dealers and croupiers and waiters; quietly unobtrusive guards; the porter who manned the strong iron-sheeted door; the link boys and chairmen who kept watch for approaching law officers.

Then there was the expense of maintaining the bank.

Plus the cost of wax candles and coal.

Romeo wearied of the honeysuckle and drifted closer, as Samson was explaining that one of the croupiers had been caught exercising a talent for cutting or turning whatever card she pleased. This practice was discouraged at Moxley's, where the customers were allowed some chance to win, unlike certain other establishments whose patrons periodically flung themselves into the Thames.

He had already found a replacement. Gentlewomen fallen on hard times could make a better living at Moxley's than by governessing, while keeping their self-respect (if not their reputations) intact.

Romeo expressed an interest in Samson's waistcoat buttons. In much the manner he dealt with recalcitrant footmen, Samson thumped the goat on the brow. Romeo curled his upper lip then withdrew to inspect the remnants of an orange tree planted in a neoclassical urn.

"The guv would be melancholy as a gib cat," said Samson, "was he to see his garden now."

The guv, reflected Mina, would have never accepted a goat as surety on a debt. Samson must think she had more hair than wit — hair that was tumbling down her back, Romeo having removed her pins.

Samson returned to the house. Romeo grew bored with the orange tree and wandered to the bench. He was a handsome fellow, as goats went, short and sturdy, his brown coat striped dark along the back, his eyes yellow with horizontal slit-shaped pupils. He possessed a plump, prehensile upper lip and tongue and a tuft of hair on his chin; a fine set of backward slanting horns and dark ears that pointed out horizontally from his head; cloven hoofs and a short upturned tail; and a very pungent scent.

"I'm told goat meat tastes similar to mutton," Mina informed him. "You had best behave yourself."

Romeo leaned against her shoulder. Mina rubbed his chest.

Grace the cat came down the path, peering warily about to make sure no enfant terrible lurked behind a bush — or the remnants of a bush — to pounce on her and pull her tail. She arrived safely at the bench, leapt up, and settled in Mina's lap. Romeo knelt so Mina could scratch the top of his head.

She surveyed the ruined garden and added the cost of fodder to her calculations. Romeo's appetite was greater than his current surroundings could sustain.

Additionally, she had Zoe to consider, and Nell. Mr. Eames had discovered that the elder Abercorn had taken himself off to Bath, but for what reason he couldn't say.

Mina had ceased scratching. Romeo nudged her knee. She frowned at him. He fluttered his sparse eyelashes in a manner absurdly reminiscent of Zoe.

Mina's smile faded. She had practically served up Devon on a platter to Zoe, who would wrap him around her finger like she did all men, having learned the trick at her father's knee, and then cast him heartlessly aside. Or perhaps she would keep him, and Mina would be invited to attend their wedding, and so what if Zoe already had a husband, because Mina had had five.

By the time footsteps crunched again on the gravel path, Mina's spirits were as flattened as her wooden fence. She glanced up. Beau was looking like a thundercloud.

Romeo clambered upright, uttering a high-pitched "Neahh!" Mina grasped the leash and collar that some overly optimistic person had placed around the goat's neck. "Hush! You must not butt or bite or nibble Beau. He is not half as handsome as you are, and you would not care for his taste."

Beau wrinkled his nose. "Since when do you have a goat?"

"That is a long story," Mina replied.

"Then I don't care to hear it. Tell me, as you would not last night, why the *devil* you think it acceptable for Dev to canoodle with Zoe."

Had there been canoodling? Mina hadn't noticed. Which, considering the already dejected condition of her spirits, was probably a good thing. "Devon is paying Zoe his attentions at my request."

Beau gaped at her. "You asked that profligate to seduce Zoe?"

Mina hadn't asked Devon to seduce Zoe. Had she? Seduction was the usual end result of canoodling, was it not? "Profligate, indeed. Listen to yourself. Our own family has turned profligacy into a fine art."

"I don't deny that I'm a profligate," responded Beau with dignity. "That doesn't mean I will stand idly by while my daughter is defiled."

Zoe defiled by Devon. Mina wondered how long it would take to banish that horrific vision from her mind. "I didn't ask Devon to seduce her, just to distract her," she protested.

Pushing Romeo aside — or attempting to; goats do not respond well to pushing, being much more amenable to a good pull — Beau sat down beside Mina. "You are a greenhead."

Mina was still caught up in horrific visions. "I suppose if Zoe *was* going to have an intrigue, there would be no one better to have it with than Devon Kincaid."

Beau eyed her suspiciously. "You sound as if you want to have an intrigue with him yourself."

Mina draped an arm around Romeo's neck and, ignoring his gamy odor, gave the goat a hug. "Don't be absurd."

Beau might in the general way of things focus his mind on selfish matters, but he was no slow-top. "*Do* you want to have an intrigue with Dev?"

"That is none of your affair." Mina's lap had grown crowded. Grace roused from her slumbers and batted the goat's nose.

Romeo bared his teeth. Beau snatched up the cat. "By God, you truly *are* a greenhead."

Mina's cheeks bloomed as scarlet as the roses that until lately had climbed the garden wall. "You haven't inquired why I asked Devon to distract Zoe. She has developed an attraction I cannot like."

Beau was much more interested in the attraction Mina had developed. "Zoe has been developing unsuitable attractions since she was in the cradle," he said dismissively. "Most memorably with the butcher's boy."

"You will not be so sanguine when I tell you Zoe has set her cap at

Quin."

"Quin?" Beau sat up straighter on the bench.

Lord Quinton was a close acquaintance. Their paths, in the pursuit of profligacy, frequently crossed. Beau wondered if the fact that Zoe was his daughter would make the Black Baron more or less inclined to corrupt her — or to allow her to corrupt him.

He gazed around the decimated garden. "Where *is* Zoe?"

"At the park. I sent her there with Meg and Nell."

Chapter Ten

Mina was mistaken. Zoe was no longer in the park. She had eluded her companions and was instead loitering on the southern side of Piccadilly, nearly opposite Bond Street, specifically outside the Egyptian Hall. On one side of this impressive example of Egyptian style architecture, complete with hieroglyphs, stood a bookseller; on the other, an apothecary's shop.

Zoe was interested in none of these structures. Her attention was fixed on a three-story building across the street, separated from Piccadilly by a courtyard. The Albany — a mansion seven bays wide, with a pair of service wings — contained sixty sets of apartments let out exclusively to bachelors and widowers. Females were denied entrance, save for the mothers, grandmothers, sisters and aunts of the occupants, none of which Zoe had been able to convince the porter that she was, and even if she *had* convinced him it would not have mattered, because Lord Quinton had issued strict instructions that though half the females in London might claim to be related to him, he'd be damned if he'd have any of them invading his rooms.

That same porter (after being subjected to a barrage of sighs and eyelash flutters and maidenly blushes) finally admitted that the Black Baron wasn't yet returned from the prior evening's carousal. Zoe settled in to wait.

It hadn't been difficult to discover where Lord Quinton resided. A man so beloved of the gossips could keep few details of his life secret from the press.

Vendors and tradesmen, shoppers and cits crowded the pavement. Street sellers shouted, cart and carriage wheels clattered, horses and donkeys neighed. A coster brushed past Zoe carrying gutted rabbits, their feet lashed together, dangling from a long pole.

She turned her head away and stiffened, much like a pointer scenting game. There in the distance was the Black Baron at last, looking devilish and disheveled and if only she could secure his interest— Well, she would have been wasted in a nunnery, after all.

Lord Quinton, staggering down Piccadilly, wanted nothing more than his bed. In furtherance of his ambition to die done up, he'd spent the previous several hours drinking hard and plunging deep.

Early in the evening, he'd told the younger Loversall she reminded him of a carp. It had been one of his better moments. The memory almost made him smile.

He glimpsed her then, as she darted out into the street, narrowly avoiding collision with a dustman and his cart — impossible *not* to glimpse her, dressed as she was in a white muslin pelisse worn over a white walking dress; a bonnet of woven straw with a ruching of lilac silk ribbon tied quite fetchingly under her left ear. The dustman cursed, his donkey brayed. The little Loversall waved a dismissive hand and continued on her way.

Quin discovered he was not as bosky as he had been mere seconds past. He narrowed his eyes at the female who once more barred his path. "You are the most abominable annoyance," he said.

Zoe recalled a recent herd of cows so terrorized they wouldn't be providing milk any time soon. "You haven't met Nell."

Had he the energy to pursue the manner, which he hadn't, Quin could have called to mind any number of Nells, and Molls, and Sues. "You waste your time, and mine. I have no intention of ridding you of your virtue."

"Why not?" Zoe had recovered nicely from her near-collision. "You've rid everyone else of theirs. I should not say so, I suppose, but I don't see any reason why we should stand on ceremony."

"Being old friends, as we are?" inquired the Black Baron. "Then I shall also speak plain, and tell you I wish you would go away."

Did he truly wish her to leave him? Zoe decided he did not. Lord Quinton was attempting to hide his true feelings. Probably he considered her above his touch. And so she was, or would be in the normal way of things, but these circumstances were not normal, and she meant to be despoiled.

The Loversall Novellas

"You fail to grasp the situation," Zoe gently chided. "Which is not surprising because you are in your cups every time we speak. If you were to try and concentrate your mind you would realize I have not even begun to explore my potential. Great-Aunt Amelia eloped with her groom to Bavaria, where she attracted the attention of a prince, and inspired a duel between that gentleman and a Greek. Third-Cousin Ermyntrude escaped an unhappy marriage by dressing as a man and fighting Red Indians in the Colonies. Gwyneth ran off with Gypsies and dwelt among them in their encampments in the woods." And Fenella had shot her faithless lover and then herself, but Zoe didn't mention that.

Lord Quinton was rapidly becoming more sober than he liked. The sun had grown damned bright. Since he didn't care to continue this conversation in the middle of the street, he grasped Whatever-her-name-was by her elbow and ushered her into a nearby coffee house. Odd in him, admittedly, but no one could predict what Quin would or would not do, including Quin himself.

They entered a large room, the front window filled with coffee cups and pots and strainers of a dozen different designs, the wooden floor worn with use, the ceiling low-beamed. Wainscoted walls were plastered with advertisements: Dr. Belloste's pills for rheumatism, Parke's pills for the stone, Daffy's Elixir, Godfrey's Cordial, Velno's vegetable syrup for the alleviation of venereal disease. Coffee-pots waited ready by the well-filled antique grate.

Lord Quinton dropped coins into a brass box, then sat down at a small round table placed near the back wall. A waiter brought two cups of hot steaming coffee in shallow delftware bowls. Quin pushed his aside and requested a brandy and water. Zoe announced that she would like a piece of almond cake.

The waiter came back quickly with their order. Quin raised his glass. Zoe took a bite of cake and considered her attack.

She and the Black Baron were going to have an amour, whether he liked it or not. Of course he *would* like it— how could any man not like making love to her?

True, Paolo hadn't approached the business with noticeable enthusiasm. Could he be one of those odd men who preferred the company of his own sex?

Maybe he would have rather made love to Cesare. Maybe Paolo was making love to Cesare even then. Maybe she would shoot them both.

"*You* don't, do you?" Zoe inquired. "Prefer your own sex?"

At least in this moment, Quin preferred no sex at all. "Man, woman or goat, it's the same to me."

Strange that he should mention goats. "You have met Romeo?"

Quin's brow began to throb. "I thought you wanted me to *be* Romeo."

"Romeo is a goat."

"I mentioned goats only because my mouth tastes as if a goat had defecated in it. Have we conversed long enough to suit you yet?" Quin beckoned the waiter to refill his glass.

Zoe said, severely, "You drink too much. People will soon start calling you a fuddle-cap."

Quin couldn't have cared less what people called him. "I'm awake, aren't I? If I'm awake, I haven't drunk too much."

"Tsk!" responded Zoe, and took another bite of cake.

She was so small Quin could have picked her up and tossed her out the window. He was briefly tempted, but too much energy would be required. "What do you wish to say to me? I want to go to bed."

"That is precisely my point!" For emphasis, Zoe waved her fork. "I want you to take *me* to your bed."

Quin had no more desire to bed Zoe Loversall than to swim naked in the Serpentine, though rumor claimed he'd done the latter, an event he happily did not recall. "Too little too late. I've just come from an orgy," he replied.

"But you said you only tumbled virgins!" Zoe protested.

"They *were* virgins," Quin informed her, and so the darlings had been: virgin sacrifices at the temple of Venus, skillfully enacted by seasoned whores.

Moreover, he doubted he'd said any such thing.

Zoe was growing tired of all this talk of virgins. She was also tired of trying to be virtuous, which didn't seem to be gaining her much ground.

Quin interrupted her reflections. "Does your cousin know where you are?"

"Don't tell me *you* are interested in Cousin Wilhelmina also!" Zoe cried.

"Also?"

"Mr. Kincaid admires her. I'm sure I don't see why."

"You fail to surprise me," murmured Quin.

Did the Black Baron not realize that, in comparison with Zoe, Mina was as old as Methuselah, if Methuselah had been female? "Cousin Wilhelmina is positively antediluvian, unlike myself. Moreover, I can be as virginal as you like, which I'll warrant Mina cannot! I should think you'd sympathize with my desire to experience passion. The wild racing of the heart. The sweet singing of the blood."

By this time, Quin's head ached so badly that his vision blurred. He saw before him not one Zoe but two. Both of them were chattering. It was almost enough to make a man swear off the grape.

He pushed his chair back from the table. "Your antediluvian cousin Mina is a mere six years older than I."

Lord Quinton couldn't leave her! Zoe grasped his sleeve. "I can hardly make a scandal by myself! That is— You of all people should understand the world well lost for love."

Quin shook her off. "What I understand is lust. It's like an insect bite that itches briefly and intensely, and is as soon forgot."

Chapter Eleven

Mina walked through the gaming rooms, regal in her gown of blue silk taffeta, cool and aloof; smiling, nodding, pausing to commiserate with a player so plucked his possessions were going to be brought to the hammer. She patted his arm, a coveted mark of favor; Moxley's patrons knew they could look but couldn't touch. Such knowledge naturally made them think about touching all the more. Gamblers who were thinking about touching weren't concentrating on their game, which was a primary objective of the attractive young women present in these rooms.

Moxley, in some ways, had been a clever man. In others, he had not. Had Moxley been more clever, he would not have taken to eating oysters with pretty opera dancers, and as a result suffered a painfully unpleasant death.

Mina could not blame him for it. It had been in Moxley's nature to be tempted by a slender ankle, as it was in her own nature to marry reckless, feckless gentlemen who died young. Peebles had not been young, but Peebles was an aberration, Mina's attempt to break her losing streak.

She arrived at the first room, without glimpsing George Eames. Mina concluded he had nothing to report.

As she was gazing at the door, and wondering if she should summon the solicitor, if for no better reason than to complain at him, a familiar tall figure entered the room. Mina's spirits unaccountably lightened, and simultaneously sank.

Devon made his way toward her. Since his progress was not rapid — Mr. Kincaid was almost as popular with his own sex as with demireps — Mina had ample time to admire the superb tailoring of his brown coat and waistcoat, the excellent fit of his pantaloons.

He'd told her to come to him when next she felt dull. Instead she'd sent him to Zoe.

Not that any of the various emotions she felt could be described as 'dull'.

Devon looked her over. "That color suits you. You are even lovelier than usual tonight."

"I don't understand," responded Mina, quelling a surge of pleasure, "why you must empty the butter dish over my head. The truth is that I am fast growing hagged."

"If you want truth—" He arched a brow. "I could suggest a little something to help you sleep."

Mina rolled her eyes. 'A little something', indeed.

In truth, she wasn't sleeping well, her dreams tormented by visions of funerals and weddings and informations laid, culminating with Zoe in her coffin, and Mina dangling from a scaffold for having put here there. "Are you avoiding us? Nell has been demanding to see her Uncle Dev."

"I would never avoid you," Devon replied. "I confess to being less enthusiastic about certain other members of your household."

Mina could hardly quibble; she hadn't recovered from the horror of learning her cousin had disappeared from the park, and her outrage when, hours later, Zoe strolled nonchalantly into the house.

Pressed for explanations, Zoe had thrown a tantrum, which inspired Nell to throw a tantrum of her own. At some point during this drama, Mina's favorite Dresden shepherdess was smashed to smithereens. She had been on the verge of locking Zoe in her room like Nell — or locking Zoe in her room *with* Nell — or tossing the pair of them out into the street — when Beau intervened.

"Beau has taken Zoe to the theater. We have a number of disappointed customers as a result, gentlemen who like to ogle Zoe. Unfortunately, Zoe can't be made to understand she shouldn't ogle them back. It is only natural they prefer to ogle her, she tells me, because she is so much younger than I."

"She *is* lovely," Devon remarked.

Mina's heart sank down to her toes. Devon was already half-wrapped around Zoe's thumb.

The Loversall Novellas

This was a disaster! Dared she tell him that she'd changed her mind? Could she persuade him to change his?

Why *should* he change his? Zoe might be an abomination, but Devon thought her lovely.

She was also, damn her, young.

At this rate Mina would soon find herself among the Loversalls who had run mad. She said, a little grimly, "I no longer want you to flirt with Zoe."

Devon frowned. "First you don't want me to flirt with you, and now you don't want me to flirt with your cousin. I wish you would make up your mind."

"I didn't realize what I was asking. That is—"

"You think I'm not up to the challenge, perhaps."

"Don't be absurd," Mina responded irritably." You know full well that you could fix the interest of a saint."

Devon was less skilled at fixing interest than his companion seemed to think. He certainly hadn't succeeded in fixing hers. "Since you bring up the subject – why are you so determined to never again gamble with your heart?"

Mina glanced around the room. "I own a gaming hell. It rather takes the glamour out of play. Do you gamble with *your* heart? Shall we have a conversation about ganders and geese?"

"I don't advise it," Devon snapped.

He was cross with her, realized Mina. But Devon was seldom cross. Or he hadn't been, before the advent of Zoe.

A horrid notion struck her. Beau thought Mina wanted Devon. Had he told Dev so? Had they shared a laugh at her expense?

She couldn't bear the thought.

Mina turned away from Devon, saw Lord Quinton standing in the doorway. He was, as usual, dressed in black.

As she walked toward him, she remembered her first glimpse of the Black Baron. Chickester had recently died. Mina had been devastated — each time a husband died she was devastated, which was why she had vowed to have no more of them — and at the same time eager to confirm that she, at least, was still alive.

Quin had obliged.

Now, years later, here he was, his feet firmly set on the path to perdition, his beautiful face refined somehow by his dissipations. So must Lucifer have looked, when tempting foolish females to toss away their immortal souls. "Quin," she said. "I wish to speak with you."

Lord Quinton surveyed his surroundings. He had no idea — again — why he had come to Moxley's. He had set out with no direction and now here he stood, confronted by Mina Loversall.

She smiled at him. Quin experienced an unfamiliar emotion. But then, to Quin, most emotions were unfamiliar. Mina added, "My cousin isn't certain but she thinks you compared her to an insect. It has made her very cross."

"She called *you* antediluvian." Quin's attention strayed to the drinks table. "And I didn't compare her to an insect, but a carp."

He was, Mina realized, not yet wholly foxed. "Quin, I beg you, don't seduce Zoe."

It was not Lord Quinton's custom to accede readily to female requests. He was the Black Baron, after all. "You misunderstand. I'm not to seduce her, but despoil her. It is an entirely different thing." And then, because he *was* London's most wicked profligate, Quin informed his companion that he wouldn't despoil Zoe if she permitted him to debauch her instead. "Granted, you're not rigidly virtuous, but I will make an exception in your case."

Mina was reminded why she had once reaffirmed herself with this man, and why she had assaulted him. "You already debauched me," she protested.

"Ah. That would explain the chamberpot," said Quin.

Chapter Twelve

The day was overcast, which was not unusual for London, and no great deterrent for anyone who wished to take the air. Devon Kincaid did not wish to take the air, but had been driven by a demon of perversity to call at Moxley House and inquire if Mistress Zoe wished to do just that. Mistress Zoe did indeed wish to, as — vociferously — did Mistress Nell. Since Devon had already been regretting his invitation, he immediately seized upon Nell's presence to protect him from Zoe. As result, neither lady was content.

Nor were either of them silent. Zoe was determined to tell Devon the story of her life — why she should think him interested, he had no notion — while Nell was so impressed with his matched team that she demanded to hold the reins. When Devon told her she could not, she pitched a fit. Devon being unable to control both the horses and the child, Nell ended up on Zoe's lap. This also suited neither lady until Devon pointed out to Zoe how pretty a picture she presented with Nell perched on her knee. Nell, he consoled with the fable of the Clever Little Tailor, and the promise of a trip to Gunter's for an ice.

His tale told to her satisfaction, Devon drew up his curricle outside Gunter's Tea Shop, centered on the east side of Berkeley Square. Customers often ate their confections in the square itself, the ladies remaining seated in their carriages beneath the shady maples, their escorts leaning against the Square's railings, while waiters dashed to and fro across the road taking orders and carrying them back.

Mr. Kincaid's curricle garnered no little attention, gentlemen of his bent not prone to frequent establishments where painted pineapples hung above the door. That he had a lovely woman with him was not surprising; Mr. Kincaid generally had one woman or another or several attached; but none of the spectators present had seen him before with a brat in tow. This circumstance led to considerable conjecture concerning the brat's parentage, and speculation that if Mr. Kincaid had one child that the world had not known about, then he might well have more, and in that case where had he been hiding them all this time?

Mr. Kincaid was, happily, unaware of all this speculation. He was wholly occupied with Nell and her ice, a large amount of which almost immediately splattered his tightly fitting coat, buckskin breeches, Hessian boots, crisp high shirt collar, hitherto flawless cravat, and curly brimmed beaver hat. Zoe — who, since her escort didn't require that she be virginal, had chosen a blue carriage dress and matching bonnet trimmed with plaited ribbon and white lace — was similarly bedecked.

The confections disposed of, one way and another, Devon took up the reins. Nell having repeatedly expressed a desire for ducks, he directed his team toward the Park.

Would Mina be annoyed that he had taken Zoe on an outing, he wondered, or pleased? Devon was uncertain which reaction had been his intent.

Mina was turning out to be as mercurial as any other member of her sex. Did she or did she not want him to distract her cousin? Was she concerned with Zoe's best interests, or her own?

Devon scowled. He'd not soon forget the moment when Mina had turned away from him to go and talk with Quin.

Really, reflected Zoe, flirting with Mr. Kincaid was very uphill work. He hadn't even commented on how fine she was today. Zoe considered her veil an especially nice touch. She was *incognita,* was she not?

She tightened her grip on Nell, who disliked to sit still, and gazed down the tree-lined avenue.

Hyde Park consisted of over three hundred acres appropriated from the monks of Westminster when Henry VIII decided to extend his hunting grounds. James I had hunted here with Jowler and Jewel, his favorite hounds. Now the park was the hunting grounds of those lovely avaricious charmers referred to as Cyprians, or the Fashionably Impure.

Mr. Kincaid was well acquainted with the Fashionably Impure. Or so rumor claimed. A person would never guess it from the way he was treating Zoe. Not that she was an impure. Yet.

Perhaps, like the Black Baron, Mr. Kincaid considered her above his touch. Perhaps he felt he was too old. Well, he *was* too old, but nonetheless—

Zoe glimpsed George Eames, standing in the shade of a distant beech tree. Impossible to clearly see the female to whom he spoke so earnestly, but she wore a sprigged muslin gown trimmed with a frill around the hem, a deep red shawl with a paisley patterned border, and a demure bonnet that boasted neither blossom nor plume. An older woman hovered nearby.

"Stop the carriage!" Zoe demanded. Devon drew his curricle to a halt. Zoe thrust Nell at him, and stood. Pleased with her new perch, Nell reached for the reins. The groom leapt down from his seat behind the curricle's main compartment and helped Zoe alight.

Zoe tripped gracefully across the grass. "Hello!" she said, causing Mr. Eames to violently start and his companion to turn her head. Seen closer, the young woman had dark hair and eyes, a prim mouth and rosy cheeks set in a plump face. "I am Zoe Loversall. And you are—"

From Mr. Eames's direction came the sound of grinding teeth. "I am Lady Anne Stuart," said his companion, before he could speak.

"I am pleased to meet you, Lady Anne. George speaks of you frequently. Are you having an assignation? Since your papa can't approve? I wouldn't let my papa dictate to me, particularly in matters of the heart, but you must know your business best." Zoe cast George a reproachful glance. "We have missed you at Moxley House. It is one thing if you neglect the rest of us, but it is unconscionable in you to abandon Nell. The poor child has missed you desperately." Zoe waved at the curricle. Nell, for once obliging, waved back. The older woman gasped.

Mr. Eames looked like he was about to have an apoplexy. Lady Anne looked stunned. Her companion looked like she couldn't wait to spread fresh gossip all around.

"But I shall say no more of that!" said Zoe. "I must return to my companions. We *will* see you soon, will we not, George?" Pleased with this good few moments' work, she bid her victims *ciao* and returned to the curricle, where Mr. Kincaid was entertaining Nell with the tale of Bluebeard, a violent nobleman with a nasty habit of murdering his wives, no fit tale for a tot, but she seemed to enjoy it well enough.

He gazed suspiciously at Zoe. "What devilment are you about?"

Zoe settled on the carriage seat. "Unfair! I was embarked on a good deed. You really don't want me, do you? How very odd."

Mina didn't want him, thought Devon. She valued him so little that she could hand him off to someone else.

He plopped Nell on Zoe's lap. "Your cousin will tell you I'm an odd duck."

"Duck!" demanded Nell.

"Yes, poppet. We're going to see ducks and geese and swans. Rabbits and squirrels. Cows and deer. We may even see a fox eat one of them. Would you like that?" Nell clapped her hands. Wildlife abounded along the banks of the Serpentine, an artificial lake created by the damming of the Westhaven River at the request of George II's wife, and so called because of its sinuous shape.

Numerous duels had been fought on these grounds. Devon hoped that, as result of this outing, Beau wouldn't challenge him to pistols at dawn.

"I am amazed," said Zoe, who was nothing if not tenacious, "that you have so low an opinion of yourself, after all those women and all those intrigues. Although you *are* growing older. I have the impression from my father that as a man grows older his fleshly prowess declines. I do not mean to indicate that Beau's prowess has declined, because I don't believe it has, but the possibility that it might do so periodically plagues his mind. It is my opinion that when a gentleman's imagination is thus being exercised, it is to the detriment of his—"

Devon ground his teeth. "Never mind!"

Zoe swiveled toward him on the seat, disarranging Nell, who squealed. "What is going on between you and Cousin Wilhelmina? Don't say nothing, like she did, because I can tell the difference between chalk and cheese."

Mr. Kincaid wasn't encouraged to hear his amatory efforts referred to as 'nothing'. "What did Mina say?"

"What does it matter what Mina says? You should be more sympathetic, because my heart has been broke." Zoe scooted closer. "Or maybe my heart was not, because I seem to be recovering nicely. Maybe I have yet to meet my own true love."

Devon inched himself, and his reins, away from Nell's grubby, grasping fingers. "'Love is a familiar. Love is a devil. There is no evil angel but love.' Shakespeare said that, I think."

"For someone who doesn't believe in love, you know a lot about it," Zoe huffed.

"One can know about something without experiencing it first-hand."

"If something doesn't exist, one can hardly know about it. You are a humbug, sir."

"Humbug," echoed Nell. Having decided she liked this new word, she repeated it several more times.

Devon recalled that the poet Shelley's pregnant wife Harriet drowned in the Serpentine. He was strongly tempted to subject his passengers to a similar fate. "I am not a humbug."

"Yes you are!" insisted Zoe. "You lust after Mina, and she lusts after you, yet you both deny it, which makes no sense to me. Although Mina's lovers don't live long, so it may be for the best."

Mr. Kincaid muttered something beneath his breath. Zoe added, "You do not want her made unhappy, in any event. Mina would be made *most* unhappy were she to discover I went to Vauxhall without an escort."

Chapter Thirteen

All was quiet at Moxley House, neither Zoe nor Nell being on the premises. The remaining residents were enjoying this brief respite, each in his or her own way. Meg was in the scullery, cheerfully scouring pots. Samson was overseeing the army of servants who cleaned the gaming suite.

Mina had taken refuge in the morning room. Grace the cat lay draped across her lap, while Romeo the goat sprawled at her feet. Romeo had tried to ingest a rhododendron bush and wasn't feeling well. Mina kept firm hold on his leash lest he revive and try to eat the furniture.

The room stank of goat.

Mina wished people would start redeeming their pledges. The watches and rings she could dispose of, if at a fraction of their worth. An umbrella, in London, could always be put to good use. Romeo, she had come to consider a member of the household. As for Nell—

She wondered what Devon was doing, and what Zoe was doing, and what Zoe was doing to Dev.

And when Abercorn was going to reclaim his hell-born babe.

Mina was annoyed with everyone. Devon, for taking Zoe up in his curricle. Zoe, for wanting to be ravished by every male she met. Beau, for playing least-in-sight. Moxley, for dying and leaving her in possession of his gaming hell. Quin for being Quin.

Romeo raised his head and made a sound reminiscent of a creaking door. Mina rubbed the sole of her slipper along the goat's back.

She regretted her behavior. Were Devon speaking to her, she would apologize. But his manner, when he came for Zoe and Nell, had been cold as the Thames in winter, when the water turned to ice.

Devon had taken Zoe up in his curricle. Mina didn't know what to think. Rather, she thought so many conflicting things that her head was in a whirl. Devon was doing as she had asked him; he was engaging Zoe. However, she had also asked him not to engage Zoe, and so he wasn't obliging her in the least.

Perhaps he meant to please Mina by occupying Zoe's attention. Perhaps he meant to drive her to distraction, in which case he was succeeding well. And perhaps he wasn't thinking of Mina at all.

Why *should* he be thinking of Mina, when he was with Zoe? Mina reminded herself he was also with Nell. She found some slight comfort in thinking of Devon at the mercy of Zoe and Nell.

He would charm his guests, of course. Devon Kincaid could charm the birds down from their boughs.

He could have, had he wished, charmed Mina out of her stays.

He might, that very moment, be charming Zoe out of hers.

Not in an open carriage. Not with Nell present to protest, and Nell *would* protest if Devon devoted so much effort to anyone else.

Mina couldn't imagine much effort would be required.

It would not have been, in her case.

Yet Devon had not expended even that little bit of effort, and Mina sat here brooding, and there was scant consolation in the knowledge she had brought this misery down on herself.

The door abruptly opened. Startled, Grace dug her claws into Mina's thigh. Romeo uttered a high pitched sneezing sound and scrambled to his feet.

George Eames strode into the room. His coat was creased and his hair rumpled, as if he'd grasped great handfuls of it and tugged.

Mina's heart sank. The arrival of one's solicitor in such a sorry state could not herald good news. "Mr. Eames! What has happened to you?" Romeo ambled forward, intrigued by the scent of the newcomer's pomade.

George sidestepped the goat and, without waiting for an invitation, dropped into a chair. "I was in the park with Lady Anne, engaged in a serious conversation, when your cousin walked up to us bold as brass. You realize, I hope, that she has maggots in her brain. She said I should make Lady Anne jealous. Jealous! Of *her*?"

Was this jealousy Mina felt, regarding Zoe and Dev? She hoped she was above such petty stuff, and feared she was not. "Surely it cannot be so bad."

"Can it not? That pestilential pig-widgeon insinuated that Nell is my child."

"Surely Lady Anne does not believe—"

"Who knows what Lady Anne believes?" George lowered his head into his hands, thereby thwarting Romeo, who was poised to nibble on his hair. "She is too well-mannered to speak her mind. One thing is certain: my hopes are all dashed."

There was a lot of that going around. Mina stroked Grace's soft fur. "What did she say? Lady Anne, I mean, not Zoe."

George replied, with loathing, "When next I see your brass-faced bacon-witted cousin, I shall have several words to say to her! Lady Anne was shocked, but only said that she must think. And what she must think is that I am a pretty scoundrel. A complete knave."

Lady Anne sounded like a paragon, and also deadly dull. Mina did not air this opinion, but asserted vaguely that things would eventually come right. She didn't believe her own words for a moment, not as regarded Mr. Eames, and not as regarded herself.

Loversalls, alas, had a long acquaintance with matters not ending well. Romola leapt off the battlements; Odo drank a fatal dose of poison; Casimir visited the menagerie in the Tower and got eaten by a bear.

On the other hand, Great-Great-Great-Great Uncle John fell into a fit of choking after eating fruit in the middle of a play at the Theater Royal, and was saved by a prostitute known as Orange Moll, who stuck her finger down his throat.

Ironic, that Mina should realize how much she wanted Devon only after she handed him to Zoe.

She glanced at the window and let out a little shriek, waking Grace, who hissed. Romeo looked up, the remnants of one of the green linen draperies dangling from his mouth.

Mina rang for a servant. Figg and a second footman wrestled the goat from the room. Grace yawned, rearranged Mina's skirts to her satisfaction, and resumed her nap.

George, during this distraction, regained control of his emotions. He had no faith that everything would turn out right — as a solicitor, George was all-too-well acquainted with instances when everything did not — but realized belatedly that Mrs. Moxley wasn't in fine fettle. He suspected she had been wrestling with troubles of her own.

"I apologize for my outburst. Your cousin's hen-witted conduct is not what brought me here. I recently discovered that Abercorn the younger's maternal grandmother resides in Bath. The old lady and Abercorn Senior have never rubbed along well together, but she dotes on the son. Senior will think Junior has gone to ask her to haul his coals out of the fire."

Mina said, "I wonder if she knows about Nell."

"If not, I daresay she will before this business is done. Frankly, I could care less." So savage was George's tone that Grace stirred, departed Mina's lap, and curled up in his instead.

George eyed the cat. He was unfamiliar with the philosophy that held most troubles could be eased by the presence of a purring feline.

"I am so sorry," sighed Mina. "About everything. You will be wishing us to Hades, and regretting you ever became involved in our affairs."

As to that, George couldn't argue. But his companion didn't deserve his censure, so far as he knew, and therefore he merely said, "Oh, well."

Chapter Fourteen

The supper box was softly illuminated by variegated lamps. On the rear wall, painted milkmaids wearing flat hats and gowns with ruffled cuffs danced to the music of a wooden-legged fiddler. Outside, in the Grove, an orchestra softly played.

It was wonderfully romantic. Rather, it might have been romantic, were Zoe there with someone else. Mr. Kincaid had consumed a remarkable amount of wine — the wines provided at the Garden were of the best vintage, even when served in a kettle and 'burnt' — while ignoring the rest of his supper (chicken and assorted biscuits, cheese cakes and wafer-thin slices of ham), along with herself.

He scowled at her. "You still haven't told me the purpose of this expedition. And spare me further drama about how dull your life has been."

Zoe widened her eyes at him. "But my life has been dull. Or it *was* dull until my wretched husband wagered me at play. Have you forgot? First I had to escape, and now that I *have* escaped, everyone is trying to keep me well wrapped in lamb's wool! Even you are suspicious of me. It is most unfair."

Devon hadn't drunk so much that he trusted his companion. "That horse is troubled with corns, my girl."

She fluttered her lashes. "Am I?"

"Are you what?"

"Your girl. I surmised I must be when—"

"Aargh."

"Are you unwell?"

Devon reached for the wine bottle, found it empty; looked for a waiter, found none. By these circumstances, his mood was not improved. "Allow me to refresh your memory. I escorted you here tonight in an attempt to spare Mina additional distress."

Zoe tilted her head so she might regard him all the better. "Mina *is* the object of your affections! She will be very jealous when I tell her you brought me to Vauxhall. Where are you going?" she added, as he pushed back his chair.

"In search of the waiter," Devon retorted. "To get through this evening, I will need much more to drink."

Finally! She had feared he would never leave. Zoe sat quietly until Mr. Kincaid exited the box, then pulled the hood of her domino over her bright curls. Beneath the domino she wore a simple muslin gown, one that would come off easily, due to the stitches she had loosened, if someone attempted to disrobe her, which she was determined someone would.

And now it was time for her rendezvous with a rakehell.

She slipped out of the box into the Grove, a square enclosed by Vauxhall's principal walks, or colonnades, and the garden's western wall. Each colonnade was lined with supper boxes, and lighted by festoons of shimmering lamps hung among the boughs, twinkling suns and stars and constellations in shades of gold and green, red and blue. In the center stood a temple, where the orchestra was housed.

The musicians struck up another selection. Zoe hurried from the Grove into a colonnade, mingling easily among the many people promenading there.

Vauxhall was crowded on this as every summer evening. Revelers strolled in all directions along the tree-lined gravel thoroughfares: the Grand Walk, a stately avenue of elms nine hundred feet long and thirty feet wide; the South Walk, spanned by three triumphal arches which were a part of a realistic painting of the Ruins of Palmyra; the Grand Cross Walk, which ran through the garden at right angles to these. Even the lesser pathways boasted exotic faux minarets and splashing waterfalls; pavilions, lodges, groves, grottoes, lawns and shadowy columned ways. If a person didn't know what she was about, she could become quite lost.

Zoe knew precisely what she was about. She had discovered at an early age that servants could almost always be bribed.

How annoying, that the Black Baron should turn up at Moxley's when she wasn't there to greet him. Zoe had accused Mina of taking advantage of the opportunity to secure his attentions for herself. Mina had in turn aired her opinion of Zoe's recent actions regarding George Eames and Lady Anne. At the conclusion of this heated interaction, Zoe had claimed a sick headache and retired to her room and from there escaped the house.

Astonishing, how certain people couldn't see beyond the noses on their face.

Like the gamesters who frequented Moxley's, who got so caught up in gambling frenzy that they played beyond their means and could not stay the course; and wound up purse-pinched, without a feather to fly with, run quite off their legs.

Zoe was immune to gambling fever. Serving as the basis for a wager left a person with a distaste for games of chance.

Still, the business was fascinating, as were all the ways in which desperate gamblers tried to cheat Dame Fortune. At Zoe's request, Samson had explained up-hills, false dice which ran high, and down-hills, their opposite; the corner- and the middle-bend and how to slip the cards; showed her the trick of sauter le coupe, by which a card placed in the middle of the pack was imperceptibly transferred to the bottom or the top. She had learned to play Quinze, a game of cards in which the winner was he who counted fifteen, or nearest to that number, in all the points of his hand; as well as rouge et noir, wherein the winning total ranged between thirty and forty points; had even tried her hand at faro, and learned about coppering a debt, and the dealer had generously demonstrated how to make the cards climb like a ladder up her arm.

Now it was Zoe's turn to gamble. If fair play did not serve her, she would fuzz the deck.

Paolo had wagered her virtue. It was only fitting that she should cuckold him in return.

A gloomy avenue of trees led to the hermit's dwelling. Zoe didn't pause to admire the scenery, which included mountains, precipices and valleys, and a large cat with fiery eyes, all worked in canvas and pasteboard; didn't wait for the old white-bearded man to emerge from his pasteboard ravine and ask her his few questions, after which he would retire and then return carrying the Future, carefully copied out on cream-colored paper, in his arms.

Zoe didn't care to discover what her future held.

She paused to savor the scented night air. The dark leafy background, the nightingales' sweet song, the fountain bubbling nearby, the strains of the roving wind players called harmonie—

Masked ladies of dubious repute dawdled along these dark and lesser travelled paths. Scoundrels lurked in wait for unwary prey. Zoe glanced around to make sure she was unobserved, ducked into a thicket of trees, and stripped off a stocking. When she left the thicket, she stepped up her pace.

The path opened onto one of the long colonnades. Zoe wove her way among the revelers who were strolling, dancing, lounging in supper boxes spaced out at intervals. She found the Black Baron in a box with a painting of *The Rake's Progress* on the back wall. He sprawled in a chair, with a female on his lap.

If that female was virtuous, Zoe would eat her domino.

Chapter Fifteen

Lord Quinton was enjoying himself — as much as Lord Quinton ever enjoyed himself – alongside several like-minded reprobates who met regularly at Vauxhall, there to sit around drinking and trading tales of their most recent depravities, some of which were made up from whole cloth, and others of which were not.

One had sold the use of his wife's body to his chief creditor. Another was the subject of a recent ribald article in the *Morning Post*. A third was relating how he had preached naked to a crowd from an alehouse balcony in Covent Garden when a stranger entered the box and approached Quin. "I was asked to tell you, guv, that a prime bit of muslin desires a private word." He held out a silk stocking, and added that the ladybird was waiting in yon dark copse of trees.

Quin hesitated. The copse lay some distance away. He would be obliged to get up and walk.

The Black Baron was unaccustomed to putting forth so much effort. However, he was in excellent spirits due to the ingestion of a double dose of laudanum and a vast amount of Arrack punch, a potent mixture of grains of the benjamin flower mixed with rum. Too, the stocking was silk, knitted in a lacy openwork stitch, and suggestive of warm, willing female. Quin hadn't indulged in any notable depravity of his own for the past several days.

Oh, why not? He stuck the stocking in his pocket and walked — or more correctly, staggered — along the colonnade. An astonishing number of lamps twisted and twinkled and whirled about among the trees, like a fireworks display.

Fireworks, or fairy lights. Quin hadn't believed in fairies even as a child. Certainly he didn't believe them now. Yet, in this moment, looking at the illuminations, he had no sure sense of what was and wasn't real.

Quin wondered much arrack punch he'd drunk. This was a rhetorical sort of musing, merely. He truly didn't care.

He stumbled into the copse, placed a steadying hand on the trunk of an ancient elm. Enough light shone in among the trees that he could see the slight figure that waited there.

She threw back her hood. Red-gold curls, sapphire eyes—

"Damnation," muttered Quin.

Lord Quinton, decided Zoe, had again imbibed more than was wise. He stood before her, gently weaving. His dark hair was disordered, as was his cravat, probably from having females sitting on his lap.

He was the most wicked of all the wicked. It made a person palpitate to think of the countless lips he had kissed, the breasts he had caressed.

Or it should have made a person palpitate. That it did not might be because the man had compared her to a carp.

Zoe edged closer. She *would* experience passion — whatever he chose to call it — at the Black Baron's expert hands.

His eyes were half-closed. Was the wretch falling asleep? "You are burnt to the socket," Zoe said disapprovingly. "It is no wonder, the life you lead."

Quin left off squinting in an attempt to bring the evil fairy into focus or, even better, make her disappear. "What if I am? Why should I explain myself to you?"

Zoe folded her arms. "I don't know why *you* should be cross. I've been put to a great deal of trouble on your behalf. May I remind you that you left me to pay the reckoning?"

Ah yes, he had abandoned her at the coffeehouse. Quin realized now that he should have kept on going, until he was well away from town.

He slipped slightly sideways, and the lights resumed their dancing. Quin braced himself more securely against the tree trunk. "You wanted the pleasure of my company. It seemed only fair that you should pay the shot."

"It was a shabby way to treat a woman prepared to give you her all." Zoe shrugged out of her domino and let it fall to the ground.

The Loversall Novellas

If ever a man needed his wits about him, Lord Quinton did so now. He attempted to speak clearly. "I don't want your all. I don't want you *at* all. I wouldn't want you if I hadn't had a doxy for a week and you showed up naked at my door."

Zoe overlooked this fine example of a gentleman saying, as gentlemen so often did, something he didn't mean. She surveyed him critically. "I have heard that excessive drink has a debilitating effect on the, um, masculine extremity."

Was she asking what he thought she was? "My extremity is not the least debilitated," Quin replied.

"I am glad to hear it." Zoe tugged discreetly at one of her weakened seams. "You need not fear for my sensibilities. I understand how these matters are conducted — how could I not, when from my cradle Beau has conducted his right under my nose? I promise I shan't hang on your sleeve."

She *was* hanging on his sleeve, Quin realized. He tried to shake her off.

Zoe felt Lord Quinton tremble. Clearly he was not as immune to her charms as he would have her believe. "I shan't allow you to behave as if there is nothing between us," she murmured, and moved closer still.

This damnable female must be even boskier than he was. She disregarded everything he said. Gingerly Quin grasped her shoulders, so that he might move her aside. "Even if I wished to — which I most definitely do not — I could not seduce you. I gave your cousin my word."

Zoe narrowed her eyes. "You are a rakehell. No one expects a rakehell to keep his word."

At the moment, being a rakehell seemed a great deal more trouble than it was worth. "I do," said Quin.

"Mina, always Mina!" snapped Zoe. "What does she have that I do not?"

Mina had had Quin, or so she claimed. A pity he couldn't recall the event. "She has a pleasant personality. A giving nature. No tendency toward romantical high flights. Shall I go on?"

Zoe's lips tightened. Her nostrils flared. Any member of her family would have recognized these ominous signs.

Lord Quinton was not a member of her family. He was astonished when she kicked him in the shin.

He cursed and released her. Zoe flew at him, fingers extended as if to scratch out his eyes. Quin caught her by the wrists. So potent was her fury, and so unsure his balance, that they fell together to the ground. Grunts and groans and curses — the sound of tearing fabric — they rolled one way and the other, her body atop his, and then his body atop hers, Zoe struggling for dominance, Quin struggling to keep the more vulnerable portions of his person from permanent harm.

Was she trying to *kiss* him? He jerked his head away. Zoe grabbed his hair and yanked it back. Quin's hand slid across smooth, bare skin. Where was her gown? Her chemise? Was she wearing no stays?

She was not. His hand encountered a breast. Quin wanted no part of it, or her, but the wench had wrapped herself around him like a Burmese python and refused to be unwound, and why the deuce would she think he wanted her tongue stuck in his ear?

He heard voices, coming closer. Quin stopped struggling and lay still. Zoe sprawled atop him, breathing heavily on his spittle-dampened skin.

She raised her head. Curious spectators crowded the copse. "Well, isn't this delicious!" cried one, a woman. "The Black Baron and Zoe Loversall."

Chapter Sixteen

The morning room at Moxley House felt different after dark, colder and less welcoming; or perhaps, reflected Mina, it was merely her mood. She had been in the gaming suite, conversing with a gentleman who'd paused by the E.O. table to watch the female elbow-shaker and went down to the tune of five hundred yellow boys in a surprisingly short time, when alerted by Samson that another crisis had occurred. Mina was tired of crises, of soothing luckless gamesters and worrying about being hauled before a magistrate.

Sometimes she wished she had never met Moxley. For that matter, she sometimes wished she'd never met Peebles, Chickester, Olmstead, and Ward.

From her place on the sofa, she watched Beau pace the floor. Devon stood at the window, and Quin by the fireplace. Zoe, wrapped in a domino, was fidgeting with the inkwell on the writing desk.

Beau paused in his pacing to glare at Lord Quinton. "I should draw your cork."

"I wouldn't advise trying," the baron responded. "Unless you want your pretty face rearranged. Since I first met your damned daughter, I have been nearly sober on more occasions than in the previous several years combined."

Beau glared. "My daughter was caught in a compromising position, damn you. Her reputation is besmirched."

"And why the deuce should I care?" inquired Quin.

"Well!" cried Zoe, simultaneously pleased that she'd caused a scandal, and displeased that she'd been ruined without deriving any pleasure from the act. "That is very callous, sir."

"Of course it is callous," agreed Lord Quinton. "London's most wicked rakehell, remember? What did you expect?"

"So much for keeping Zoe's presence here a secret," sighed Mina. "Come daybreak, all London will be enjoying the tale of her reappearance, in such a condition, and with the infamous Black Baron. How *could* you, Zoe?"

Zoe drew the domino tighter about her. "I was overwhelmed with passion. You wouldn't understand."

Mina experienced a passionate desire to box Zoe's ears. She studied her hands.

"What's done is done," Beau interjected, correctly interpreting the expression on Mina's face. "We must decide what to do next. Zoe is already married, so she can't marry Quin."

"I may also be married," Quin remarked.

"If you are married, where is your wife?" demanded Zoe.

Quin propped himself against the mantelpiece. "I have no idea."

Devon crossed the room, sat on the sofa beside Mina. She regarded him without favor. "What were you thinking, to take Zoe to Vauxhall?"

"You may not believe this, but I was trying to help. She told me you would worry if she went there alone."

Mina looked skeptical.

Beau had overheard this conversation. "You *meant* to encounter Quin?" he demanded of Zoe.

"To waylay me, you mean," said Quin. "Had I known she was going to be at Vauxhall, I wouldn't have gone near the place."

"She slipped away," Devon continued. "By the time I found her, the damage was already done."

"Why is no one concerned about my reputation?" inquired Quin. "Caught *in flagrante delicto*, by God."

"Like the greenest gapeseed," said Beau, momentarily distracted. "You may never live it down."

Devon wasn't feeling sympathetic, having seen a caricature of himself in a shop window earlier that day. "At least nobody's saying you have an astonishing number of byblows hidden around town."

"Some rakehells you are," muttered Zoe. "As concerned about your reputations as any debutante."

Samson interrupted, bearing a bottle of brandy and several glasses. Quin appropriated the bottle and drank.

He lowered it and squinted. Either a goat had just ambled through the door, or he was not nearly as sober as he'd thought.

"This is Romeo," explained Mina. "He has learned to unfasten the kitchen latch."

"Ah," said Quin, as bits of memory coalesced. "Wherefore art thou..."

Zoe's nostrils quivered. Romeo was prodigious pungent in so confined a space.

Romeo's nostrils quivered also. A symphony of tantalizing scents emanated from the small woman's cloak. He moved closer to investigate.

She backed away, and came up hard against the desk. Romeo followed, snuffled at the fabric, bit down on an edge, and tugged. Zoe resisted. Romeo tugged all the harder. She jerked the cloak away. Romeo eyed her retreating figure, lowered his head, and charged.

"Oh, Lord," said Mina. The gentlemen stared.

Caught off-balance, Zoe stumbled, fell to her hands and knees. Romeo butted her upthrust derriere. Zoe was sent sprawling. She hung on grimly to the cloak. Romeo caught the fabric between his strong teeth and spun her in a circle until, dizzy, she let go. He retreated, dragging his prize. Zoe pushed her hair out of her eyes and climbed slowly to her feet.

Beau took in his daughter's gown, which was barely held together with a few threads here and there, leaving a great deal of creamy flesh exposed. "Where is your other stocking?" he inquired.

Quin thrust his hand into his pocket, pulled out the article in question. "A fellow brought it to me. Said a ladybird was wishful of a private word."

Some papas might have found this explanation lacking. Beau, however, had been gifted with innumerable silk stockings in the course of his career. He frowned, stuck by the realization that he'd been sent no stockings for some time. Samson, meantime, thwacked Romeo on the head, relieved him of the cloak, handed it to Zoe, and led the goat away.

Beau snatched the stocking from Quin's hand. "Don't bother trying to talk your way out of this, damn you. You'll meet me at dawn."

"No," objected Quin. "I'll *not* meet you at dawn. If I met you at dawn, I'd have to kill you. If I kill you, I'll be stuck with your daughter. I'd rather be dead."

The Black Baron would rather be dead, would he? Zoe picked up the inkwell and hurled it at the wall. The desk chair followed. Then she kicked the long case clock. These measures having failed to ease her temper, she set to screeching, and drummed her hands against the wall.

Her face turned bright red. She let out one last howl, and held her breath.

Devon watched this display with alarmed fascination. "You're not concerned?" he asked Beau.

Beau tossed the stocking on a table. "She'll either start breathing again, or she won't."

"We Loversalls are victims of our tumultuous passions," Mina explained.

"Not even for you," said Mr. Kincaid, "will I seduce that tiresome little twit."

Lord Quinton raised the brandy bottle, discovered it was empty, wondered if Samson could bring another without also bringing the goat.

A twit, was she? Zoe inhaled, crossed her arms beneath her bosom, and accused Mina of having designs on the Black Baron herself.

"Me?" said Mina, startled.

"Do you?" inquired Quin.

Mina shot him a severe glance. "Before Quin showed up at Moxley's, we hadn't spoken in years."

Lord Quinton contemplated the empty bottle. "I consider conversation vastly overrated, myself."

Zoe pulled her cloak more tightly around her. "You seem to think highly of Cousin Wilhelmina still, even if she's not rigidly virtuous, though I'm beginning to suspect that virtue business was a hum."

"Rigidly virtuous?" Mina was confused.

Quin set down the bottle. "I was prepared to make an exception in Mina's case. I even told your cousin I wouldn't debauch you if she allowed me to debauch her instead."

"And *did* you debauch her?" Zoe asked.

All eyes fixed on Lord Quinton. With dignity, he said, "A gentleman doesn't debauch and tell."

"*Perdio!* You aren't supposed to be a gentleman!" cried Zoe.

The Loversall Novellas

"Whatever Lord Quinton did or didn't do," Mina interrupted, "has no bearing on the present case."

Zoe scowled at Devon. "If *you* are going to debauch Mina, you should do it soon, before you're both too old."

It occurred to Beau that if he was going to shoot someone, it should probably be his daughter. He grasped her arm. "That's enough. Have your bags packed. You're coming with me."

Zoe struggled to break his grip. "Where?"

Beau responded, grimly, "You expressed a desire to enter a nunnery."

Quin detached himself from the mantle. The events of the past several hours had reminded him why he preferred to pass his time in the steamier haunts of London, amongst thieves and other low-lifes. "What an excellent idea."

Mina rose, held out her hand. "I am so sorry. This is my fault. I told Zoe she should avoid you."

Quin smiled at her. "Like the plague, I believe you said. Was I so bad?"

The Black Baron's smile was rare, and definitely sinful, but also a poignant reminder of the man he once had been. Mina replied, for his ears only, "You were very bad indeed, and it was very good."

Quin raised her hand to his lips. "You set my mind at ease."

Chapter Seventeen

The next day dawned, to Mina's thinking, far too soon. It found her closeted with Zoe and Nell in the morning room.

"I'm not a tiresome little twit," repeated Zoe, for what seemed the millionth time. "I'm not, I'm not, I'm not!"

"Twit!" echoed Nell, who was embarked upon an exploration of the chamber, and currently attempting to climb the writing desk. At least she could not overturn the inkpot. Zoe had already done that.

Merely watching Nell exhausted Mina. The child was a perpetual motion machine. Mina gave up all effort at containing her, and collapsed into a chair.

Zoe made a face at Nell. "And *you* are an odious brat."

Nell thrust out her lower lip and echoed, "Brat!"

Pot, meet kettle, Mina thought. Zoe's bags were packed. All that remained was for Beau to return and take his daughter away.

Where he meant to take her, Mina neither knew nor cared.

Figg tapped on the door. He did not announce Beau, however, but Mr. Eames.

George entered the room. Accompanying him were a stout gentleman in his middle years, with luxurious side whiskers and thinning russet hair; and a younger gentleman, obviously related, whose sartorial splendor — light brown swallowtail coat with lapped pockets and gigot sleeves; a violet waistcoat; nankeen pantaloons buttoned at the ankle with two gold buttons; yellow stockings with large violet clocks; shoes with buckles of polished cut steel — dazzled the eye.

Mina set down her chocolate cup. "Abercorn!" she said. Nell saw him at the same time. "Da! Da, da, da, da, da!"

The younger gentleman scooped her up. "Here's my Nell."

The elder Abercorn started. "Her name is Eleanor? In honor of your ma? She resembles her, by God."

"It is, and she does," replied his son. "As you would know had you not refused to set eyes on the child."

The elder man was still staring. He extended a cautious hand. Recognizing an easy mark, Nell grabbed his thumb and grinned.

"Junior and Senior have come to an agreement," George explained to Mina. "His maternal grandmother wants the keeping of the girl."

Within the next few moments, Mina was relieved of Nell and presented with five thousand pounds. She couldn't say which she appreciated more.

The Abercorns departed. Mr. Eames remained. "Lady Anne has agreed to marry me," he said, with a dark glance at Zoe. "She believes it the only way to save me from your cousin's fell designs."

"And her father?" Mina asked.

"Sir Ian was amenable, once I pointed out the Stuart bloodlines are not as unsullied as he would like the world to believe."

"Blackmail!" Zoe had been silent far too long. "How clever you are."

"I am a solicitor," George responded coolly. "This is what solicitors do."

After all her efforts, the ungrateful wretch offered her not a single word of thanks! Zoe plopped down on the sofa.

"Would you care for chocolate?" asked Mina. "Coffee? Tea?"

Zoe muttered, "I don't see why he doesn't just leave."

George eyed the long case clock. "My business here isn't done."

Figg returned. "The Conte de Borghini and Signore Cesare Rizzoto."

"You cad! You bounder! You—" Zoe leapt to her feet. She glared first at Mr. Eames, and then at the two gentlemen who stepped through the door.

They were a study in contrasts, one slender and fair, with ivory skin and amber eyes and golden hair; the other squat and swarthy, with thick black curls and a magnificently Roman nose. Paolo was handsome as Adonis. Cesare was not.

Moreover, Cesare smelled of garlic. Zoe announced, "I won't go home."

Her spouse glowered. "Very well."

Zoe glowered back at him. "You'll give me a divorce?"

"There will be no divorce," replied Paolo. "Nor will I murder you, though it is a great temptation. An annulment can be arranged."

"An annulment?"

"On the grounds our marriage was never consummated."

Not consummated? Zoe was horrified. She hadn't managed to be despoiled — she hadn't even managed to be kissed! And now the world would think even her husband hadn't cared to bed her. "It's not true!" she wailed.

"Just consider," offered Mina. "You will be the first Loversall to ever be annulled."

Zoe picked up a pillow from the sofa and flung it at her cousin. Mina caught the pillow and set it safely aside.

Cesare Rizzoto stepped forward. "*Abbastanza!* I have won a wager. A man of honor pays his debts," he said, in heavily accented tones.

"I am not a man!" retorted Zoe. "And Paolo is no more honorable than that—" She looked wildly around her. "Than that clock! Anyway, you are too late. I am ruined. You should go away."

"I do not believe you." Cesare took another step. "And I am resolved to have you, even if the bloom is off the rose."

"Bloom?" echoed Mina.

"Bloom," repeated Cesare, with a dramatic gesture of his hands. "As when a blossom first opens, before the petals begin to wither and fall away."

"I beg your pardon!" interrupted Zoe, indignantly. "My petals are intact."

"*Perfetto.*" Had he a moustache, Cesare would have twirled its tips. "You will come with me and—"

"No!" said Zoe. "I won't."

Cesare glanced at Paolo, who shrugged. "Ah, but you will. The husband says do this, and the wife obeys."

"Not in this instance, I think," George put in. "If I may offer a word of advice, a wise man would write off his loss."

"Ah, you English," sneered Signore Rizzoto. "You do not understand the fever in the blood. When first I saw *la bella donna*, I vowed that I would have her. And now—" He snapped his fingers. "Now she is mine."

Zoe also glanced at Paolo, who lounged in the doorway, brooding. "I shall enter a nunnery!"

George remarked to Mina, "Would the nuns have her, do you think?"

"Certainly you may go to a nunnery," said Cesare. "After I have had my way with you." He advanced.

Zoe reached for another pillow. A poor thing with which to defend oneself, admittedly, but all that lay within reach. She lifted the pillow — and found beneath it the pistol Mina had placed there, days ago. Zoe snatched up the gun, pulled back one of the hammers, closed her eyes, and fired.

The gunshot briefly deafened her. When her ears stopped ringing, Zoe heard a gasp — that had been Mina; and a bit-off exclamation — Mr. Eames, she thought; and *"Diavolo!"* uttered in astonished tones.

Zoe opened her eyes. Cesare remained upright, his dark complexion turned chalk-white. Paolo sprawled on the carpet, clutching his left thigh.

His bleeding left thigh. Zoe cried, "I wasn't aiming at you!"

"It's only a flesh wound," George soothed a horrified Mina. He raised his voice. "I am uncertain how matters stand in Italy, but in this country it is illegal for a wife to shoot her husband. As your solicitor, I advise you—"

"You advise him nothing!" Zoe dropped to her knees beside Paolo, pulled off his cravat, and wrapped it tightly around his bleeding leg.

He stared at her. "You have shot me, *cara*, and with my own gun. No one has ever shot me before. You should put down the gun before you shoot me again."

Zoe lowered the weapon. "I didn't mean to shoot you. Al-though I *should* have shot you! You wagered me at play."

"I didn't mean to wager you," protested Paolo. "I'd taken too much to drink. Matters got out of hand. As I would have explained, had you not run away."

"What do gentlemen find so alluring about drunkenness?" Zoe inquired. "Or gambling, for that matter? It quite blights one's spirits to hear them talking about being on the rocks and bleeding very freely and threatening to blow out their brains. In case you don't know it, Cesare tried many times to persuade me to be unfaithful. I refused."

Cesare was fast recovering from his shock. He pounded his fist on his chest. "No one refuses Cesare Rizzoto!"

"*Cretino!*" Zoe raised the pistol. "If you don't go away, I will also shoot you."

The Loversall Novellas

Mina rang for her servants. "Spoilsport," muttered Mr. Eames. Nonetheless, he suggested it was time Mr. Rizzoto took his leave. Mr. Rizzoto disagreed. Samson and the footmen removed him, forcibly, from the premises.

Zoe and the Conte ignored these distractions. They were staring deep into each other's eyes. "I have perhaps behaved a little badly," Zoe admitted. "I was devastated to discover my true love is a toad."

Paolo grasped her hand. "Am I?"

Zoe pouted prettily. "Only a toad would have lost me to Cesare."

"*Si, si!* Admittedly I am a toad. A *cazzone*. But, *carissima* , am I your true love?"

Zoe was encouraged by the way he clutched her. "I thought you were. But then—"

"Because," Paolo interrupted, "I see now that you are mine. I realized it when you shot me. *Naturalmente,* I should have understood before, but—"

"But you are very spoiled!" cried Zoe. "I perfectly understand. And you were annoyed that I had run away."

"No one has ever run away from me before," agreed Paolo. "It angered me."

Mina said, "Should we do something?"

Suggested George, "Shoot them both?"

"I have not truly been ruined," admitted Zoe, with lowered lashes and a becoming blush. "I tried to be, but no one would oblige. It is for the best, because—" She awarded Paolo her most melting glance. "The person I truly wish to explore the baser side of my nature with is you."

Paolo looked both intrigued and appalled. "*Caspita!* One does not do that sort of thing with one's wife."

"If one's wife is a Loversall, one does." Zoe leaned closer, until mere inches separated them, and her soft breasts pressed against his arm, and her sweet perfume stirred his senses. She whispered a naughty suggestion. "*Per favore?*"

Beau walked into the room then, to find his daughter embracing her estranged spouse, who wore a bloody cravat wrapped around his thigh. "*Now* what the devil?" he wearily inquired.

Chapter Eighteen

Mina was alone in the morning room, save for Grace the cat, who crept out from beneath the sofa to curl up in her lap. Beau had departed, along with Zoe and her Conte. Mr. Eames had taken his leave also, and gone to share these latest developments with his Lady Anne.

Mina surveyed the bloodstained carpet, the ink-stained wall. She was staring blankly into space when Figg appeared in the doorway and announced, "Mr. Kincaid."

Devon strolled into the room, carelessly elegant in riding coat, breeches, and top boots. A casual observer might not have noticed the weary lines around his hazel eyes.

Mina was not a casual observer. "Loversalls cannot help our bad behavior. It is in our blood."

"Is that an apology?" He glanced cautiously around. "Has Zoe really gone?"

"She's gone, but not with Beau. The Conte set out for London immediately upon discovering his wife had fled. Apparently — astonishing notion — he knows how she thinks. Meanwhile Mr. Eames had sent word that Zoe was here." Mina related the events that had taken place earlier, including George's suggestion Mr. Rizzoto be bought off to ensure he would trouble them no more.

Devon did not comment. Mina remained uncertain how he felt. "You said Zoe was lovely. I thought you wanted her."

He picked up the empty inkwell. "I took Zoe driving in an attempt to annoy you. Or to please you. Or both. You had just left me to go and talk to Quin. No one seeing the two of you together could doubt there was something between you once."

"It's true that I'm not rigidly virtuous," Mina admitted. "And if you had intrigued with Zoe, I would have withdrawn from the world myself."

"She is too young. Too slender. Too everything." Devon set down the inkwell. "*Did* Quin debauch you?"

"Then or now?"

"Point taken. I've been a bloody fool. But in my defense, you were always getting married, and never seemed to either want or need my company."

Mina put Grace aside, rose and moved to the window. "I am an excellent actress. A woman has to be, when she's had as many husbands as I've had. As for Quin, you and I had quarreled. I feared Beau had told you— Well."

"You feared Beau had told me what?"

"That I wish to have an affaire."

Devon also moved toward the window. "You wish to have an affaire with Beau?"

"Don't act the innocent. Beau realized I wish to have an affaire with you." She shrugged. "I am usually rather more subtle about such matters, but there it is."

He rested his hands on her shoulders. "I came here today to try and persuade you to gamble one last time."

Mina leaned back against him. "This is truly terrifying. I find myself dithering like the greenest girl. And then I remind myself that you are faithless, and that I don't want my heart broke."

"I'm not the one who's wed five times." His breath was warm against her cheek. "I understood everyone but Peebles. He was almost thrice your age."

Mina turned to face him. "I was trying to change my luck."

"You of all people should realize that one must play the cards one's dealt." Devon caught her hand in his. He had removed his gloves.

"Is that what you're doing?" she murmured. "Playing the cards you were dealt?"

He trailed his thumb along her wrist; clasped her fingers, kissed the tips and then the knuckles; pressed his lips against her palm. "I am."

Truly, thought Mina, this business was much simpler when no troublesome emotions were involved. Simpler, and far less profound. She abandoned both finesse and common sense and threaded her fingers though Devon's thick hair; kissed his chin, his jaw, his earlobe, and finally his mouth. Devon pulled her hard against his body and kissed her back, deeply and so thoroughly that her senses spun.

Her hands slid over his arms, his shoulders, found their way beneath his jacket. Devon picked her up, carried her across the room and tumbled her atop him on the sofa. Grace leapt hastily aside.

Mina yanked on his shirt, pulled it free from the waistband of his breeches. Devon laughed and then groaned as she raked her nails across his back.

His mouth claimed hers again. Pleasure curled through Mina as he explored her with his lips, tasted the curve of her cheek, the pulse-point in her throat, then moved lower, and lower still while his hands — oh, those skillful hands — stroked down her side to the swell of waist and hip and—

Mina gasped, "Maybe we should continue this upstairs."

Devon drew back. "Reservations, my sweet?"

"We forgot to lock—"

The door swung open. Romeo ambled into the room. Dangling from his jaws were the remnants of a high-crowned beaver hat.

Devon rose, held out his hand to Mina. She stayed seated on the sofa. "Are you certain, Dev? I have believed for some time that I must love you, but—"

She was tall and lush and tousled from his kisses. Devon had never seen a more glorious sight. "I am glad to hear it, because I have believed for some time that I must love you too." Horrified, he saw a teardrop brim in her blue eyes, trickle slowly down her cheek. "Don't weep, my darling. I promise I won't break your heart."

"It's not that!" cried Mina, as a second tear followed the first. "Must I remind you: Moxley, Olmstead, Chickester, Peebles, Ward? People say I am to blame. I couldn't bear to lose you, too."

Devon offered her his handkerchief. "Moxley ate spoiled oysters, Olmstead came to grief beneath the hoofs of a half-broke horse, Chickester swallowed a fatal dose of laudanum after unsuccessfully speculating on the Stock Exchange, Ward overturned his carriage driving at a breakneck speed along the Bath Road. I suppose you may be fairly said to have some responsibility for Peebles succumbing to a spasm of the heart; having married a gentleman so elderly, you probably should have tried to dissuade him from engaging in amatory acrobatics. However, that also was his choice. People say a great many excessively stupid things, my sweet peagoose. You are not the kiss of death."

Mina was immensely cheered, whether by his comments or his endearments she couldn't say. She took the handkerchief and dabbed at her nose. "I have asked Mr. Eames to find a buyer for Moxley's. I want to be well away before some other member of my family decides to take refuge here."

Devon grasped her hands and drew her to her feet. "Where will you go?"

Mina's heart beat faster. "I had thought that I might travel, but I do not care to encounter Zoe, which rules out Italy and France. Perhaps I will retire to the country, where Romeo may have sufficient room to forage, and a female goat or two for company."

Devon glanced at the goat, which had ingested not only his hat but his cast-off leather gloves and was currently looking about for a postprandial snack. "I concede, my darling. You have brought me to my knees."

"Your knees, is it?"

"I am quite at Point Non Plus."

"And that means?"

"I own a home in the country." Ruefully, he smiled. "I also own a herd of goats."

Epilogue

Moxley's was doing a brisk business. The supper room was crowded. Lord Quinton set aside the remnants of his pickled salmon, swallowed the last of his iced champagne.

He strolled through the rooms, eyeing the thick carpets and marble fireplaces, the rich upholstery and comfortable furnishings; listening to the rattle of the dice, the clatter of the roulette wheel and ball, the murmurs of players and croupiers. Faro, E.O., hazard, rouge et noir— Punters gathered around the tables, laying stakes against the bank. The private alcoves were filled. Overseeing the evening's business were Samson and his sharp-eyed guards.

Quin paused by the E.O. table, mentally tallied the piles of markers by the bank. He had frequented hells beyond counting without considering, for example, the astronomical cost of wax candles and green peas.

He left the gaming suite behind and entered the private portion of the house. In the morning room, he poured himself a liberal splash of brandy from a decanter sitting on the desk.

The chamber still stank faintly of goat.

The items Mrs. Moxley had held in pawn were no longer on the premises. The umbrella had been redeemed by its owner, the watches and rings sold.

Though their mistress had departed, the household staff remained. As did the gaming room employees, among them a number of virtuous young women ripe to be introduced to depravity.

Samson had sternly informed Quin that the females were off-limits. Quin had suggested Samson also inform them.

Hazard was a game well named. It made a man or undid him in the twinkling of an eye. George Eames had approached Quin one evening when he was drunk as a wheelbarrow and playing for high stakes. Owning a gaming hell, Mr. Eames suggested, was an excellent way to lose a fortune. Or to gain one, or both. That Lord Quinton should purchase Moxley's, George informed him, had been Mina's idea.

All London was still reeling. Following a whirlwind courtship during which both parties conducted themselves in an outrageously moonstruck manner, Mina Loversall-

Chickester-Ward-Olmstead-Peebles-Moxley had added Kincaid to her string of names.

Quin had not yet decided if Mina had done him a favor, or the opposite, in saddling him with Moxley's. However, one thing was clear: whether or not the Contessa de Borghini contrived to continue the Loversall tradition, her cousin was engaged in loving fully, with complete abandon, and great style.

Quin

Chapter One

Play was deep at Moxley House, and the stakes were high. Gamblers flocked to try their luck at hazard, faro, rouge et noir, E.O; to discover what changes the new owner had put into effect (none, to date); and to speculate upon how much time would pass before he abandoned the place altogether, the gentleman not known for sustained interest in anyone or anything.

That new owner stood, just now, in the supper room, which was fitted out with crystal chandeliers and a thick carpet, small tables set with silver and fine china and pristine linen cloths. The patrons were feasting on boiled fowl with oyster sauce, washed down with liberal amounts of champagne.

Lord Quinton was, as usual, dressed in black. He was a devastatingly handsome man in (or so the ladies said) a deliciously diabolic way, with black hair worn unfashionably long and eyes as dark as his transgressions, ascetic features stamped with dissipation and ennui. No less memorable was the gentleman with whom he was engaged in conversation (or rather, to whom he was listening, with a disinterested expression), who was athletic of figure and angelic of feature, with red-gold hair and sapphire eyes.

The Black Baron was the most wicked rakehell in all of London. His companion was one of the legendarily libidinous Loversalls.

Quin led the way into the next chamber, where amber-eyed Daphne was casting the dice at hazard. If Daphne nicked, or called her main, the house would win the stake.

Beau raised his voice to be heard above the gamesters crowded round the green baize table. "A face that could launch a thousand ships. A mouth made for sin. A body—" His hands sketched a sinuous shape in the air. "I can't say when I've been so taken with a female."

"I can't say when you haven't been," Quin responded drily. Beau maintained a stable of sweethearts, most notable among them the languishing Mrs. Ormsby and the volatile Mrs. Thwaite, which in no way deterred him from acquiring a new *petite amie* approximately every other week. "Last month, it was that pretty equestrienne who performed bareback at Astley's. You vowed she had the most neatly turned ankles you had ever seen."

Beau smiled in reminiscence. The artiste's name had been Nanette, her specialty a rousing variation on the traditional handstand. However, Nanette's ankles could not compete with the fair face and lips, etcetera, of Miss Mary Fletcher, newly employed at the Opera House further down the street, and so he said.

Quin turned a deaf and not entirely sober ear to these renewed rhapsodies.

Indeed, Lord Quinton hadn't been entirely sober since he took over the hell. Truth be told, he hadn't been entirely sober for a long time before that. Idly, he wondered when he *had* last been sober. After a brief cogitation, he gave up the attempt.

The world, in Quin's opinion, was a much more pleasant place when viewed through a narcotic haze.

He raised his glass, and found it empty. A female attendant hurried forward with decanter in hand.

Quin sipped his whiskey. There were distinct advantages to owning a gaming hell, one being that a man could lose a fortune without leaving his house. Though Quin had not thus far managed to rid himself of a farthing, he was not discouraged. His luck would change.

Of this much he was certain, sober or no. Dame Fortune was a fickle bitch.

He entered the third chamber, accompanied by Beau, who continued to blather on about Miss Fletcher, annoying as a buzzing gnat. The noise level was higher here. Dice rattled, the E.O. ball clattered, the players conversed among themselves while the dealers announced results and called for wagers to be made anew.

Gamblers were gathered around a faro table covered with green baize cloth. Behind the table stood the banker, statuesque brunette Adele. In an honest faro game, the punter's chances were slightly more than even of coming out ahead. On the other side of the room, the E.O. table was being set in motion by russet-haired Rosamond. The odds were less inclined to favor the players gathered there, intent on the turn of the table, or alternately admiring Rosamond's décolletage. Moxley's employed more women than any other London hell.

Quin grew weary of Beau's continued exaltations. "So tumble her," he said.

Beau stared in astonishment. "Are you grown so jaded that you no longer savor the excitement of the chase?"

Quin considered the question. He could not recall when he had last embarked upon a pursuit. More often than not, females pursued him. Recently he had been waylaid and damn near ravished at Vauxhall by a young woman determined to be divested of her virtue. The memory was so unpleasant that he drained his glass.

"Caught *in flagrante delicto*," said Beau, who had an unnerving — and annoying — ability to sometimes guess a person's thoughts. "Like the most callow youth. You must redeem your reputation. If you will take my advice—"

Quin regarded him with faint curiosity. "Why should I?"

"Because I am seven-and-forty, whereas you are only thirty-five. And you remind me of myself at your age."

Quin was briefly appalled by the suggestion he might spend his dotage ogling opera dancers' ankles. However, at his current rate of dissipation dotage was not likely to be achieved. He glanced into one of the private alcoves that opened off this chamber, where a disgruntled exclamation indicated that another unfortunate transaction (from the player's point of view) had just taken place.

The front room was dominated by the rouge et noir table, which was marked with two red and black diamond-shaped spots on which the players placed their stakes. On either side a croupier waited with rake in hand, her task to watch the cards and gather in the money for the bank. A passing attendant noted and replenished Quin's empty glass.

As the banker called *'Le rouge perd!'* indicating that the first card was red, the bank thereby rendered safe, a bald brawny individual entered through the outer doorway. Samson looked every inch the bruiser he had been before allegations of misconduct resulted in his banishment from the ring. Now, in his retirement, he oversaw the gaming rooms, a comedown perhaps from the days when he had remained on his feet against Jem Ward for one hundred thirty-eight rounds spread over one and one-half hours, but a comedown for which he was extremely well-paid.

Whereas Quin might find it mildly diverting to own a gaming hell, he wasn't interested enough to involve himself in the running of the place.

Samson beckoned. Leaving Beau to appreciate the croupiers' considerable assets, Quin stepped into the relative quiet of the hall.

Candles burned in sconces along the long narrow corridor. At the far end stood Liliane, one of the attendants, a shapely young woman with masses of honey-blonde hair.

To her bosom, Liliane clutched a bust of Voltaire, fashioned from black basalt ware. At her feet, curled in a fetal position, a slender man lay groaning, his hands cupped around his genitals.

The hell had been doing a brisk business ever since Lord Quinton took possession. His fellow profligates flocked to inspect the gaming rooms, expecting to discover the bawdiest of whores on the premises, the lewdest of posture women, private rooms where all manner of depravities might take place; and stubbornly refusing to accept this was not the case.

Quin strolled down the hallway. "Hallo, Coffey. Why are you lying on my floor?"

Gingerly, Coffey uncoiled himself and staggered to his feet. He was a slender man with abnormally pale skin and hair and, currently, a bloody nose. "I like a bit of pepper in a pullet. It adds spice to the game."

Liliane brandished the basalt bust. "This *salaud* placed his hands on me. It requires a punishment, milord."

Quin held out a handkerchief. "From all appearances, punishment has already been dealt out."

"You do not take this seriously!" Liliane stamped her foot. "Me, I am no doxy. I should not be treated so."

Coffey took Quin's handkerchief and dabbed his damaged nose. "All women are doxies. A man needs only find their price."

Few knew better than Lord Quinton that there was no point attempting rational conversation with a drunkard. Still, he felt obliged to try. "I

The Loversall Novellas

fail to understand why you should seek a doxy here. You must have mistook the address."

"So you say," scoffed Coffey. "But I know a doxy when I see one, and I'm looking at one now."

In point of fact, Coffey was looking at Lord Quinton. Nonetheless, Liliane snarled, "Go to the devil, pig!"

"It's you as should go," interrupted Samson, as he removed the bust from her grasp and replaced it on its stand. "Back where you belong. Before I start inquiring why you was where you shouldn't be." Liliane huffed, turned on her heel, and flounced down the hall.

Coffey watched until she disappeared into the gaming rooms. And then he staggered, stumbled to his knees, and emptied the contents of his stomach out onto the floor.

Chapter Two

Kate peered through the window of the hackney coach. The vehicle had seen finer days, its paint scratched and faded, its interior leather stained and torn. As, she thought, had she. As had the Haymarket itself. The broad, long street, which connected Pall Mall with the eastern end of Piccadilly, was lined with hotels and cafes, stable yards and inns.

Lights flared by the entrance to the King's Theater for the Italian Opera, located at the southwest end of the street; a handsome edifice cased with stucco and adorned with an elegant colonnade constructed of cast-iron Doric pillars supporting an entablature and balustraded gallery. The front had been redesigned since Kate last visited London, and was decorated with a beautiful relievo representing the origin and progress of music, or so the newspapers explained.

There had been many entertainments in the Haymarket when Kate was a child, most popular among them human curiosities and animal prodigies. She recalled the ox with six legs and two bellies; the skeleton of the Irish Giant who measured nearly nine feet tall. The Cat's Opera had been her favorite, second only to the tricks performed afterward by a horse, a dog, and some monkeys. In addition to the organ-grinding and rope-dancing performances, the monkeys had taken wine together, and rode on the horse, before one of them danced a minuet with a dog.

Now Kate was a human curiosity herself, in her unadorned black cloak and bonnet and severe bombazine gown. A country mouse. A quiz. A dowd.

Further along the street, on the eastern side, carriages and pedestrians thronged the pavement adjoining the Corinthian columns and pedimented portico of the Theatre Royal. Ladies glittered in extravagant gowns and expensive jewels. Gentlemen were darkly dashing in their evening attire. Street venders of every description, pickpockets and prostitutes threaded their way through the fashionable crowd.

The hackney rattled by. Kate glimpsed a perfume shop, shuttered at this late hour. A wine merchant. A coffee house. Taverns beyond counting. The lights of the various establishments shone out into the street. The stench of the city was as she remembered: a noxious combination of coal smoke and fog, rotting vegetables left over from the weekly markets held since Elizabethan times, the stink of other less definable waste.

The interior of the carriage smelled only marginally more sweet. The clatter of wheels on cobblestone was deafening within these close confines. Through the window, Kate watched a bosky young buck attempt to haul his companion from the gutter, lose his balance and land on his backside, earning a hoot and a jeer from the whore loitering beneath a street lamp.

The street grew quieter as the hackney neared the northern end, passing a succession of house fronts, some wide, some narrow, three or four storeys high; all with shop-fronts below save the last, which was two structures linked together with separate facades but built as one.

The hackney halted. "Moxley House," the driver announced. "Are you sure you want me to leave you here, miss?"

Kate was sure of nothing, save that she'd been told Lord Quinton resided at this address. The house was made up of the usual basement, three storeys and a garret, all in dull red brick work, its doorways framed by molded architraves and triangular pediments fashioned of stucco. A plain iron railing guarded the basement area. Light blazed from the large widely spaced windows. The owner must spend a fortune on candle wax.

Clutching her battered valise, Kate climbed down awkwardly from the coach, handed the driver a coin. The horses' hooves clattered against cobblestone, wood and metal creaked as the vehicle moved away.

Her courage wavered. Seventeen years had passed since she'd last seen Quin. What would he think of the person Kate had become? What would *she* think of him?

The front door of the house swung open. Quin stood on the threshold. As a young man, he had been extraordinarily handsome. Now on that

The Loversall Novellas

once-flawless face was writ the tale of his excesses. He looked to have enjoyed them well.

Accompanying Quin were an individual who had the appearance of a prize-fighter and a third man who was slender, fair-haired and none too steady on his feet.

The men were arguing. Rather, the third man was arguing. The pugilist remained silent. Quin seemed disinterested. Kate remained in the shadows so that she might watch them unobserved.

The pugilist took hold of the third man's collar and jerked upward. "Save your breath to cool your porridge. You know the house rules. A man can stare until he's cross-eyed, but he's forbid to touch."

The third man's voice rose an octave, perhaps due to the circumstance that his lapels now resided in the vicinity of his earlobes. "You're not blackballing me!"

Quin said, in tones of utter boredom, "I rather think we are." The pugilist applied his other hand to the waistband of the third man's breeches, hefted him, and pitched him down the steps.

The man hit the pavement, tumbled wrong end foremost. He rolled to a stop, cursing, at Kate's feet.

Kate moved away from him, and limped slowly forward. Eyes narrowed as if he found it difficult to focus, Quin watched her approach. "Here now," said the pugilist, as she climbed the steps. "Who are you, and what do you want? This is no place for you, miss."

Kate had not expected Quin would recognize her. Still, his lack of recognition stung. "Don't you know me?" she inquired.

Quin regarded her blankly. "Have we met?"

"His lordship," put in the man called Samson, "can hardly be expected to recall every female he—"

"Every female who has crossed my path," Quin interjected. "Let us not be crude."

Every female he had tumbled, Kate amended. "Perhaps his lordship may remember this." She drew back her hand and slapped his mocking face.

Chapter Three

Lord Quinton sprawled on the sofa in his morning room, a pleasantly proportioned chamber located at the back of Moxley House. Green linen draperies softened the sash windows. Green and white striped paper hung on the walls. The floor was polished oak, the furnishings rosewood.

It was a surprisingly feminine chamber, reminiscent of its previous owner. Quin sometimes thought about turning the room into a more masculine study, but had not drummed up sufficient ambition to undertake the project.

He stretched out his long legs, swirled the brandy in his glass. His visitor wandered around the room, inspecting the long case clock, the writing desk with its beaded drawers and tapering square legs, the ink stain on the wall.

Now that she had his attention, Kate seemed uncertain how to proceed. Not inclined to make matters easier for her, Quin raised his glass.

And then he lowered it. Kate Manvers was in his morning room. He needed to regain the full use of his wits.

She was a tall slender woman, with hair as dark as midnight, eyes as grey as morning mist. More years ago than he cared to count, those wine-red lips had ravished his.

Kate caught his gaze and flushed. It was the curse of such perfect pale flesh: no emotion could be hid.

Ignoring her discomfort, Quin continued his inspection. Thick dark eyelashes, sharply marked brows. High cheekbones, aquiline nose. His fingers recalled the feel of that long slender neck.

She had removed her cloak. The severe black of her gown suited her, if the style did not: high necked and long sleeved and fashioned in a manner that failed to flatter the body hid beneath it, which was particularly fine.

Quin marveled that he hadn't known her. Once he would have known Kate Manvers anywhere. But such was his reputation that women frequently presented themselves at his front door on the flimsiest of pretexts.

Had Quin not been present, Kate would have been denied entrance, there being no rational reason for a respectable woman well past her first youth to arrive on his doorstep clutching an old valise.

What a coxcomb Samson had made him sound. *His lordship can hardly be expected to remember every female—*

And then Kate slapped him, and Quin realized who she was.

It wasn't the first time Kate had slapped him.

She hadn't limped then.

Recollection, if slow to stir, was simmering now. Quin suspected — the curve of a bare breast, sunlight gleaming in dark hair — this was not a good thing.

Disconcerting to discover that he wanted to know the details of Kate's injury. To learn how far she'd traveled. And why she had come.

Quin rose, crossed to the decanter, poured brandy into a second glass. "Sit down before you fall down. How did you hurt your leg?"

Kate accepted the brandy, sank down awkwardly on an upholstered chair. "A riding accident."

He frowned. She had been a superb horsewoman. "How unlike you to be careless. Was the horse also harmed?"

Her fingers tightened on the glass. "Arabella had to be put down."

"I'm sorry to hear it." Kate had loved her dappled mare.

She brushed aside his sympathy. "It was a long time ago. Tell me, do you often have your guests tossed into the street?"

"Certainly, when they misbehave. I do have standards, though they are not high." Quin smiled, without humor. "As you may have heard."

She cast him an ironic glance. "The whole world has heard of the infamous Black Baron. As I daresay was your intent."

Quin had believed himself beyond annoyance, but discovered he was not. "Take care lest you begin to bore me, Kate."

"Or you will toss *me* out into the street?" Uncowed, she raised her chin. "No matter what I say or don't, you will do as you please. Do you truly care so little what people think?"

"I care for very little."

"Then I am sorry for you, Quin."

Quin was further affronted by this comment. Had he not seduced a thousand women (or allowed them to seduce him), wagered a fortune (and won three), visited the field of honor with men who did not survive to duel again? Yet here sat Kate, with something akin to pity in her gaze.

"You cannot think I give a damn for your opinion," he said coolly.

Kate placed her drink, unsampled, on the small sofa table. "I'm not here to quarrel, Quin."

He raised an eyebrow. "No?"

"Appearances to the contrary," she said wryly, and shifted in her chair. "Believe me, had I any other choice, I would not have come to you."

Quin didn't doubt it. He imagined Miss Manvers would be more eager to encounter the plague — if she remained a miss, and wasn't instead a ma'am, in which case her spouse should be shot for allowing to enter this house. Unless she had run away from said spouse, and wished Quin to protect her, which was an even more unsettling notion, Quin being more in the habit of avoiding irate spouses than facing them head-on.

What the devil *did* she want from him? Were he to ask, he'd hand her the advantage. Kate already had more advantage over him that Quin cared her to realize.

"Yet here you are," he said, determined to disconcert her at least half as much as she had disconcerted him. "Showed up on my doorstep like a strumpet searching for a tumble. Shall you find out for yourself if what the scandalmongers say is true?"

She scowled, "No, I shan't! Pray don't try and provoke me further. I have already behaved badly enough for one evening."

Kate had not behaved half as badly as he would like. Quin recalled various occasions on which he had been bit and scratched and bruised, result of no excess of temper, but passion of a different sort. He disliked these memories, wished they would go away.

He wished *she* would go away.

Or alternately that she would stay, and toss aside her bonnet, and rip off her gown, and bite and scratch and bruise him one more time.

Which was even less likely than a visitation of levitating swine.

Kate was watching him, more closely than he liked. "Shall I apologize?" she asked.

Quin turned away, rang for a servant. "Why bother, when we both know you won't mean a word? The hour grows late, and I have things to do. Tomorrow is time enough for talk. You'll stay here tonight."

She stiffened. "And if I don't care to spend the night beneath your roof?"

"I said beneath my roof, not in my bed." Quin glanced pointedly at her valise. "Did you not already tell me you have nowhere else to go?"

Kate bit her lip, then sighed. "Thank you. I suppose."

She thanked him, she supposed? He *should* have her tossed out. "Your gratitude is premature," said Quin, as he strode toward the doorway. "The infamous Black Baron does nothing without expecting payment in return."

Chapter Four

The last of the gamesters had departed, exhilarated by gain or disheartened by loss: some in partial possession of their faculties and therefore remaining upright; others unable to ambulate without assistance; the more sodden among them stuffed by footmen into their carriages and sent home. Servants scurried about, setting the gaming rooms to rights. Liliane paced the supper room, awaiting her audience with her employer.

She disliked being made to cool her heels. As if she were a supplicant and Quin some high-and-mighty feudal lord.

Patience, she told herself. Her goal was in sight. Before Lord Quinton suspected her intentions, he'd be caught fast in her web.

And wouldn't the pusses hiss and spit then? Rosamond, Adele, Daphne and the others would turn pea-green with envy upon learning Liliane had managed a tête-à-tête with Quin

Yes, and she meant to make the most of it. Liliane inspected herself in a looking-glass. Honey-blonde curls and creamy skin and big green eyes, perfect teeth, a luscious lower lip, and a straight little nose. Gown of raspberry silk with a tightly fitted bodice that clung to her curves, rounded neckline that exposed her shoulders and a great deal of her chest, sleeves puffed and tapered, skirt embellished with large tucks and a broad hem. The gown wasn't hers to keep, of course. The garments worn by the girls during working hours remained on the premises when they left for the night.

Liliane smoothed her skirts. She was a diamond of the first water, if she did say so herself. And a clever enough actress that she should tread the boards, Samson in the usual way of things not one to permit the wool to be pulled over his eyes. Yet she had persuaded him to hire her by claiming to be something she was not, him being partial to females of good character fallen on hard times as opposed to misses barely out of the schoolroom, not that Liliane had ever seen the inside of a schoolroom, but she was a quick study nonetheless, could mimic the manner of an impoverished gentlewoman as well as anyone, and mouth break-teeth words better than most.

Life was a curious business. Here she was pretending to be the sort of female who when nose-to-nose with trouble would feel a spasm coming on, her constitution not being strong; who in a ticklish situation would require a nice lie-down, and her temples bathed with lavender water, and calves' foot jelly served up to her on a silver spoon. In truth, Liliane considered silver spoons better for the selling of them, and wouldn't recognize a maidenly spasm if it nipped her on the nose.

However, a nice lie-down was in her future, providing she was clever with her cards.

At least, she supposed it would be nice enough. His lordship had tossed up sufficient skirts that he should know what he was about.

Liliane turned away from the mirror. Her nerves were in a jangle, now the moment drew nigh. Still, how difficult could the business be? Everybody knew the Black Baron was a sot.

Lord Quinton entered the supper room at last, beckoned an attendant to his side. As his eyes flicked over her, Liliane discreetly tugged her neckline lower. His lordship, alas, appeared more interested in the brandy fetched him than in her creamy flesh.

Ladies and ladybirds alike flocked to the Black Baron like moths to a candle flame, drawn by his reputation, curious to discover for themselves how well he was equip't. Liliane wondered if those other hopefuls found it this difficult to catch his eye.

She drew in a breath so deep the seams of her bodice creaked, and cleared her throat. Quin frowned, as if puzzling why she was still here. "*Tiens!* That Coffey pig— The incident was of the most distressing." Liliane clasped her hands beneath her breasts, plumping them up further in case his lordship was too fuddled to remark what was right under his nose. "Although it is not the first time I have found myself the object of unwanted attentions, you comprehend."

The Loversall Novellas

Quin sampled his brandy. "I didn't imagine it was."

He had barely glanced at her bosom. The man was jaded beyond belief. Liliane was strongly tempted to inform Lord Quinton that he might kiss her arse.

Instead she touched a lace-trimmed handkerchief to the corner of one eye. "He said he desired to speak with me about a private matter. I did not expect one of your friends would behave so shabbily."

"More fool you," murmured Quin. "Curious, is it not, that a man would try and force himself on an unwilling female when there are so many willing females to be found?"

Matters weren't progressing as Liliane had anticipated. For one thing, her employer was — despite his reputation — far from being foxed.

Needs must when the devil drove. Mam would have her guts for garters if she didn't soon have some progress to report.

"Who can explain a drunken swine?" Liliane allowed a second tear to trickle down her cheek. "I beg you, don't turn me off! It's a harsh world for such as me, should I lose my place."

Unmoved by her tears, Lord Quinton gestured. The attendant hastened forward, decanter at the ready. She poured. Quin studied the brandy, then raised it to his lips, and drank.

Only when his glass was empty did he look at Liliane. "Samson wants me to dismiss you, being of the opinion you wouldn't have wandered into the hallway in the first place if you were up to any good. However, I've decided to give you the benefit of the doubt."

"*Vraiment?*" Liliane dabbed her eyes with the scrap of fabric before tucking it into her bodice, which — though there seemed little enough point in doing so — she nudged lower still. "You are of a kindness unsurpassed."

"Ah yes, I am all indulgence," Quin said sardonically. "Therefore, I will tell you that even if you drop your neckline to your navel, you'll catch no more than a cold."

He thought so, did he? Mam thought otherwise. Liliane thought she'd like to be shut of the pair of them. This behaving like a hen-hearted little ninny without a ha'porth of spirit went against the grain.

Delicately, she shuddered. "You mistake, milord. Me, I am much afraid. What if the Coffey lurks in ambush, waiting to revenge himself? I beg you permit me to remain tonight beneath your roof."

Quin did not immediately answer. Liliane crossed his fingers behind her back. Would he, or would he not?

He beckoned the attendant. "I might as well be running a blasted hotel."

Chapter Five

Lord Quinton was preparing to break his fast — the morning newspapers spread out on the mahogany table in front of him, alongside a pot of coffee and a plate piled high with boiled eggs and cold roast beef, although he had no appetite, and was wondering why anyone would choose to be awake at this ungodly hour — when his ruminations were interrupted by the arrival of Beau Loversall. Beau was dressed for riding in dark blue coat and buckskin breeches and tall top boots, buff waistcoat with black stripes wide asunder, cravat tied in the Trone d'Amour. His golden curls were tousled, his expression reminiscent of the cat that had got into the cream.

"An early rendezvous?" Quin ventured. "With Miss Fletcher, I presume?"

"Miss Fletcher is holding me at arm's length. Mrs. Thwaite, however, enjoys a brisk morning ride." Beau examined the sideboard where food had been set out in chafing dishes. There were no servants in attendance, Quin preferring (result of his usually fragile condition) to greet the day in solitude. "What are you doing up so early? I was sure I'd find you still abed."

And so Quin would have been, had not sleep proved damned elusive. "In that case, why are you in my house?"

"May I remind you Moxley's previously belonged to a member of my family? It is practically a second home, and in some ways even better than my own." Beau settled himself on an upholstered chair. "While Mrs. Ormsby rubs along well enough with Mrs. Thwaite, she dislikes Miss Fletcher's manner. I suggested she might be more tolerant of a damsel half her age."

"Ah. Yet here you sit. Apparently unscathed."

Beau reached for the coffee urn, which was decorated with a rustic landscape populated by shepherdesses and sheep. "Appearances are deceptive. The lady has exceedingly sharp fingernails."

A brief silence descended on the chamber, while its occupants reflected upon the damage done their respective persons by their various amours. It was a pretty room, tinted pale blue with cornices a slightly darker shade, the ceiling embellished with relief mouldings in papier-mâché, the wallpaper lush with foliate scrolls and a small-scale repeating pattern of flowers and leaves.

Quin raised a hand to shield his eyes from the bright morning light. He fancied he was sober, and didn't fancy it at all.

The door opened. Liliane was wearing her own clothes this morning, a day dress of figured calico, doves' breast with black flowers, the sleeves puffed at the top and fitted to the wrist. She was not, Quin noted with displeasure, wearing a cloak or a bonnet or any other item of clothing that might suggest her imminent departure. He inquired, "Why haven't you left?"

"More to the point," said Beau, "why is she here at all? I distinctly recall you telling me the women who work at Moxley's are not to be enjoyed. But you own the place, do you not, and ownership has privileges." He rose. "Do join us, *chérie*."

Privileges, had he? Quin wished someone would tell him what they were.

Liliane approached the table and seated herself as close as possible to him while remaining out of reach. "You mistake, monsieur," she explained to Beau. "I am not here because his lordship and I have the intimate connection, but because of the *cochon* Coffey, who will desire to revenge himself because I damaged his manly apparatus. It was no more than he deserved, for misusing me."

"The cad misused you?" echoed Beau, enjoying himself far more than Quin found seemly. "You must tell me all. But first— Am I *de trop*? Do you wish to be private with Quin?"

Liliane glanced at Quin. He scowled, lest she mistake his dislike of the notion, and she said, "*Mais non!* I came for the coffee. Unless milord desires I leave before I break my fast?"

The Loversall Novellas

"Don't be a goose!" Beau scolded, before Quin could express his regret that Liliane had not departed at the break of dawn. "Of course you must stay." Liliane reached for the sugar bowl, a maneuver that invited her companions to gaze down the neckline of her dress.

Beau's gaze drifted to her bosom. Liliane leaned forward to afford him a better view. Quin raised his coffee cup. Trial enough that he had forgone his morning whiskey. Watching flirtation enacted at his breakfast table was more than a man should have to bear.

"May I bring you some toast?" asked Beau.

"Yes, please. *Merci!*" Liliane glanced again at Quin. "Are you angry with me, milord? I am sorry I slept so late. I lay awake almost all the night, tossing and turning and fretting myself to flinders about what the pig person may do."

Although he suspected she had ulterior motives — in Quin's experience, females almost always had ulterior motives — Liliane also had a valid point. Coffey was of a vindictive bent.

He pushed away his untouched plate. "You have misplaced your accent, mademoiselle." Liliane had also rested her elbows on the table. She flushed and snatched them back.

Beau returned from the sideboard, carrying a plate of cheese and toast. He set the food in front of Liliane. She thanked him prettily. He resumed his seat.

The door again swung open. Kate hesitated on the threshold. "I'm sorry to interrupt. I didn't realize you weren't alone."

"It's a marvel to me how seldom I *am* alone." Quin stood.

Liliane stared at the newcomer. "Who is that? What is she wearing? Someone should recommend to her the so-clever Mme Dubois."

Lord Quinton felt like recommending Liliane take herself to Hades. "Do join us, Kate. You must pay no heed to Liliane, who has no manners. Furthermore, she was just leaving. Weren't you, Liliane?"

"But I have not—"

"You have overstayed your welcome. Go, before I call Samson to render you assistance." Cheese and toast in hand, Liliane pushed back her chair. Kate limped toward the table, her gait more awkward than the night before.

"By God! The rumor's true," said Beau. "You *do* prefer rigidly virtuous females." Halfway to the doorway, Liliane turned to gape.

Quin crossed the room and opened the door; pushed Liliane through the portal, and closed it in her face. "Kate, this reprobate is Beau Loversall. Beau, you will not be rude to Miss Manvers."

"Rude?" Beau echoed, wounded. "I was merely pointing out—"

"I don't think I am rigidly virtuous." Kate looked reflective. "Though I daresay I once was."

Beau poured coffee into another cup. "Before you met Quin, you mean. Witness me proven correct."

"Witness you an idiot." Quin reclaimed his seat. "Kate and I were betrothed."

Beau widened his blue eyes. "The most wicked of all the wicked had a fiancée?"

"I was a mere eighteen. And I didn't have her long."

Kate sipped her coffee. "That would be because he also got himself betrothed to Verena Wickersham."

Beau tsk'd. "Miss Wickersham was an heiress, I suppose? Immense dowry, lands marched apace, that sort of thing? Did she additionally have spots? A hairlip? A squint?"

"I couldn't say," said Kate. "We were never introduced."

Sobriety, decided Quin, was highly overrated. All in all, he'd rather be nursing a sore head.

Chapter Six

Moxley House was busy. Countless people were flitting about, whispering behind their hands, casting curious looks at Kate as Quin hustled her down the hallway and through the door.

They were puzzling over who she was, of course, and why she'd been allowed to stay. The latter, Kate was puzzling over herself. Quin could only be inconvenienced by her presence in his house.

Once outside, he released her. Kate surveyed the garden, or what remained of the garden, as she rubbed her abused wrist. Naked honeysuckle bushes, the ruins of morning glory and camellias and various shrubs, trees stripped of vegetation to the height of a man's head—

Wisteria drooped forlornly. The remnants of an orange tree protruded from a neoclassical urn. "Good Lord. What happened here?" she said.

Quin motioned her toward a shell-shaped bench. "The previous owner kept a goat. I brought you outdoors not to enjoy the scenery but because this is the only place I can be relatively certain we won't be overheard."

Kate conceded that it would be difficult for anyone to hide in the sparse shrubbery. "Precisely what *is* Moxley's?" she inquired.

"You don't know?"

"Brothel, bedlam, bachelor establishment — I can't make up my mind. Mademoiselle Liliane gives every appearance of being bachelor's fare."

"Mistress Liliane," corrected Quin. "The lady — and yes, I use the term loosely — is no more French than you and I. In answer to your question, you've taken refuge in a gaming hell."

A gaming hell? It needed only that.

Kate wondered, though she surely shouldn't, how many mistresses

Quin had.

She wanted Quin herself, if the truth be told, which was shocking in her, because if anyone should know better, it was Kate.

Harsh unforgiving daylight deepened the lines in his face, revealed threads of silver in his dark hair.

The skeleton of a rambling rose spread over the old stone walls. Quin snapped off a withered branch. "Cat got your tongue? Or have your delicate sensibilities been overcome?"

Kate refrained from remarking that her delicate sensibilities had not survived the occasion when he'd spread his jacket on a bed of fragrant straw. "It is beneath you to amuse yourself by baiting me," she said.

Gravel crunched beneath Quin's boots as he moved toward the bench. "If anything is beneath me, I have not yet discovered what it might be."

He was angry with her. But why? Surely she was the one with a right to bear a grudge? Kate longed to ask him, and at the same time was reluctant to venture down that particular conversational path.

Still holding the rose branch, Quin sat down beside her. Kate had not realized the bench was so small.

She took a sudden intense interest in her hands, which were folded in her lap. Beside her sat a philanderer who had corrupted countless women and fought numerous duels, a man of libertine propensities who had engaged in every vice not once but many times, who had driven at least one lover to suicide; the sort of scoundrel damsels were warned against, lest they find themselves with their skirts around their ears and minus a maidenhead. But he was also Quin, who long ago had held her heart in his hand, and she glimpsed traces of the boy he had been at eighteen in the tilt of his head, the twist of his mouth, a fleeting expression in his dark eyes.

Kate didn't think she could bear that Quin should touch her now.

And yet she wished him to, intensely.

She was the worst kind of fool.

And Quin was watching her. "You are quiet," he remarked.

Kate felt her cheeks redden. "I was remembering."

"Memory frequently eludes me," said Quin. "I am more often grateful for it than not."

Kate supposed she should be grateful he no longer shared this physical

The Loversall Novellas

attraction. "You do not mind that you cannot recall portions of your life?"

He shrugged. "Why should I? The past is dead. Liliane is right about one thing: that is a dreadful dress. Have you nothing else?"

"I— No. If you are determined to insult me, I will take my leave."

"You are insulted by the truth? In that case, I declare a truce. Now perhaps you will explain why you are here."

Kate hesitated. How best to proceed? "I've been residing with my Aunt Dorothea in Yorkshire."

Quin stretched out his long legs. "Dotty Aunt Dorothea, mother to the odious Edmund — I have not forgot quite everything, you see. Why aren't you with your aunt now?"

So small was the stone bench that his thigh brushed against hers. Kate refused to give him the satisfaction of edging away.

Nor would she crawl onto his lap, no matter how strong the temptation. "Aunt Dorothea fell down the hall stair. Her heart wasn't strong."

"My condolences on your loss." Quin began stripping the thorns off his rose branch. "Even though it's obvious the damned woman didn't feed you half enough."

In contrast to the voluptuous Liliane, Kate must seem as dry and brittle as the stick he held. "Aunt Dorothea was kind, in her way."

"But not kind enough to provide for you, I'll warrant," Quin remarked.

Kate considered the various violent uses to which one might put a denuded rose branch. She inhaled a deep, calming breath. "Edmund was jealous of her fondness for me. My cousin in his tantrums was something we both were eager to avoid. We went on well enough, until Edmund debauched the vicar's wife."

Quin was looking contemplative. Kate wondered if he had ever debauched a vicar's wife. "It made a dreadful scandal," she hastily continued. "Aunt Dorothea had hysterics, and threatened to cut Edmund out of her will. Not long after, she had her mishap on the steps. There was an inquiry, of course. Her death was deemed an accident."

Quin turned sideways on the bench. "You don't believe it was?"

Kate met his gaze. "Aunt Dorothea had a new will drawn up and witnessed during one of Edmund's absences. Once he learns of its existence, I'd not lay odds on my continued good health."

Chapter Seven

Quin strolled through the gaming rooms. Moxley's might be located in the raffish Haymarket, but these chambers were as elegantly fitted out as the finest gentleman's club.

The same could not be said, alas, for the clientele. Quin was growing tired of pouring inebriated acquaintances into their carriages. It made a man reflect upon the countless occasions when he had been the one being poured.

And upon the company he kept.

Near-sobriety was an uncomfortable condition. Quin contemplated his half-filled glass of whiskey, only his second of the night. He felt restless, unsettled, craving he knew not what.

Solitude, for one thing, Lord Quinton decided, as amber-eyed Daphne shot him a smoldering glance. Ever since Liliane had remained overnight in the house, the other women aspired to do the same. Statuesque brunette Adele claimed to feel a spasm coming on, if not outright palpitations, but was certain her health would improve immensely if she could only gain a comfortable night's sleep, preferably in his lordship's bed. Russet-haired Rosamond insisted she had come down with a case of snuffles and only a monster would send her out into the damp.

Quin was surrounded by conniving females. Including, he suspected, Kate.

Was Kate truly in danger? Or had she spent the past seventeen years plotting her revenge?

Verena Wickersham. He hadn't thought of her in years. His father's candidate for the next baroness had possessed no finer moral standards than the stable cat.

It hardly mattered. For whatever reason Quin had set out sowing his wild oats, he had long ago become an unrepentant sinner determined to each every step of his journey to eternal hellfire.

Now here was Kate, and what he was to do with her, he had no idea.

Samson touched Quin's elbow, drawing his attention. "That Coffey cove is raising a rumpus, saying he must speak with you and threatening informations laid."

Welcoming the distraction, Quin set down his glass.

He walked along the carpeted hallway, descended the broad stair. At the bottom stood a door sheeted with iron and covered with green baize, in its center a small aperture through which visitors could be scrutinized.

Quin put his eye to the peep hole. Coffey waited in the small foyer, one arm gripped by the porter and the other by a footman, neither of whom seemed interested in what he had to say, which had to do with his determination to try his luck at hazard, and their inexplicable refusal to admit him to the hell. What, demanded Coffey, was wrong with his blunt? Granted, he'd possessed more coin when he set out this evening, before he'd tried to catch the smiles of fortune by risking a few pounds he could ill afford to lose. Curious, was it not, how a man started out placing a few cautious wagers and wound up punting recklessly on the spin of the ball, tossing money on the table in competition with his companions as if the lot of them were caught up in some passing lunacy?

Quin closed the aperture. Generally euphoric when intoxicated, Coffey wanted always to be intoxicated, on one substance or another, or preferably several substances at once. From all appearances this evening he was not yet drunk as an emperor, or even drunk as a lord, which was ten times less; but instead merely drunk as a wheelbarrow, and not even David's sow.

David had been a Welshman who possessed an alehouse, a tippling wife, and an especially fine sow. The wife had lain down to sleep herself sober in the sty, where she was observed by company, who declared her the drunkest sow they had ever beheld.

How he knew all this, Quin couldn't imagine. If indeed he *did* know it. He might not be as sober as he'd thought.

He opened the iron-sheeted door and entered the foyer, which boasted

The Loversall Novellas

wainscoted walls and a checkered tile floor, and not a single chair or bench where a caller might comfortably cool his heels. Coffey burst into renewed complaints on sight of him. His nose was still slightly swollen, and there was noticeable bruising around one eye.

"Enough," said Quin. "Release him." The servants obeyed.

Coffey straightened his sleeves, adjusted his lapels. "That French trollop lured me into the hallway, and not the other way around. Whose word are you going to take, hers or mine?"

Quin placed himself, casually but firmly, in front of the green baize door. "Neither, I think. You're not barred because of Liliane."

Coffey's pale gaze narrowed. "What, then?"

Quin leaned against the door jamb. During his frequent forays into the less savory sections of London, he had rubbed shoulders with countless *chevaliers d'industrie* and Greeks and therefore recognized the breed. "This is an honest house. No false dice, no marked decks. No such tricks as the Dribble or the Long Gallery or the Stamp. No lambs damp behind the ears waiting to be fleeced."

"You accuse me of being a Captain Sharp?"

"I accuse you of nothing. But if you think me a pigeon for your plucking, you have feathers in your head."

Coffey looked less cast away than he had mere moments past. "You'll regret this, Quin."

The footman stepped forward. The porter opened the door. With a last furious glower, Coffey stepped out into the night. Rather than returning to the gaming rooms, Quin made his way to the private portion of the house.

His valet was waiting in the hallway, nodding in a chair set outside the bedroom door. Wibbert was a thin brown-haired man of some sixty years, with a slight paunch and a receding hairline. Quin grasped his shoulder. "Why are you sitting out here in the hall? You should be in bed."

Wibbert jerked awake. "Oh, sir. I mean, my lord! I meant to tell you that—"

"Tell me tomorrow. When did I become so harsh a master that you feel you must sit up half the night?"

"Oh no, my lord! Not harsh! But—"

"Wibbert. Are you trying to make me cross?"

The valet wrung his hands together "No, my lord! Not cross! Very well,

I'll go! But pray remember you said—"

Impatiently, Quin gestured. With one last anxious glance, Wibbert scurried away. Quin entered his bedroom, shrugging out of his snug-fitting coat.

The curtains had been drawn, the fire let die down until mere embers glowed on the hearth. The chamber's gloom was broken only by the single lighted candle on the shaving stand. Wondering whether his valet might have got into the whiskey, Quin tossed his coat in the general direction of a chair. He pulled off his cravat, unfastened his trousers, sat down on the edge of the bed to pull off his shoes—

And paused. His nostrils twitched. The hair on the back of his neck stirred. Before he could collect his wits, small strong hands grasped Quin's shoulders and pulled him down on his back.

The hands seemed determined to remove more of his clothing. The hands' owner smelled as if she'd rolled through a particularly pungent flower bed.

No wonder Wibbert had been jumpy as a cat on a hot bake-stone.

Quin's eyes had grown accustomed to the shadows. He made out the shapely form of his assailant, who was clad only in a thin shift, and struggling with one of his boots.

He jerked his foot away and said, "Give over, Liliane." The boot thudded to the floor.

"*Oui, c'est moi!*" Liliane flung herself atop him, effectively hampering his escape. Her plump breasts flattened against his chest, a not-unpleasant sensation, as noted by a portion of Quin's anatomy not directly connected with his brain. They lay thigh to thigh, belly to—

She wriggled. "You see? We are *très sympathique*! I suggest—"

"*I* suggest," growled Quin, as he grasped her arms and pushed her off him, "you pray to *le bon Dieu* that I do not strangle you."

"*Voyons!*" Liliane hurled herself at him, scrabbling for a hold. "Oof! Ah, now I have you, milord."

She had him, indeed. Quin froze.

"Ooh, là là!" cooed Liliane, giving him a none-too-gentle squeeze. "You are *magnifique*! *Splendide. Formidable*—"

"Whereas you are *inapproprié*." Kate stood in the doorway of the adjoining chamber, a lighted candle in her hand. "Unhand my fiancé, mademoiselle."

"Your fiancé?" Liliane shot off the bed as if she'd been stung by hornets. "*Merde!*"

Chapter Eight

Quin grasped Liliane by the elbow, snatched up her clothing from the chest where she had neatly placed it, and propelled her into the hallway. Kate heard their quiet voices but could not make out the words.

She raised her lighted candle and inspected the room. It was a remarkably ordinary chamber, from the tall wardrobe to the short chest of drawers to the corner shaving stand fitted out in Spode blue and white. A mahogany wing armchair was drawn up in a cozy manner near the hearth. A Turkey carpet covered the wooden floor.

These were hardly the sort of surroundings in which one imagined orgies taking place. Kate eyed the canopied bed. Some manner of activity had been about to take place, and without Quin's cooperation, judging from the conversation she had overheard.

Honestly, she'd just meant to take a peek.

Curiosity was a character trait not limited to felines.

Quin returned, closed the door and leaned against it. Kate spun round to face him, mortified at having been discovered staring at his bed. The man should have looked ridiculous, rumpled and disheveled, his shirt pulled out of his breeches — which may or may not have been unfastened, she didn't dare look — and wearing only one boot. He did not. Kate's mouth went dry. Quin in disarray was temptation personified.

Meanwhile, she was swathed in a voluminous night garment that covered her from head to toe.

Not that she had come here to be ravished, which was a good thing since Quin clearly had no interest in ravishing her. Doubtless she failed to meet the Black Baron's standards. Kate felt like smashing her candlestick over his rakehelly head.

"This has set the cat among the pigeons," he said, as he moved away from the door. "Why the devil did you tell Liliane we are betrothed?"

He was cross, realized Kate, and for good reason. Whereas she had no right to be annoyed at finding a female in his bed. "My apologies. Clearly, I wasn't thinking. The presence of a fiancée will impede your usual pursuits."

Quin passed by her, so close she felt the heat of his body; sat down on the edge of the bed and took hold of his remaining boot. "I assure you the presence of a fiancée would make no difference whatsoever to my 'usual pursuits'. However, it doesn't suit me to have you known as such. We can only hope Liliane will keep her tongue between her teeth."

Kate watched him wrestle with the boot a moment before she set down her candle, stooped, grasped the heel and tugged. The boot came off in her hands. As she set it aside she asked, "Do you think she will?"

"'Close as oysters, milord,'" Quin quoted. "'So long as you pay my price.' You're freezing, Kate. Come here."

The room *was* cold. Warily, Kate approached the bed. Quin pulled off the coverlet and wrapped it around her shoulders. His touch was impersonal. Kate couldn't decide whether she was resentful or relieved.

He settled himself against the carved headboard. Kate arranged herself facing him, her back against a bedpost, trying not to contemplate what sort of bargain Quin might have struck with Liliane. "I'm sorry if I've created problems. It sounded like you needed assistance. I couldn't think what else to do."

"Assistance? My dear."

Despite herself, Kate smiled. "I take it Liliane aspires to be your mistress."

Quin settled more comfortably among the pillows. "I don't take mistresses." Light from the candle on the bedside table only faintly penetrated the thick shadows cast by the bed hangings. Kate could not make out the expression on his face.

She drew the coverlet more tightly around her. Her aunt had subscribed to the London papers, regarding outdated scandal as better than no scandal at all. Kate had snatched up the newssheets after Dorothea discarded them and pored over the pages in the privacy of her bedchamber, searching for mention of Quin.

More often than not, she found it. "I've heard otherwise."

Quin regarded her sardonically. "The word 'mistress' indicates a relationship lasting longer than one night."

Kate wondered if he too was thinking of how many nights they'd had. Or if not nights, then stolen moments. Lazy afternoons.

Seventeen years, thought Kate. Seventeen years gone, though hardly in the blinking of an eye. Now here she was, alone with Quin in his bedchamber.

In his bed.

At the opposite end of his bed, to be precise. Kate cleared her throat. "I have heard it suggested that a man may be allotted a finite number of indulgences in one lifetime. I pass this theory along in case you might care to pace yourself."

Quin reached out and clasped her ankle. "And you?"

"Me, what?" Kate asked, rather faintly, distracted by the warmth of his fingers against her skin.

He pulled off her slipper. "Have you been chaste? Or shall I have distraught admirers pounding on my door?"

His fingers stroked the top of her foot, toe to ankle. It was an old familiar ritual, relaxing and rousing at the same time. Kate managed to respond, "No one is likely to come looking for me here."

"That's not what I asked you." He moved his thumb and fingers in circular motions over the sole of her foot. "If you tell me about your conquests, I'll tell you about mine."

How many slippers had Quin removed during the years since he'd last removed hers? "I've no desire to hear about your conquests," Kate snapped.

He released one foot to pick up the other, tossed aside the second slipper to join the first. "It's just as well. I would find it difficult to be precise. As with anything done in overabundance, the details tend to blur."

Kate tensed. He held her injured leg. She tried to draw away, but he refused to release her. She closed her eyes as his fingers traced her scars.

Quin said nothing. Nor did she. His hand returned to her foot, rubbing, soothing her into a curiously calm intimacy that transcended time and thought. She was only vaguely conscious of the lateness of the hour, the quietness of the house, the sheltered depths of the huge bed—

The clock chimed, and the mood shattered. Kate knew the exact instant when Quin realized the ankle he so deftly caressed was hers.

He replaced her slippers. Kate drew her feet up beneath her on the bed.

Quin rose, moved to a chest, picked up a decanter. "You believe your cousin means you harm."

Kate accepted the glass he offered her. "Edmund set the kitchen cat afire, after it merely scratched him. Anyway, it wouldn't be the first time."

Quin frowned. "Your accident?"

"The girth had been cut half through."

He cursed beneath his breath.

Kate did not care to remember those dark days, when she had lost both Quin and Arabella within the space of a few weeks. "Aunt Dorothea refused to believe her son might have been responsible. Edmund as much as admitted to me that he had. His disposition has not improved with time."

"Let me understand this." Quin sat down beside her on the edge of the bed. "You have no family left, no friends you care to expose to Edmund's malice. And so you came to me."

Kate felt her cheeks redden. "Not to expose you to his malice. I hoped that in you Edmund might meet his match."

"In malice, you mean? I had no inkling my father was going to make an announcement, Kate."

Kate stared into her glass. She had been fool enough to believe Quin's promise they would wed. How many times had he made the same promise to some other woman? And broken it as well?

Quin said, quietly, "I didn't know where you'd gone."

He hadn't been meant to know. Kate was an orphan, with no real home of her own. When she told her scholarly uncle she wished to leave, Harlan had been relieved to pass her along to some other relative.

"I made a dreadful scandal," Quin continued. "My father threatened everything from disinheritance to dismemberment. He could force me to do nothing. I was of age."

Kate placed her glass carefully on the bedside table. Quin could have found her, easily enough, had he made the effort. But that was water well under the bridge.

He was watching her, an odd expression on his face. "What?" she said.

Quin reached out and touched her hair. "Kate by candlelight. I was admiring your nightdress." His fingers moved down her throat, came to rest against her pulse. "So modest and demure, yet infinitely more enticing than the most diaphanous shift."

Her heart was beating frantically. As Quin must realize. Kate leaned toward him, as entranced as any reptile by a snake charmer's flute. And then she recalled this charmer's countless nameless conquests, and drew back.

He quirked a quizzical eyebrow. Kate rose, limped across the room and paused in the doorway to her own bedchamber. "I am not naive. You would like to banish me to the ranks of those other women whose details you have forgot. I shan't let you, Quin."

He made no move to prevent her leaving, said not a word in his defense. Before her good sense could desert her altogether, Kate closed and locked the door.

Chapter Nine

"*Mais non!*" protested Liliane. "This is a terrible mistake. I would never have on purpose entered milord's chamber, *je t'assure!*"

"Oh, aye. Especially not wearing just your shift." Samson grasped her by the elbow and marched her up the stair. "Don't bother to try and explain how you came to mistake his lordship's chamber for the one given you on the servant's floor."

"But *naturellement* I wear my shift! What would you, have me sleep in a state of nature?" Liliane shuddered, dramatically. "A girl could catch her death — I mean, could take a chill."

Samson beetled his brows at her. "You'd be wise to watch your step."

"Watch my step? But why?" Liliane glanced down at the stair. "Oh, you mean I must beware of the *cochon* Coffey. But this is why I must spend another night—"

"No," said Samson. "You *won't* spend another night. Maybe you've discovered you can bamboozle some of the people a great deal of the time, but you won't bamboozle me."

Samson wasn't half so downy as he thought himself. "What is this bamboozlement? I do not comprehend—"

"You have five minutes to get dressed." Samson shoved Liliane into the small room where she had previously slept. "Before I toss you out into the street."

The door closed behind him. Hastily, Liliane gathered her possessions, pulled on her clothes. In the usual way of things, her invasion of her employer's bedchamber should have led to her being immediately dismissed. But that was not the case. Samson would try and ferret out why Quin had made an exception for Liliane.

Who *was* the dark-haired woman who'd set all her careful plans at naught? Lord Quinton had eyes for only her at breakfast that morning, even though Liliane had been wearing her finest garment, which might have been sackcloth for all the attention he paid.

He had not been noticeably more impressed by her shift.

Liliane struggled with the fastenings of her gown. No small feat, this inducing a cove to dance the feather-bed jig while at the same time playing the part of an innocent in case what Beau Loversall had said was true, and the infamous Black Baron preferred not to dab it up with an impure.

Be that as it may, or not, he hadn't wished to dab it up with *her*. Mayhap his appendage had become jaded as result of overuse. Mam had all manner of remedies for such things. One might utilize the bile of a jackal, or asses' milk, or melt down the fat from the hump of a camel and rub it on a cove's pizzle just before he set to swiving. Liliane contemplated boiling a ram's testicle in milk, adding sugar, and forcing it down her employer's uncooperative throat.

She might have succeeded — mightn't she? — had they not been interrupted. Who would believe Quin had a partiality for a particular female? A female he didn't want the world to learn about, judging from the amount of blunt he had promised Liliane to keep the information to herself.

"Time's up," said Samson, as he re-entered the room. Liliane crammed her bonnet on her head. "Being as you're suddenly afraid of your own shadow, Figg here will see you home."

Liliane eyed the footman, who didn't suit her notion of the breed, having neither good looks to recommend him, nor broad shoulders or strong thighs. He was only a few inches taller than she, with brown hair, nondescript features, and a slender frame.

Under her scrutiny, he blushed. *"Nom de Dieu,"* she sighed.

"Don't be misled," Samson assured her. "Figg has a black belt in Japanese jujutsu."

Liliane didn't quibble. That appearances were deceiving, she knew better than most.

Figg escorted her down the servant's stair, and opened the outer door. "Where to, miss?" he asked.

"Covent Garden," Liliane replied.

The Loversall Novellas

The hour was late, or early, depending on one's point of view; the fog thick and the lamplights dim. The streets were empty of traffic save for the occasional watchman passing on his rounds, the night-soil cart clattering over the cobblestones. "And so," said Liliane to Figg, "what is this jujutsu?"

Japanese jujutsu was a martial discipline developed around the principle of using an attacker's energy against him, instead of directly opposing it, Figg explained; he had learned the science from a sailor met several years ago when his lordship passed a debauched interval in an establishment of less-than-stellar reputation near the London Docks. As he kept watch on their surroundings, Figg went on at some length about throwing, trapping, joint locks, holds, gouging, biting, disengagements, striking and kicking, and other grappling techniques.

"It is of a fascination," commented Liliane, who rather than listening was deciding what she dared tell Mam, which wouldn't be that his lordship was betrothed. Nor would she be blabbing about the bargain they had struck, lest Mam demand her cut.

Claws scrabbled on slippery cobblestones. A cat, decided Liliane; or a large rat, or some other less appealing creature of the night. She stepped closer to Figg, slipped her hand through his arm. Beneath the fabric of his coat, she felt solid muscle. Definitely, there was more to the footman than met the eye. "Is this jujutsu something I could learn?" she asked him. "So if someone was to attack me, I could fling him arsy-varsy — er, head over heels?"

Figg blushed, whether at Liliane's language or her proximity it was impossible to say. She moved closer, so he could take in a good whiff of her seductive perfume.

At least, Mam said it was seductive. Quin had not seemed to find it so. Mayhap there was also something wrong with his nose.

"Have you worked for Lord Quinton long?" she asked. Figg allowed as he had. Further inquiry revealed, however, that the footman knew nothing about anything, or if he did, he wouldn't tell.

Liliane suspected that, with her decision to bamboozle the Black Baron, Mam might have gnawed off more than she could chew.

The streets were no less empty here near Covent Gardens, resurrection men having temporarily abandoned their quest for corpses, and whores for customers, and footpads for drunken lordlings with more brass than brains. A vast variety of buildings made up this neighborhood: shops and townhouses and tenements, high and low public houses; theaters, taverns and coachmen's watering houses, all closed at this hour.

Figg was explaining how Japan's first martial art had originated in 23 B.C., when Emperor Suijin ordered wrestling champion Tomakesu-Hayato to fight Nomi-no-Sukene, who then kicked Tomakesu-Hayato to death in a unique fighting style that developed into jujutsu. An alternate theory suggested jujutsu had its origins among the samurai between the eighth and sixteenth centuries as an unarmed fighting style, kicks and punches having little effect if a warrior had to defeat an armed and armored opponent without the advantage of a sword; and so pins and throws, chokes and joint locks on unprotected targets like the neck and wrists and ankles had evolved.

Liliane halted on a street corner. "This is far enough." She'd not be bringing Figg within arm's reach of the nanny house where she lived with Mam.

He looked as if he might argue. Liliane raised up on her tiptoes and brushed her lips against his cheek. "*Merci.* You have been most kind to escort me." Figg blushed and bowed and fled.

Liliane stifled a giggle. For all his skill at jujutsu, the footman had almost tripped over his own feet.

She heard a sound behind her. No scrabbling of claws, this, but shoe leather on cobblestone. Slowly, Liliane turned around.

Coffey stood beneath a street lamp, swathed in a greatcoat with as many capes as any coachman, the faint light making a halo of his fair hair. "Thought you were going to give the lad a tumble. It was you as lured me into that hallway with your artful glances, no matter what lies you told Quin."

"It was no lie to say you put your hands where they weren't invited," Liliane responded, edging backward. "And I did nothing of the sort."

Coffey begged to differ. He knew a short-heeled wench when he saw one, or so he said; and he saw in Liliane just the sort of female who needed only the slightest nudge to roll over on her back.

"Crackbrain," hissed Liliane, indignant. "Have you already forgot I kicked you in your cullions and knocked you in the nose?"

The Loversall Novellas

Coffey reached into his greatcoat and pulled out a fistful of banknotes. "Come down off your high ropes. I've a bit of business to suggest."

Liliane eyed the money. True, Coffey was a pig. However— "Talk to me, *mon chou.*"

Chapter Ten

Kate sat at the breakfast table, sipping chocolate and trying to impose order on her chaotic thoughts: her cousin wished to kill her; Quin wished to ravish her for all the wrong reasons; and she couldn't say which circumstance disturbed her more. Seated across the table from her, Beau Loversall was enjoying a hearty meal of kippers and eggs.

Kate stiffened as Quin entered the room. Beau made a welcoming gesture with his fork.

Quin moved to the sideboard. "To what do we owe the pleasure of your presence, Beau? Another early morning ride?"

He was going to pretend nothing had happened between them, Kate decided. Well, to be fair, nothing *had* happened, save that Quin had rubbed her feet and then tried to seduce her, but of course she hadn't let him, and damned if she didn't want to dissolve into tears.

"Mrs. Thwaite has become rather too demanding. I'm letting her cool her heels. Since Mrs. Ormsby is currently engaged with her spouse, I find myself at loose ends." Beau glanced at Kate. "*Does* absence make the heart grow fonder, do you think?"

'Fonder' didn't come near describing the condition of Kate's heart, which from one moment to the next could not decide whether to break or burst. "I daresay it depends on the situation. A case could as easily be made for 'out of sight, out of mind'."

"There's a pretty setdown." Quin pulled out a chair. "I am uncertain which of us it was intended for. Speaking of setdowns, how proceeds your pursuit of the divine Miss Fletcher?" He, too, glanced at Kate. "'Divine' being Beau's word, not mine."

"You must need spectacles," said Beau. "Only a man with failing vision would deny Miss Fletcher is sublime."

"Divine, sublime, perceptive." Quin reached for the coffee urn. "Beau's pursuit of the lady isn't proceeding apace."

"So it may seem on the surface," Beau admitted. "However, was I a betting man—"

"Are you not?" Kate inquired.

Quin poured coffee into a cup. "Beau prefers to wager on the game of hearts. Females afford him a more gratifying return on the investment of his funds than do cards and dice. That is, they once did. Alas, how the mighty are fallen. Never did I think to see the day when Beau Loversall dangled at an opera dancer's slipper strings."

"I am *not* dangling!" Beau insisted.

"Of course you're not," soothed Kate, and nudged the jam pot beyond his reach.

"Of course he is," Quin differed. "However, I have a solution to his predicament that will serve us all."

Beau abandoned his kippers. "Why is it I mistrust your intentions? I am not usually the suspicious sort."

"Perhaps," suggested Quin, "you are more intelligent than you generally admit. Kate can't keep hiding in her bedchamber. We need an explanation for her presence here."

Kate suspected she might be perfectly content remaining unseen in her chamber. As for her presence, she couldn't explain it satisfactorily herself. Any female with a grain of sense would take her chances with murderous relatives rather than risk her heart with Quin.

How often, she wondered, did he find uninvited women hiding in his bed?

What would he do if *she* slipped between his sheets?

Kate pushed away her cup. Most likely, he would shove her out onto the floor. Where Edmund would be waiting to strangle her. At least then the business would be done.

"Since when does the Black Baron need to provide explanations?" Beau asked. "Your past relationship is reason enough."

"You alone are aware of our past relationship." Quin reached for the butter dish. "I prefer it remains that way."

The Loversall Novellas

Of course he did, thought Kate. "You and Liliane."

Beau looked startled. "Liliane?"

"She was attempting to ravish Quin. I came to his defense."

"Never did I think to see the day," Beau murmured ironically. "Far be it from me to belabor the obvious, but in that case the cat must be well out of the bag."

"So long as I supply the cat with sufficient cream," said Quin, "she will keep her claws sheathed. If I may continue? The servants realize there is a stranger in the house. I propose we explain Kate as one of your conquests. You have so many conquests no one will find it of especial interest if you acquire one more."

"But Miss Fletcher!" protested Beau.

Quin spread butter on a slice of toast. "Miss Fletcher's interest will be piqued."

"Excuse me," broke in Kate, not best pleased by this cavalier disposal of her person. "If I am to be Mr. Loversall's latest, ah, light o' love, wouldn't I be more likely to be residing beneath *his* roof?"

"But this is my roof!" argued that gentleman, entering into the spirit of the thing. "Or it was, as near as doesn't count. I think too highly of you to introduce you into a bachelor establishment, you see. And under the circumstances, I think you should call me Beau."

"*This* is a bachelor establishment," Kate pointed out.

"No," retorted Beau, "this is a gaming hell. And you, it would appear, are a *fille de joie*. In which case, I question why I would leave my *fille de joie* beneath the same roof as Quin."

"You trust me?" Quin suggested.

"In a pig's eye," snorted Beau.

Kate stared at the linen tablecloth. Truth be told, she wanted to be beneath no roof save Quin's. But Quin had neither mistresses nor relationships lasting more than a few hours. Was that what she desired for herself?

If only she could forget the feeling of his fingers stroking her foot. The memory made her squirm.

Both men were watching her. "I could have had an *affaire* with Quin at some point in the past," Kate offered. "Immoral creature that I am. Consequently we are both immune."

Beau said thoughtfully, "It might serve. Quin retains some vague fondness for you — oh yes, I grasp the reasoning behind this subterfuge — while I am quite *épris*." Head tilted to one side, he studied Kate. "No one will believe I am *épris* over anyone dressed as unfashionably as you are. I shall take you to Mme Dubois, which will give additional credence to our tale."

"But I am in mourning!" Kate objected. "Under the circumstances, it is hardly proper for me—"

"Under the circumstances," Quin broke in, "it is beyond hypocritical for you to preach propriety."

Kate clenched her hands in her lap, lest she hurl the jam pot at his head.

Chapter Eleven

Quin might have, had he cared to do so, counted numerous instances of ill-judgment made during the course of his career. None had been so momentous as his purchase of a gaming hell. With Moxley's had come responsibilities. People depended on him for their livelihood.

He stopped by the hazard table where, to the astonishment of everyone assembled, he went down fifty pounds. It was not Quin's custom to lose. Nor was it his habit to care one way or another whether Dame Fortune smiled or frowned.

Rather, it had not been his habit. Lately he had come to think he preferred to keep his fortune intact.

Quin suspected this about-face had to do with Kate. Precisely *what* it had to do with Kate, he could not say.

Did not care to say.

He was not accustomed to so much introspection.

Sobriety was not for the faint of heart.

He was called away from the hazard table by an altercation at the front door, where a band of drunken bucks were belligerently demanding feminine companionship, result of Coffey having told them whores of great skill and inventiveness worked within. It was damned mean-spirited of Quin to refuse to share, they stated, lightskirts being in the habit of serving themselves up to him on silver platters, while lesser mortals were expected to pay the going price. The bucks were persuaded to depart, at length and with lust left unslaked, only after Samson rolled up his sleeves and announced he was of a mind to break some heads. As result of this and other irritations, the hour was later than usual when Quin made his way to his bedchamber.

He opened the door. A fire burned on the hearth. A figure was curled up in the comfortable wing chair.

A female figure. But all the females were safely off the premises, or so he had believed. Quin realized he hadn't actually seen Liliane depart.

She had been all conciliation since they struck their bargain. Quin didn't trust her the merest fraction of an inch.

The figure stirred, sat up. Firelight gleamed in Kate's dark hair.

How had he forgotten for a moment that Kate was in the house? He certainly had not forgotten what happened the last time they were alone together in this room.

She'd accused him of meaning to banish her to the ranks of his forgotten women. It wasn't true. Quin hadn't set out to seduce Kate, or if he had it was without ulterior intent, or with no more ulterior intent than usual, and probably less.

He closed the door behind him. Kate's recent purchases hadn't included nightwear, unless she fancied voluminous neck-to-toe attire. Around her shoulders she wore a Norwich shawl.

Quin pulled off his coat, his waistcoat, unwound his cravat. Kate watched without expression. He wondered how far he'd have to go to wring a reaction from her.

And then he wondered if he truly wanted her to react to him, and why, or if this aberrant notion was result of the annoyances and frustrations of the past several hours.

"Nice shawl," he observed. "Did Beau purchase it for you?"

"Did you purchase it, you mean? The shawl suited my coloring, he said." Kate rested her dark head against the back of the chair. "Mr. Loversall introduced me to Mme Dubois as Kate Manvers. I daresay it hasn't occurred to you that I might have a care for my reputation, Quin."

Lord Quinton was hardly in the habit of concerning himself with female reputations. Feeling vaguely guilty, he moved to the fireplace. "Being as you are residing beneath my roof, your reputation is already tarnished beyond repair." He paused before he added, "You are safe here, Kate."

Wryly, she regarded him. "It's you who are safe, from other women, so long as I am on the premises. Or so you may think. You have not succeeded in making yourself ineligible, you know."

The Loversall Novellas

Quin rested an elbow against the mantle. "*Touché.*" Was Kate as aware as he of the huge bed looming in the shadows? Her feet were bare.

And very pretty feet they were. Quin knew every crease and curve. His fingers tingled with the memory of caressing her, tracing the length of her scar.

If only those once-perfect feet had grown callouses and thickened nails.

Quin left off thinking of Kate and bunions, a futile effort at any rate since it was proving no deterrent to his desire.

Thought of his eligibility, however, was. The Quintons were an ancient family, mentioned in the Domesday Book; they had been granted lands in Essex and Dorset by Duke William of Normandy following the Battle of Hastings in 1066. The title of feudal barony became one by patent — 'and for Us Our heirs and successors do appoint give and grant until him the same name state degree style dignity title and honour of Baron to have and to hold unto him and their heirs male of his body lawfully begotten and to be begotten' — issued by King John as result of some covert activity concerning the Magna Carta. In the ensuing centuries the Barons Quinton had successfully managed to curry favor and feather their nests, generation after generation, until the present day.

The current holder of the title had no heir nor was anxious to acquire one. Quin hoped his father was rolling in his grave.

Kate was observing him, more closely than he liked. "You never married?" he inquired.

"I lost my taste for the business," she retorted. "After Verena Wickersham. What became of her? I never heard."

Quin eyed the brandy decanter, which was on the other side of the room. "I couldn't say. She attempted to arrange a compromising situation. I refused to cooperate."

"And so she was truly compromised." Kate's tone made it clear she understood exactly what he had omitted. "Have you no conscience, Quin?"

If ever Quin had possessed a conscience, he'd done his best to root it out. "That is a foolish question. But I'm not surprised you ask. Whereas men seldom waste pondering motivations, women are forever desirous of determining what makes a man tick."

Kate made no response. Quin crossed to the brandy decanter, raised an inquiring eyebrow. She shook her head.

The devil with her. Quin filled a glass, and drank. Kate said, "You must surely realize that all those women want to bed you because of your reputation and not because of the man you are."

Quin didn't immediately reply, a facile response not suitable to the moment, and any other manner of response unthinkable, much as he might like to turn Kate over his knee.

Sex was, to him, a simple biological function. He enjoyed it in the moment, and performed his part with no small skill, and then dismissed the business with an indifference apparently irresistible to the opposite sex.

Irresistible, that was, until recently.

This member of the opposite sex had locked her door against him. Quin didn't recall any female locking a door against him before.

Or fleeing from his touch.

Usually it was the other way around.

Not that he took flight, precisely. Quin preferred to think of it as beating a prudent retreat.

And indifference, in this instance, was no good word for what he felt. "What did you think of Mme Dubois?"

Kate pulled the shawl closer around her. "I did not realize how countrified I have become. Skirts, Mme informs me, are conical in silhouette with various types of decoration, sometimes large and ornate and padded with cotton wool. Sleeves are alternately puffed at the top with a tapering lower sleeve, puffed in a huge billow from shoulder to elbow, puffed only at the elbow, puffed from shoulder to wrist; and known variously as the 'Marie' sleeve, the 'Demi gigot', and the 'Imbecile'; all these kept distended by down-stuffed pads or linings of stiff book-muslin and buckram, or in the most extreme cases, whale-bone hoops. As for necklines: the lower the better, so far as Mme Dubois and Mr. Loversall are concerned." She broke off, uncomfortable. "You spent a small fortune on me today. I will repay you after I meet with my aunt's solicitor."

"No need." Quin didn't recall Kate was prone to nervous chatter, and was curious as to what had caused it now. "Consider it a compensation for our broken betrothal vows."

Kate looked as if she wished to comment on that broken betrothal. Instead she bit her lip. "You are under no obligation. I am in your debt."

Quin could think of a means by which she might repay her debt, reprobate that he was. He experienced a vague disappointment Kate didn't seem similarly inclined.

Nonsense, he told himself. This odd emotion must be relief.

There was a long silence before Kate spoke again. "Edmund will know by now that he has lost his inheritance. He'll be looking for me in hope of getting it back. Yet you tell the world I am staying here. What are you playing at, Quin?"

Chapter Twelve

In so large a metropolis as London, amusements of every variety could be found; and if gambling houses such as Moxley's fixed themselves up in imitation of the more exclusive gentlemen's clubs, lesser hells were not so nice. Edmund Underhill found himself in one of those lesser places now. The long low-ceilinged room was furnished with chairs and small tables and dimly lit by small lamps, the air pungent with stale perfume and unwashed bodies and tobacco smoke.

Edmund gestured for another bottle. He had not recovered from the shock of learning that what he'd believed his fortune was, in fact, earmarked for Kate. The family solicitor — unaware himself until recently of the changes made in the disposition of the Underhill estate — apologized but explained that, legally, there was nothing to be done. Edmund left the office in a temper, deriving scant satisfaction from the knowledge he had frittered away a fair amount of Kate's windfall.

The remaining funds had been meant to finance his come-about. Edmund had arrived in London intending to present himself as a young gentleman newly in possession of a fortune, who would be welcomed everywhere. But matters had turned out otherwise, as was clear from his surroundings, and where the deuce *was* Kate? Not in Yorkshire, where she should be, which suggested her suspicions might have been aroused.

She had seen nothing, surely? Edmund stared into his glass. Sometimes in memory he heard his mother's head thudding against the steps. Sometimes he wakened, drenched in perspiration, from dreams of dead eyes. It was her own fault, he informed Dorothea on those occasions. She should have been more sympathetic to his needs.

Whatever she had seen, or hadn't, Kate must be located. Edmund was her next of kin. It was unlikely she had already made a will.

He turned to his companion, a friendly sort of fellow if unsettling in appearance, with pallid skin, pale eyes (one set off by a fading bruise) and colorless hair. They had met at the hazard table, where Edmund had gone down heavily, then spent the next hour matching each other drink for drink. "Thing is," he confided, "I'm hunting a female."

"What sort of female?" The pale-haired man, as it turned out, had vast knowledge of the prostitutes who plied their wares in nearby Covent Garden, including the details of their age and appearance, and the specialties for which each was known. One excelled at the game of schoolmistress, with the aid of a brace of youthful pupils; another was deemed a fluent linguist due to the agility of her tongue; a third was noted for her enthusiastic application of the amatory arts, which frequently resulted in teeth marks left on her admirers' anatomy. Discipline, by means of green birch brooms and cutting rods, was a favorite overall.

Edmund filed away these details for later consideration. "Not *that* sort of female. What did you say your name was?"

Coffey hadn't said, but saw no harm in it. "Charles Coffey, at your service," he replied, not without some truth; he had already helped this greenhead part with a goodly portion of his coin, encouraging him to attempt to recover his gaming losses by doubling his stakes, a stroke of ill judgment which would not go unrewarded by the house. A man of Coffey's standing didn't receive a fixed income for luring young men of fortune into places such as this for the purpose of plundering them of their property, but instead from time to time was permitted to borrow large sums from the hell-keepers, it being understood on both sides the loans would never be repaid.

Coffey was, as Quin had so aptly put it, always on the hunt for pigeons ripe for plucking, with plump pockets and more hair than sense.

His current pigeon, Coffey suspected, hadn't many feathers left.

Quin had himself been an excellent source of income until just recently; so inebriated in general, and so wealthy, that he hadn't missed, or at least begrudged, the occasional pound or ten.

Now Coffey wasn't permitted to pass through Quin's front door. Damned if the Black Baron wasn't turning into a dull stick.

The Loversall Novellas

Ah, well. A man couldn't expect to win each hand. Coffey felt philosophical tonight, due to the ministrations of a medical student with an unfortunate addiction to vingt-et-un.

And speaking of doxies, as he had been so recently: Coffey watched Liliane enter the room and gaze around her with distaste. He raised his hand and beckoned. Liliane's disdainful expression did not change.

She sauntered toward the table, ignoring the admiring glances cast in her direction. Damned if she wasn't a fine saucy piece. She was also damned expensive, and proving less than helpful about matters at Moxley House.

Coffey pulled out a chair. Gingerly, Liliane sat down. "This place is not at all *comme il faut*," she sniffed. "Me, I do not see why you insist I meet you here."

Coffey raised his pale eyebrows. "If you would prefer a tête à tête—"

Edmund roused from ruminations involving scheming cousins and usurped inheritances. "Not this sort of female, either," he protested. "A *particular* female. Thought I saw her in New Bond Street today but when I turned back she was gone."

"What sort of female do you think I am?" Liliane indignantly inquired.

"Don't mind him," said Coffey, before Edmund could respond. "What have you found out?"

"Precious little. I can't exactly search his lordship's rooms." Liliane eyed Edmund. "Who is this man?"

"Nobody," said Coffey. "Otherwise known as Edmund Underhill."

"It's not as though she's the sort of female as ordinarily catches the eye," continued Edmund. "Dark-haired. Skinny. Walks with a limp."

Coffey experienced a moment of that clarity which sometimes comes to persons who are under the influence of pharmaceutical substances. Damned if his ignominious expulsion from Moxley House hadn't been witnessed by a skinny dark-haired female who walked with a limp. Casually he inquired, "What's so important about this wench?"

Edmund's face contorted. "She has something of mine and I mean to have it back."

Coffey fell silent, mulling implications.

"Bugger!" muttered Liliane, under her breath.

Chapter Thirteen

Kate gazed with curiosity around the gaming rooms. Her previous experience with play had consisted of joining Aunt Dorothea at piquet. With no less interest did the gamesters inspect Kate. Inspired by the promise of largesse, Mme Dubois had exceeded all expectations. Kate was in possession of several gowns originally intended for someone else.

This particular gown was black, a lovely creation fashioned of bombazine silk with two bands of roses adorning the hem, puffed sleeves of a variety whose name she had forgotten, and a dramatically plunging neckline. Around Kate's throat and wrists and dangling from her ears were exquisite jet beads, courtesy of Quin, and she was spending far too much time wondering where he'd come by the set. Her dark curls were fashioned in an intricate looped knot.

Beau drew her arm through his. He was almost as splendid as she. Dark trousers correct for evening wear, blue dress coat with gilt buttons, white marcella waistcoat, snow white stock— Beau Loversall had no need of padding to broaden shoulder or calf, or corset to nip in his waist. He escorted Kate through the chambers, relating scandalous on-dits about the people present, plying her with champagne. He always plied his women with champagne, Beau informed Kate when she protested at being presented with more of the effervescent beverage. People would think it odd she didn't become mildly tipsy, he said, and winked.

"Rogue," responded Kate, positioning her glass so as to partially prevent the nearby gentlemen from staring down her décolletage, as they were staring at every other female present, of which there were more than a few. If this was the way *filles de joie* normally went about, it was a marvel they didn't all catch their deaths of cold.

Beau was explaining the various ways in which a gamester might influence the outcome of play. An experienced cardsharp could easily slip an old gentleman from the deck, an old gentleman being a card somewhat larger and thicker than the rest of the pack, while an old lady was a card broader than the rest. "To be used sparingly and with discretion," he added. "A man has to take care not to become notorious for the regularity with which he wins. No one wins regularly at Moxley's. Samson keeps close watch."

Kate hoped Samson was on the alert for more than cardsharps. Quin had promised Kate would come to no harm beneath his roof.

Pointless to wonder who would keep her safe from him.

Where *was* Quin? Kate had not seen him for some time. It seemed almost as if he was avoiding her. And who could blame him, were that true? Kate either assaulted or insulted the man each time they met.

One of the dealers demonstrated how to make a deck of cards march up her arm and down again. Politely, Kate smiled.

"If you want people to believe you are my inamorata, you will have to do better," Beau scolded. "My inamoratas are never bored."

That, Kate could well believe. "I am not used to being the cynosure of all eyes."

"You may blame your neckline," Beau said bluntly. "Not that the rest of you isn't equally sublime. I myself was struck speechless. You are in high bloom."

"I am unveiled, you mean."

"You are bait. Now, where was I? Ah, yes! I was being thrown into a transport of passion. If not struck entirely speechless, at least head over heels."

Despite her discomfort, Kate's lips twitched. "You needn't try and flimflam me."

"But I must. It is expected." Beau raised her hand to his lips. "To continue: I am smitten. I should have seen it before. But you have been hiding your light beneath a barrel." His eyes twinkled. "As it were."

Kate couldn't help herself; she laughed. "What's most shocking in all this is that I'm almost tempted to believe you."

Beau grinned. "Well, yes. I *am* quite good."

The Loversall Novellas

"You should laugh more often, Kate. It suits you," said Quin, at her elbow. "However, I suggest you try and remember why you're here." Kate swung round to protest but he had turned from her and was strolling through the crowd.

"I'm good," repeated Beau, reclaiming her attention, "but I beg you *won't* believe me. Quin has killed his man three times in a duel. I do not care to make a fourth."

Over which forgotten females had those duels been fought? There could be no question but that females had been involved. "I doubt he would feel compelled to defend my honor," Kate replied, all amusement fled.

"I don't think honor is a consideration, when it comes to Quin." Raised voices broke into their conversation. Two women — one fair, one dark, wearing modish gowns and identical irate expressions — were bearing down on them.

"Mrs. Thwaite and Mrs. Ormsby," sighed Beau. "I suspect they have heard I am dressing, and therefore most likely also undressing, another female; and have consequently suffered a revulsion of feeling so profound there is nothing for it but they must tell me so." There was no time for further explanations. The ladies were upon them.

Beau was correct; they had much to say. 'Curst rum touch' was mentioned, and 'coxcomb' (to which Beau took exception), as well as 'worm' and 'cur'. Mrs. Ormsby lamented that she had been treated in so cavalier a fashion; Mrs. Thwaite expressed great disappointment that the object of her affections should behave so shabbily; both ladies agreed that whatever Mr. Loversall may have been in his grasstime, he was a cod's head now. Moreover, he was a worse profligate than even the Black Baron, because the Black Baron broke only one heart at a time.

Beau listened, politely, until they paused for breath, at which point he remarked the ladies had known from the beginning that he was the most faithless creature in creation, so why in Hades were they kicking up such a dust?

As Mrs. Thwaite and Mrs. Ormsby erupted with further indignation, Kate escaped to the supper room, where she sank down gratefully on a chair. After so long standing, her lame leg ached. There were two suppers served each evening — tonight's fare a substantial repast of cold chicken, joint and salad; sherry, brandy, and the like — but the room was empty save for the servants passing through the discrete doorway that led to the nether realms of the house. Kate set down her champagne glass, hoping for a few uninterrupted moments in which to catch her breath.

She was not granted them. Liliane swept into the supper room, eye-catching in a crimson gown so low-cut that in comparison Kate felt positively demure.

Liliane pulled up another chair to the small table. "Aren't you fine as fivepence? Mme Dubois makes all our gowns. Which brings to mind what I wish to say to you. Gentlemen are predictable creatures, in the nature of asses and geese. If one doesn't want you, another will; and once the second does, the first will follow suit. And as to that, his lordship has many enemies."

Kate didn't doubt Quin had enemies. How could he not, after the life he'd lived? But she was not among them. "What's that to do with me?"

"You can't be so beetle-headed," scolded Liliane. "It's everything to do with you. I'll admit I cast my eyes in his direction, but that was only cream-pot love."

"You cast more than your eyes," Kate retorted drily. "Or *my* eyes played me false."

"His lordship probably *will* play you false, if he hasn't already, but I'll say as shouldn't that you have the wrong sow by the ear." The conversation degenerated into an incomprehensible jumble of ladybirds and lickspittles and females who tried to suicide themselves, interspersed with an occasional *Zut* and *Mon Dieu!*

The sound of a throat clearing brought Liliane abruptly to her feet. "Me, I was just taking a breather," she explained to Samson, who stood scowling in the doorway. "Until the contretemps died down."

"Mr. Loversall has departed, and the ladies with him." Samson jerked his head toward the door. Liliane muttered, "You'll remember what I said."

Alone again, Kate tried to decide what, precisely, Lilianne *had* said. That Quin clothed a harem? That he had enemies?

And how on earth were they to convince the world she was Beau's latest flirt when he was always off flirting with some other female?

Or, in the current instance, more than flirting, she conjectured.

The Loversall Novellas

"Excuse me, miss!" came a voice from behind her. Kate turned to see a gaunt grey-haired woman hovering in the servants' doorway. She was wearing a dark dress of the sort favored by upper servants.

Kate hadn't known Quin had a housekeeper.

Obviously, she didn't know a great many things about Quin.

"If you please, miss, his lordship says—" The woman's words were slightly imprecise, as if she wore an ill-fitting set of false teeth. Her hands twisted in the fabric of her skirts. "Would you mind coming closer? Himself wouldn't want this to be overheard."

Kate wondered who might overhear conversation held in a deserted room. Still, the woman was clearly anxious, and so she stepped out into the passageway. "What is it his lordship says?"

"It's not what he says now, but what he will." The woman raised her hands. With one, she beckoned. In the other, she held a gun.

Chapter Fourteen

"What do you mean, Kate is missing?" demanded Quin.

Samson didn't gulp, exactly, but he did swallow hard. "No one has seen Miss Manvers since she went into the supper room."

Quin surveyed the supper room — filled with diners sitting down to the second serving — and cursed himself for not keeping closer watch on Kate. He had removed himself from her vicinity after discovering that watching patrons gape at her décolletage made him all out-of-reason cross. The owner of a successful gambling establishment didn't go about breaking his customers' heads.

He really was quite spoilt. So accustomed to females pursuing him that it put him out of sorts when one did not.

But this was no moment in which to ponder his numerous deficiencies of character. "You're certain she's not in the house?"

Samson remained a prudent distance from his employer. "Aye."

"And she didn't leave by the front door?"

Samson shook his head.

"Then," said Quin, through gritted teeth, "she must have gone out through another. Which she would hardly have done of her own accord. Was there anyone who shouldn't be in the other areas of the house?" And if so, how had that been allowed to happen, he didn't say aloud, but Samson nevertheless turned pale.

"I don't see as how anyone could have slipped in unnoticed," he answered. "Everybody was told to be on the alert. Rosamund did say as she glimpsed an older female when she went down to the kitchen, but figured it must be Miss Manvers' abigail."

Kate *should* have been assigned a maidservant. Why hadn't Quin realized before? In his defense, he was hardly in the habit of acquiring maidservants for the various ladies of his acquaintance, said acquaintance seldom lasting more than a few hours. Still, his failure to provide for Kate was yet another indication of his tendency to think only of himself.

Exposure to Miss Manvers was rapidly shattering what few self-delusions he had left.

The kitchen, Quin discovered, was a spacious room with a lofty ceiling and a stone flagged floor. Cookware of all descriptions — copper pots, bronze cauldrons, pottery bowls, salt boxes, spice holders, butter stamps, graters, and a number of items he didn't recognize — were displayed on the numerous dressers and open shelves that lined the white-washed walls. Servants bustled back and forth between the large scrubbed elm table and cast iron kitchen range. When Quin entered the room, they stopped to stare, as astonished as if their realm had been invaded by a kangaroo.

Enquiries elicited the information that yes, a strange woman had been glimpsed in the house. One person thought she was this, and another that, but all agreed it wasn't their place to question which of his females their employer chose to have on the premises, or why, even when the female didn't seem at all his sort. This attitude further annoyed said employer, who had made it a point *not* to have extraneous females on the premises, save Kate, who could by no stretch of anyone's imagination be called his.

And furthermore, Figg the footman was also no longer on the premises.

"Come with me," Quin said to Samson, and strode toward the back door. The kitchen staff watched in silence as they exited.

Samson hailed a hackney. "You suspicion where she's gone to, guv?"

"I do." Edmund Underhill, Quin had discovered, owned no London house. When in town, he stayed at Richardson's in Covent Garden, a well-known hotel.

Mr. Underhill was not to be found at Richardson's, however. After accepting a generous gratuity, the porter allowed as the gentleman could most likely be located at a certain establishment in Maiden Lane, which was to his way of thinking a low sort of place and not to his lordship's taste. If the porter were to make a suggestion, which he would be happy to do, for an additional small stipend—

But Lord Quinton had returned to the hackney, and was rattling away.

The porter had misjudged him. His lordship was acquainted with the establishment in Maiden Lane. He gained entrance without difficulty, having visited this and similar establishments more times than he could count. A brief conversation with an individual of singularly sinister appearance, Sprowl by name; another exchange of coins; and then Lord Quinton and Sprowl were moving through the rooms, Samson at their heels.

They found Coffey seated at one of the small tables in a low-ceilinged anteroom. Beside him brooded a dark-haired man.

Sprowl nodded toward a doorway on the far side of the chamber and then took his leave of them. Samson raised his eyebrows. Quin inclined his head.

Samson approached the table, grasped the dark-haired man by the collar, and hauled him upright. "Edmund Underhill? His lordship is wishful of a word."

Edmund choked, sputtered and struggled. His chair fell over with a crash. Such was the nature of the establishment that none of the other patrons so much as glanced his way.

Samson forcibly escorted his captive over to where Quin waited. "Who the devil are you?" Edmund snarled.

"Nemesis," responded Quin. "Take him outside."

'Outside' was a narrow alleyway, illuminated by light coming through the windows of the adjacent buildings, redolent with sewage and refuse. Samson propelled Edmund through the doorway; released him so abruptly he staggered and almost fell. Quin demanded, "What have you done with Kate?"

Edmund straightened his lapels. "Kate who?"

"Kate Manvers. Your cousin. If you've the sense God gave a goose, you'll not waste my time."

"I have no idea what you're talking about." Edmund took in his surroundings with one quick assessing glance. "As it turns out, I have a few things to say to my cousin. If you come across her, perhaps you could persuade her to stop playing least-in-sight."

Quin said, grimly, "You want to more than speak to her, I think."

"Mr. Underhill is hunting a particular female," offered Coffey, who had wandered outside in their wake. "One who limps."

Quin removed his jacket and handed it to Samson. "Edmund is hunting the limping lady because she is aware he pushed his own mother down the stairs."

Coffey stared disapprovingly at Edmund. It wasn't at all the thing to go around pushing mothers down the stairs.

Quin unbuttoned his waistcoat. "He is responsible as well for the accident that left the lady lame."

"I didn't!" growled Edmund. "If Kate says otherwise, she lies."

"I don't think I'd take his word," said Coffey. "The man's a blackguard."

Quin grabbed Edmund's lapels and shook him hard enough to dislodge what brains he might possess. "Damn you! Where is Kate?"

Edmund jerked out of Quin's grasp. "I wouldn't tell you if I knew."

Scowling at each other, the men took up a pugilistic position. Samson placed a heavy hand on Coffey's shoulder, lest he be tempted to interfere.

It was, as Samson later described to a group of fascinated footmen, as neat a bit of cross and jostle work as a man could hope to see. Had he been giving odds on the outcome of the encounter — which he might have done, but Coffey hadn't survived so long without being fly to the time of day — he would have wagered Mr. Underhill had no more chance of planting Lord Quinton a leveller than a cat in hell surviving without claws. Although the other gentleman displayed well enough, his lordship was not only fast on his feet but had the most wicked of left hooks. Quin landed Mr. Underhill a facer and in so doing drew his cork — "That's for Kate" — followed by a blow to the bread-basket — "And that's for Dorothea" — ending with a clout on the jolly nob —"And *this* is for the kitchen cat!" Quicker than a cove could say Jack Robinson, Mr. Underhill landed on his bumfiddle in the muck.

"Now," said Quin, who despite his various dissipations was barely breathing hard. "Tell me where she is."

Edmund dabbed at his swollen mouth. "Damn you, I don't know."

Quin turned aside in exasperation. Quick as any adder, Edmund drew a dagger from his boot and lunged. Quin spun round, caught Edmund's wrist and turned the blade toward him. Edmund could not halt his momentum. His eyes widened as the knife plunged into his heart.

Widened, and then clouded. Quin released him. Edmund crumpled to the ground.

Samson withheld comment. Coffey muttered, "Bloody hell."

"There you are! I have been searching for you everywhere." Daintily, Liliane picked her way toward them through the refuse. She twitched her skirts away from Edmund, who lay in an ever-widening pool of blood. "Is that man dead? *Alors!* I can tell you where your Kate has gone — but it will cost you dear, milord."

Chapter Fifteen

Kate saw no means of escape from the small parlor, which was furnished with a surprising degree of luxury, and located in the rear of what seemed to be a large and very busy house. Only one door opened into the chamber, and that door was firmly closed. The windows, behind their elegant damask hangings, were barred.

At least the pistol was no longer pressed against her ribs, although staring into its muzzle was little more reassuring. "This is a lovely room, Miss— Ah. We have not been properly introduced. What do you prefer I call you?" Kate inquired.

The woman gazed at her mockingly. "How polite we are. Shall I offer you refreshment? Is sherry to your taste?" Kate inclined her head. The woman reached for a decanter and poured, maintaining her grip on the pistol all the while. "In answer to your question, I'm known here as Mam."

Gingerly, Kate took the glass. "Where is 'here'?"

Mam laughed, revealing an unexpectedly fine set of teeth. "You're in a house of civil reception. A nunnery. Where anyone sufficiently flush in the pocket can make the beast with two backs."

First a gambling hell, and now a bordello, mused Kate. Her experience of the world was advancing at a startling pace.

Judging from those teeth, which Mam was displaying in a most unnerving manner, the woman was younger than she had first appeared. Kate took a deep swallow, felt the sherry course through her, warming her throat and belly. "And so you are—"

"Laced mutton?" suggested Mam. "Haymarket ware? I am the abbess of this fine establishment as well."

Wonderful. Kate was being held prisoner by a bawd. She hoped Quin would soon rescue her.

But why should he think to search for her here?

And why *was* she here?

Kate took another swallow, trying not to think what might be going on in other parts of the house. "What do you mean to do with me?"

Mam looked her over, critically. "Sell you, of course. Maybe at auction: I haven't yet decided. There's some as like a cripple. To each his own, I say."

Kate might have said several things, all of them unwise, had not a sudden horrendous suspicion caused her to clench her teeth.

Was *Quin* familiar with this place?

"Are you ill?" Mam inquired, with mock solicitude.

Kate had been too nervous to eat dinner. She had nothing in her belly but champagne, sherry, and butterflies.

The sherry packed a particularly potent punch. "You've drugged me!" Kate gasped.

"Naturally I drugged you, ninnyhammer. What did you think, I snatched you up so we could have a comfy coze?"

Came a tapping on the door. Eyes fixed on Kate, Mam called out, "Who's there?"

Liliane strolled into the room. Her eyes narrowed at sight of Kate. "Moxley's closed early due to a spot of trouble. What's *she* doing here?"

Mam aimed her pistol, briefly, at the doorway. "She's the cheese in my trap. You should have told me the minute she showed up at Moxley House."

"Why should I have done?" Liliane came closer. "What's this one have to do with the price of peas? And how did *you* know she was at Moxley House? If there was others about your business, you should have said, so we wouldn't trip all over each other and ourselves. Or mayhap you're forgetting it was you as told me too many cooks spoil the broth."

"I had no one else at Moxley's." Mam gestured toward Kate's gown.

"Mme Dubois?" Liliane frowned. "Beau Loversall bought those clothes."

"Beau Loversall is a notorious nipfarthing," Mam said impatiently. "Quin paid the reckoning. And now he's going to pay another that is long past due."

Liliane looked blank. "She means to sell me," Kate croaked.

"Sell you?" Liliane echoed. "But you are quite old!"

"Keep a civil tongue in your head," snapped Mam. "She's no older than I am. The Black Baron's partiality for her will compensate for any shortcomings she may have."

"What partiality? Quin holds me in no fondness." Difficult to converse rationally, Kate discovered, when one's tongue didn't fit properly in the confines of one's mouth. She tried to lift her hand, discovered she could not, and gurgled a protest.

"It sounds like a crack-brained scheme to me," Liliane said severely. "We're waiting for him to put in an appearance here?"

Mam oozed exasperation. "No. We're waiting for this one to grow properly pliant. His lordship's invitation hasn't yet been sent."

Liliane looked doubtful. "You must know your own business best."

Kate wasn't feeling at all pliant. She wanted nothing more than to give Mam a good kick. Still, she couldn't find it in herself to be especially afraid. It was as if they were actors playing out a scene, the others strutting and declaiming all around her, while she squatted on the sofa like a broody hen.

Mam shifted in her chair. Liliane moved aimlessly around the room, touching this, picking up and discarding things.

Kate had never before been inebriated. Her current condition gave her a better understanding of Quin. It was rather pleasant to be so detached from her surroundings, her thoughts bouncing like a rubber ball from this to that and back again. If she was in a bordello, did that mean Liliane was a *fille de joie*? If so, was Liliane a *fille de joie* by choice or by force? If by force, what hold had Mam over her? Kate imagined any number of potentially extortive situations might arise in the course of an evening's enterprise. Perhaps Liliane had inadvertently killed one of her customers in an excess of passion and Mam disposed of the corpse.

Would someone be obliged to likewise dispose of Kate?

She'd have a few words to say to Quin about his promise she'd be kept safe, when next they met.

If next they met.

Kate marveled at her imagination, which was not usually so lurid. And surely she was hallucinating, because suddenly Quin was standing in the doorway, a pistol in one hand. Kate blinked — she was pleased to discover she could still blink — but he didn't disappear.

Instead he walked into the room, pistol pointed straight at Mam, and said, "Put down the gun."

"Or you'll shoot me? I think not." Mam raised her own gun, aimed at Kate. And then she tossed aside the spectacles, spat out the plumpers that distorted her cheeks, pulled off her wig to reveal faded blonde hair.

Kate stared, struck speechless by more than the drug that she'd ingested. Even Liliane blinked. Quin said, slowly, "So. Kate has naught to do with your vendetta. Let her go."

"She's everything to do with it," retorted Mam, much more distinctly. "Can you deny you would have married *her*?"

Kate might have denied it, could she have untied her tongue. Quin was not the marrying sort of gentleman.

He scowled. "You know damned well, Verena, that I never said I'd marry you."

"No, but you seduced me easily enough," Mam — Verena — spat. "I expected any moment you would make an offer. Instead you showed me a clean pair of heels."

Quin had seduced this woman? A bolt of strong emotion burned through Kate's mental fog. A sun-drenched afternoon, the feeling of hands against her flesh, the smell of new-mown hay— If Quin had taken Verena Wickersham to and in that stable, Kate would stick a pitchfork in them both.

Verena gestured toward Liliane. "That isn't all you showed me. Say hello to your by-blow." Quin and Liliane regarded each other with mutually appalled astonishment. "So you see," Verena added with relish, "Miss Manvers is merely the icing on the cake."

This was like watching a melodrama. Kate decided some audience participation was required. "If you refer to Liliane being in Quin's bedchamber," she whispered with an immense effort. "Nothing happened. I was there."

Verena scowled at Liliane. "Nothing happened? But you said—"

"*You* said he was an elbow-crooker who was full of juice," interrupted Liliane, scowling in her own turn. "And that he'd die of barrel fever soon enough, but in the meantime he'd bleed freely, and so I should ingratiate myself. But it was all a bag of moonshine. Just look at him! He's as sober as a judge."

"He always was a damned unpredictable devil." Verena sighed. "I daresay his people have taken over my house. There's nothing for it. We'll have to shoot them both."

Liliane moved out of pistol range. "*You'll* have to shoot them. I'm not aiming to dance the sheriff's jig."

Verena kept her gun trained on Kate. "Take care I don't shoot you too. How sharper than a serpent's tooth it is to have a thankless child."

"*Thankless?* You were going to have me debauched by my own father, you mad old bat." Liliane snatched up the sherry decanter and brought it down, hard, on Verena's head.

Chapter Sixteen

Quin hesitated in front of the door leading from his bedchamber into Kate's. Behind the barrier, he heard sounds of movement. Steeling himself, he turned the knob.

Kate was wrapped in a voluminous nightdress. Her valise sat open on the bed. Quin wore the same clothes he had the night before, since he hadn't yet retired.

Without waiting for an invitation, he entered the room. "I would offer my condolences, save that even your aunt's solicitor agrees your cousin is no great loss. Fitting, I think, that he should have inadvertently died by his own hand. As for our other villain, Verena Wickersham is being restored to her family. An account of recent events will be provided them, along with my strongly worded suggestion that she be confined in a private asylum somewhere, which I suspect they will find preferable to the public embarrassment of her imprisonment and trial." And Coffey, as result of these recent misadventures, had decided to pursue his pigeon-plucking in another part of town.

Kate leaned against the bed. Her dark hair tumbled loose over her shoulders, and her face was pale. Quin would never forget the fear he'd felt at seeing a pistol trained on her. He said, "How do you feel?

"Like some large unpleasant spider has spun cobwebs in my brain." Kate brushed loose curls back from her face. "How did you discover where I was? Were you familiar with that place?"

"I was not. Which is why Verena went to such lengths. Liliane glimpsed 'Mam' at Moxley's, and grew alarmed. When you turned up missing she sent Figg to watch the bordello, suspecting Verena would take you there.

Liliane had the devil of a time tracking me down, else we would have come for you sooner. I was convinced Edmund was to blame."

"Doubtless Edmund would have been, had he known I was here," Kate said. "But why was Liliane so helpful? I mean, if she wasn't aware you and she were, um, related? I didn't realize she was so young."

"Nor did I," responded Quin, with feeling. "Or she would have never got past the front door. As for her helpfulness, we had struck a bargain. Liliane, it seems, isn't one to go back on her word. Moreover, she informs me, it isn't *sporting* to go around snatching people off the street."

The bawdy house had been a fortress. Verena had not expected to be taken by surprise. However, her staff proved easily seduced by silver, collectively displaying no more loyalty than a louse. Any lingering reluctance was dispelled by a dazzling exhibition of Figg's prowess at jujutsu, which inspired a number of tarts and customers alike to abandon their mutual exertions and marvel at how this and that were done. At the same time, Samson had distracted Mam's bully boys with an account of how he managed to remain upright against Jem Ward for one hundred and thirty eight rounds and one and one-half hours, which wasn't something often heard straight from the horse's mouth.

"Beside," Quin added wryly, "my pockets are deeper than Mam's."

Kate lowered her gaze to her hands. "Verena expected that even the Black Baron must be devastated to discover he had defiled his daughter. She underestimated you."

Quin shouldn't have been surprised Kate held him in low esteem. Had he not gone to great lengths to prove he gave a damn for nothing and no one? "Having never defiled a daughter, I cannot say how I would have felt. There might have been a certain piquant perversity involved. I was certain I had managed to indulge in every depravity at least once. Not it turns out I have not."

"You are a failure," Kate said wryly. "If you bribe enough people, you may prevent word getting out. When I said Verena underestimated you, I meant you had no interest in Liliane." She fell silent for a moment. "When you and I — were you and she — damn you, Quin, you know what I mean."

Damn him indeed for his curst reputation. "No. That is: yes, I do know what you mean; and no, I was not. Verena and I were history by the time I met you. At least, *I* thought we were. Verena, as it turned out, intended otherwise. When all else failed, she went to my father and told him I'd taken her virginity. You know the rest."

"Not even the half of it, I'll wager." Kate's tone was less censorious than curious. "*Were* you her first?"

"Hardly. Nor was she mine." Quin watched as she picked up a garment, folded it, placed it in the valise. Of course Kate was leaving. Why would she care to stay?

"Where are you going?" he inquired.

"I haven't decided. Other than that it won't be Yorkshire." Kate moved away from the bed. "You said there would be a price for your assistance. I've been thinking what your price might be."

Quin watched her walk toward him. "I promised you'd be safe with me. It was not the case. Any debt you might owe me is canceled out."

"I pondered your rakehelly ways," Kate continued, as if he had not spoken, "and wondered what you would ask of me, and if I would agree. You expressed a curiosity about my other lovers. I will tell you about them now."

"I would prefer you did not."

"There have been none."

Quin stared at her. "None?"

Her eyes fixed on his face. "No one has touched me since you last touched me. I wish very much you would touch me now."

She stood so close Quin could have easily reached out and touched her. He told himself he must not. Quin had touched a thousand women. Kate had touched only him.

Ah, but he was a sinner, and bound for damnation. Quin raised one hand and gently traced the outline of her face.

Kate turned her cheek into his palm. "You broke my heart."

Quin raised his other hand and brushed back a loose tendril of her hair. "You badly damaged mine."

"Then perhaps we are even." Kate straightened her shoulders. "About that price—"

Quin set her away from him. "This is madness. You can't still want me, Kate."

She smiled at him. "Oh, but I do."

Lord Quinton was not in the habit of self-denial, or considering what was best for another person. He was uncertain if he had ever before attempted to put another's needs above his own. Still, it was obvious Kate did not grasp the enormity of his iniquities, else she would not be offering herself to him.

He must disabuse her of her delusions. "I am a bad man."

"I know you are."

"Women tend to think they may redeem me."

"Not I."

Quin folded his arms so he could not crush her to him. "You believe me beyond redemption, then?"

Kate shrugged, and the nightdress slipped off one slender shoulder. "I believe each man must redeem himself. Providing he is so inclined. On the other hand, I hear the pathway to perdition can prove surprisingly pleasant. I have been lonely, Quin."

How could he refuse her? Quin had been lonely, too. Furthermore, he owed Kate a debt, or she owed him one, or they were in each other's debt for events that had transpired today and yesterday and seventeen years ago— He was a little muddled as to who owed what to whom.

Quin lifted Kate into his arms and carried her across the room. He placed her on the bed and paused, allowing her this last opportunity to change her mind. She drew her nightdress up over her head and dropped it on the floor.

Well. What was a man to do?

His breath on her flesh, her lips and teeth against his skin; a caress here, and there, and oh yes, *there*. Quin took his time, kissing her slowly, thoroughly, with infinite patience and pent-up passion, and found it oddly difficult to breathe as she did the same to him; kissed her and caressed her until she had lost all reason, and he had as well. It was the first time again, both his and hers, though he could not recall precisely when his first time had been; the first and also somehow the last, because for all his women, Quin had made love to no other, and never would.

It was not the pathway to perdition he travelled with Kate, but to paradise.

The Black Baron was not known for a tendency to cuddle following the amorous congress, or before it for that matter, but after he had divested

The Loversall Novellas

Miss Manvers of what little virtue he had left her, they lay entwined, his cheek resting against her breast.

Quin found all this quite pleasant. So pleasant indeed he thought he might like to do it frequently, and for a long time. "What now, my Kate? I am yours to command."

She was too wise to ask him for how long. "The south of France, I'm told, is particularly nice this time of year."

And because she did not ask him, Quin answered her unspoken question. "I never forgot you for a moment. I have always loved you, Kate."

Epilogue

"Married!" Beau stared aghast at Liliane. "Surely you jest."

"It is true, *je t'assure*," Liliane informed him. "I witnessed the ceremony myself." She half-expected Beau to ask why *she* should have been present, but he was too stunned.

The gaming rooms were doing a brisk business. Gamblers were losing vast sums at faro and E.O. Adele eyed Liliane speculatively, as did Rosamund, from across the room. Doubtless they were wondering how she came to be acting as hostess in Lord Quinton's absence, albeit under Samson's shrewd skeptical eye; concluding her rise in status was result of blackmail; speculating how Quin had been caught out, and what misstep he had took.

Beau, meanwhile, was brooding. What was the world coming to when the most wicked of all the wicked stepped into parson's mousetrap? Love changed a man, and not for the better. He vowed to make bloody sure the malady never afflicted him.

"So now you are the most wicked rakehell in all of London," remarked Liliane, a little wickedly herself.

"Profligate in residence," Beau murmured. "It has a nice ring. What is it you're keeping from me? Could I persuade you, do you think?"

Liliane winked at him. "I am no tell-tale, monsieur."

He laughed and pinched her cheek, and then excused himself. Miss Mary Fletcher having at last succumbed to his charms, Beau currently had his eye on Signorina Alfonsina Giordano, a tempestuous Italian actress newly arrived at the Theater Royal.

Liliane watched him make his way through the crowd. Lord Quinton's marriage wasn't common knowledge, but unless she'd mistook her mark, it soon enough would be.

She entered the next room, where hazard was the game of choice, caught a curious glance from Daphne, who was casting the dice. Liliane moved among the guests, stopped to speak with this person and that. Tonight she wore a blue silk gown made high up to the neck, one of the advantages of her new status being she no longer need put her assets on view, which resulted in the patrons flocking round her, men being the contrary creatures they were.

In the front room, croupiers waited on either side of the rouge et noir table, rakes in hand. They, too, would be conjecturing what she had on Quin. Liliane exchanged a nod with Samson and stepped out into the hall.

She paused there for a moment, savoring her solitude. Though few knew it, Moxley House now belonged to her. Since she was too young to own property outright, Quin would act as her guardian until she came of age.

Whenever that might be. Liliane wasn't certain of her birth date.

Just think, she might be a baron's side-slip.

Or she might not, Mam having scant acquaintance with either virtue or the truth.

Liliane had never particularly wanted a father. She had no higher opinion of the opposite sex than she had of her own.

On the other hand, Quin was much more generous than Mam. He had been so appalled by the possibility of parenthood that he made generous provision for Liliane despite their mutual reservations, and then immediately removed himself from the vicinity, which suited her just fine.

She walked down the long narrow corridor, gave the black basalt bust of Voltaire a passing pat, entered the private portion of the house. In her bedchamber — not the chamber assigned her in the servants' quarters, but the one recently occupied by Kate — Liliane removed her gown and folded it tidily away; pulled on white cotton drawstring trousers and a matching jacket, and drew the sash tight around her waist. Barefoot, she slipped into the adjoining room.

The furniture had been pushed back, leaving a large clear space in the middle of the floor. Thick mats were spread on top of the rug.

Figg was waiting in one of the mahogany armchairs. He wore a costume similar to hers.

As Liliane entered he rose to his feet and stood silently staring straight ahead, the perfect footman, able to open doors and perform other small services while at the same time appearing deaf, mute and blind.

Able, also, to instruct a young woman in what he called the Art of Yielding and Pliability.

They bowed to each other. Liliane approached until she stood only an arm's length away. *Take his balance,* she silently recited. *Remember your timing. Position. Leverage.*

She turned her back on him, bent her knees, ducked under his arm. Right foot in front of his right foot; her left arm across her body to grasp his right. Hip and buttocks tight against the front of his thighs. Bend forward and pull and—

"*Voilà!*"

"Well done, Miss Liliane," said Figg, from his supine position on the mat.

"Arsy varsy," agreed Liliane, and grinned.

A Respectable Female

Chapter One

The wickedest rakehell in London (true, he had not had the title long, and only held it now because his predecessor had, against all good advice and common sense, retired from the field) strolled through the gaming rooms at Moxley House. He exchanged flirtatious glances with the pretty croupiers stationed at the rouge et noir table; the tall brunette who stood banker at faro, the amber-eyed minx who cast the dice at hazard, the russet-haired beauty who presided at E.O. Loversalls were notorious for their amorous adventures, the gentlemen renowned for the number and quality of their mistresses, the women for their inclination to love unwisely and too well. Beau had done his damnedest to live up to the Loversall tradition. Of late he'd secretly begun to wonder why.

Moxley's had once belonged to a member of his family. Beau considered it a second home, the difference between this and his primary residence being that here no one expected a man to do more than he felt like doing, save game away a fortune, and everyone knew Beau Loversall was more inclined to play at l'amour than the board of green baize cloth.

He paused, his progress interrupted by a voluptuous young woman with masses of honey-blonde hair, a straight little nose and big green eyes, who was wearing a high-necked, long-sleeved emerald silk gown that clung to her enviable curves. She had placed herself smack in his path.

Beau raised a brow. She lowered hers. "*Zut!* I'll thank you to leave off casting sheep's eyes at the staff. It distracts them from what they're supposed to be doing, which is to make sure that it's the customers and not the house that's being fleeced."

"Don't work yourself into a fidget." Beau knew that, despite her accent,

Liliane was no more French than his boot. "There's no harm done."

She looked him over — lean muscular figure clad in an excellently fitting corbeau colored coat, white marcella waistcoat, cream-colored kerseymere breeches that fitted snugly to calf and thigh; face of such wicked perfection as to make an angel weep; red-gold hair worn slightly longer than was fashionable, and disheveled as if from an amorous caress; eyes the deep blue of fine sapphires — and sniffed. "Clearly you have no notion of the cost of champagne and green peas."

"No, nor do I care to." Beau tucked Liliane's hand through his arm. She permitted him to escort her into the supper room, where crystal chandeliers illuminated small tables laid with silver and fine china set on pristine linen cloths.

The supper room was empty of company at this hour, save for the solitary gentleman brooding at a corner table in company with a half-empty bottle of brandy, which as they watched he hoisted with an unsteady hand. Deeply, he drank. A lock of dark hair tumbled forward on his marble brow.

"Young Tremaine," murmured Liliane. "Luck smiled on him at the faro table, but abandoned him at hazard. Now he doesn't know how he's to come down with the derbies without applying to Messrs Howard and Grubbs."

Beau wouldn't have been surprised to learn his companion received a commission from the local moneylenders. Moxley's held out irresistible allure to impressionable young greenheads eager to prove they were men of the world. Liliane was the mistress of Moxley's, the hell's titular owner — the afore-mentioned previously most wicked — having recently removed himself from Town. "What will you do?"

"Give him the opportunity to buy back his vowels. Beyond that—" She shrugged. "A cove who can't afford to pay, shouldn't play. Why are *you* playing least-in-sight tonight?"

"I'm not avoiding anyone," Beau retorted, with perfect truth; much as he might like to, a man could hardly avoid his own reflection in the looking-glass. Lately he'd taken to bypassing mirrors altogether whenever he could. In a mere three years, Beau would turn fifty, and upon attaining half a decade (or seeing it looming on the horizon, which wasn't far enough away by half) had been inspired to stop and not only take a good look in the mirror but take stock of his life. What had he accomplished? How much time did he have left? If he turned up his toes tomorrow, would anyone care? His daughter might, for a moment, but Zoe's primary focus would always be herself. His various relatives might mourn a few moments longer, but not many, while his mistresses—

Beau winced. His latest *inamorata*, Signorina Alfonsina Giordano, a tempestuous Italian actress employed at the Theater Royal, had at the climax (or anticlimax) of their last encounter hurled a vase at his head.

It was deuced unfair. If a man was allotted a finite number of indulgences in his lifetime, he should bloody well be warned of it before the hourglass ran out.

Liliane nudged Beau, reclaiming his attention. "You might try the bile of a jackal. Or melting down the fat from the hump of a camel. I hear it's a bang-up remedy for a shaft that refuses to rise above half mast."

Beau cast her a quelling glance. "There's nothing wrong with my mechanics, thank you very much. It's my enthusiasm that has flagged."

"You have that look about you, like a brat whose favorite toy is broke." Liliane tapped one slender gloved finger on her chin. "The head being shaved and anointed with mustard, is recommended for the lethargy. Or, alternately, a spoonful of mustard in the mouth. Which should at least distract you from feeling mopish, *n'est-ce pas?*"

"You're enjoying this entirely too much," Beau growled.

Before she could goad him further — Liliane had many more remedies to suggest, involving soup made from animal genitalia, powdered rhinoceros horn, skink flesh and sparrow brains — a burly, black-clad, bald-headed man entered the room. His eyes were cold as the depths of winter, his nose as flattened as his ears. A noted bruiser before allegations of misconduct resulted in his banishment from the ring, Samson now preserved his pugilistic efforts for the gaming hell. Woe betide any patron caught doing what he shouldn't. He'd find himself summarily snatched up by the waistband of his trousers and tossed out into the street.

Altercations at the entry were not unusual events at Moxley's, Liliane having barred any number of choice bloods from the house. The current choice blood, one Roderick Kilpatrick, otherwise known as Randy Roddy, was demanding to speak with his brother Beau.

"Half-brother," Beau amended. The Loversalls in general were not noted for carnal circumspection. His own father having been a prime example of the breed, Beau had numerous half-siblings, most of whom he'd never met. Randy Roddy was not among those strangers, alas.

"*Merde alors!*" said Liliane. "You might find it easier to play at bo-peep if the whole world didn't know where you were hid." She glanced at the burly Samson. "If the blighter raises a further rumpus, feel free to break his head."

If Beau didn't persuade Roddy to cease haunting the front door of Moxley's, Liliane might put *his* head next in line to be broke. Therefore, he accompanied Samson through the gaming rooms, along a carpeted hallway, down the broad stair and through the iron-shielded green baize door into the foyer, through the front door and down the steps into the cobblestone street. Moxley's stood on the west side of the Haymarket, at the northern end; two residences combined behind a red brick facade, each with basement, three stories and a garret, four chambers to each floor.

Roddy was leaning against the iron railing that guarded the basement area of the house. The handsome looks that in his youth had brought him a brief success upon the stage had long since faded. His golden hair was thinning, his skin puffy from excess; his double-breasted coat showed equal signs of wear, as did his breeches and top boots.

He straightened and stepped away from the railing. "Damned if you aren't a buck of the first head, brother," he sneered. "Adding Miss Liliane to your stable of whores."

Beau owned no such stable. True, he numbered Mrs. Ormsby, Mrs. Thwaite and Miss Mary Fletcher among his admirers, and aspired half-heartedly to acquire Signorina Giordano, but they were hardly whores.

As for Liliane, he would rather bed a barracuda. "Want me to crack his napper?" Samson inquired.

Sorely tempted, Beau resisted. "I'll reserve that privilege for myself."

"Have it your way, guv." Samson took up a position at the bottom of the steps.

Beau regarded Roddy without enthusiasm. "What do you want now?"

Roddy pressed a hand to his chest. "Is that any way to talk to a member of your family? And family we are, even if one of us is full of juice while the other don't have sixpence to scratch with."

This was a refrain heard far too often. "Been drawing the bustle too freely, have you?" Beau asked.

"'The quality of mercy is not strained'," quoth Roddy. "The gentle rain from heaven blesseth both him that gives and him that takes." Beau refusing to respond, he gave up playing Portia. "It's no easy thing, living hand-to-mouth. Being as we're related, I'm giving you the opportunity to help me raise the wind."

Beau wasn't one to waste the wherewithal. Especially on improvident half-siblings, as Roddy should know from previous encounters of this nature. With mild curiosity he inquired, "Why would I do that?"

Roddy raised one hand and beckoned. From the shadows emerged a slight, cloaked figure, obviously female. "Behold! Prime goods. If you don't snap her up, some other gent will."

A skilled player, whether at games of heart or chance, learned to prevent his feelings from being writ across his face, in this instance a foreboding that sent Beau's stomach sliding toward his toes. "I can't imagine why you believe me to be in need of female companionship," he drawled, and for good measure flicked a fleck of nonexistent lint from his coat sleeve.

Roddy smiled, revealing a missing lower tooth. "Ah, but she ain't just any female. Izzy, show us your face."

The girl halted in front of them. Clutching the edges of the cloak together with one hand, she pushed back her hood.

Hair was as golden as Beau's own. Wide dark-lashed sapphire eyes. Her features were as divine as any goddess's, her skin fair and fine as the most priceless porcelain, her cheeks pink with cold.

Or with embarrassment. Roddy flipped back her cloak to reveal a garish scarlet gown. Beau could not help but notice that the girl had a splendid bosom, most of it on display, and a figure so enticing that any man who saw her would wish to whisk her off immediately to bed.

Rather, almost any man. Beau felt not the slightest stirring of desire.

She bit her lip. Beau glimpsed a dimple. He experienced a burning sensation in his chest.

Chapter Two

Beau whisked his new acquaintance through the doorway, up the stairs, and into a pleasantly proportioned chamber with rosewood furnishings, a polished oak floor, green and white striped paper hung on the walls. He retreated to the fireplace, rubbing the bruised knuckles of his right hand.

"*Eh bien!*" said Liliane, who had followed them into the morning room. "That must be some conversation you and Randy Roddy had. Who is she, other than a Loversall?"

"She's too young to be my sister," muttered Beau. "Beyond that, damned if I know."

Liliane studied the young woman, who was gazing wide-eyed around the morning room, which was far from fascinating, save for the bloodstain on the carpet and the ink stain on one wall. Beau raised his voice. "I am Beau Loversall. This is Miss Wickersham. You are in her house. Roderick called you Izzy. Is that your name?"

The young woman started, then curtsied awkwardly, due to the valise she was clutching to her chest. "Everyone calls me Izzy, though my real name is Iseult. After the legend of Tristan and Iseult. Have you heard it, sir? Iseult's husband King Mark, who was also Tristan's uncle, came upon Tristan and Iseult as he was playing the harp for her under a tree— They had accidentally drunk the love potion prepared for Iseult and Mark, so it wasn't their fault if they committed adultery! The cruel king stabbed his nephew in the back with a poisoned lance, and Tristan, at Iseult's request, crushed her in a fatal embrace as his final act. They were buried side by side. Two trees, hazel and honeysuckle, grew out of their graves. King Mark tried to have the branches cut three separate times but each time they grew back and intertwined. Eventually he gave up and let them grow. Isn't that a moving tale?"

Liliane had listened to this account with fascination. "*Voyons!* They both died."

"Yes, but they died for love!" protested Izzy. "And it is only a story, after all. From what I have seen, people don't do things like that in real life. My mama certainly did not. Though if she and my father had drunk a love potion, perhaps things might have worked out other than they did. Mama was a parson's daughter, you see. Papa was an actor, playing Romeo. Mama no sooner set eyes on him than she tumbled violently in love. Papa must have been smitten also, because they ran off together within a fortnight. But pretty is as pretty does, and Papa didn't act as pretty as he looked, and so Mama took me and left him when I was two years old. Grandfather let her return to the rectory, after he'd given her a dreadful scold, though no one could call her a fallen woman, because she had her marriage lines."

Beau roused from the stunned stupor that had struck him. "Roddy is your *father?*" Badly as Loversalls generally behaved, this was a new low.

Izzy nodded vigorously. "Mama seldom spoke of Papa; she said that if one can't say anything good about a person, one should say nothing at all. And now that I have met him, I understand what she meant. Although I didn't have a chance to know him well, and do not wish to be judgmental. No doubt he has many fine qualities."

"If so," Beau commented drily, "he hasn't chosen to share them with the rest of us."

"Maybe if he had," said Izzy, "you wouldn't have broke his face. Not that I mean to criticize! I'm sure you meant it for the best. But he seemed so *diminished* lying there in the street."

Roddy had deserved to be diminished. Selling off a family member. Beau had been so annoyed at being forced to play knight errant that he'd popped him in the nose.

Liliane gestured Izzy toward the sofa and sat down beside her. "You do realize your father meant to sell you?"

"He *did* sell me!" Izzy responded. "I never claimed he was a nice man. But he is still my papa, even though I cannot like him, which I realize is unChristian of me, because 'needs must when the devil drives' and I

The Loversall Novellas

daresay Papa *wouldn't* have sold me, if he hadn't been in need of funds. Or maybe he would have, because I don't think he liked me much. Which makes me even sadder! Since I have lost my mama, he is the only family I have left. I'm running on again, aren't I? Mama used to say that I'm a dreadful gabster. You must do as she did, and tell me to leave off. 'Maidens must be mild and meek, swift to hear, and slow to speak'."

Beau broke into this monologue. "Slow down! Your mother is deceased?"

"There was a contagion in the village." A tear trickled down Izzy's cheek. "Both Mama and Grandpapa took sick and died, and though it is not for me to question the ways of our Creator, it seems a shabby way for Him to repay His servants' good work." Guiltily, she flushed. "I did not mean that, of course! But it has been very hard. Mr. Addington, the curate, said I could stay with them, but his wife didn't like the notion because she already has too many mouths to feed. So when I found Papa's address among Mama's belongs, I took it as a Sign, because surely a father would long to know his daughter, or so one would think. We composed a letter, and Papa sent me the money to come to London, but now he has gone off and left me here and I am truly all alone in the world." A tear trickled down one pretty cheek. "It is very sad to stand on bad terms with one's only parent. Even if he is, though I should not say it, a shocking loose screw. You needn't look so surprised! Just because a person chooses to find the best in other people — in the case of Papa, I *try* to at any rate — doesn't mean that she can't see what's right in front of her."

Not unacquainted with weeping females, Beau pressed a handkerchief into Izzy's hand. "You aren't alone. You have various relatives, most of which, unfortunately, are not in Town."

Izzy dabbed her little nose with the linen square. "How kind you are! I cannot understand why my mama wanted nothing to do with the Loversalls. Maybe she assumed you are all like my papa, which clearly you are not! You *do* look a little bit like him, sir, but I see no signs of meanness around your eyes and mouth. You will think I am a goose but I have to ask: who *are* you? I don't like to appear pushing, but you haven't explained how we are related."

Liliane raised her eyebrows. "You went off with Beau without knowing who he was?"

Izzy looked puzzled. "What else was I to do? It would have been cowardly to run away. Yes, and ungrateful also, because Mr. Loversall had just given money to Papa. You should not have, sir. But it was very generous of you, and I'm sure you meant it for the best."

"*Incroyable!* Beau Loversall paying for a female," marveled Liliane. "Who would have thought to see the day?"

Beau shot her a quelling glance. "If you wish to see many more days you'll keep a still tongue in your head. Your father is my half-brother," he explained to Izzy, and then there was nothing for it but he must expound upon the family tendency toward amorous excess.

"Perhaps Papa *did* love my mama," Izzy ventured.

Liliane snorted. "And perhaps frogs may learn to fly."

Izzy eyed her with interest. "It is unusual, is it not, for someone as young as you to have an establishment of your own? Maybe you are a harlot. 'The lips of an adulteress drip with honey, and her mouth is smoother than oil; but in the end she is bitter as wormwood, as sharp as a two-edged sword.' I've never seen a harlot, so I wouldn't *know*. Oh dear, I shouldn't have said that, should I? And after you have been so kind."

Beau and Liliane remained silent, both struck temporarily mute by the notion that Liliane was 'kind'. "I didn't mean to insult you," Izzy added earnestly. "I only thought maybe you were — that! — because you are so pretty that you must shine every other lady down."

"*Merci,*" murmured Liliane. "How old are you, miss?"

"Sixteen," Izzy replied.

Beau groaned.

"Do you have the headache?" Izzy asked sympathetically. "'A cheerful heart is good medicine, but a crushed spirit dries up the bones'."

"No, I do not have the headache!" snapped Beau. "What I have is you, and what the deuce am I to do? Mine is a bachelor establishment. I can hardly take you home. Nor can I leave you unprotected. You are legally your father's property as long as you are underage." Liliane, meantime, was recalling when she had been sixteen, which wasn't that long past, and what she had been doing, which was in some ways preferable to what she was doing now.

Liliane hadn't risen so far in the world that she'd left off assessing every new situation for potential advantage to herself. *This* situation was rife with possibilities, not least among them an entertainment for herself. "I have a solution. Izzy can remain here while you decide what is to be done. She'll be safe enough at Moxley's until you can find a respectable female to act as her chaperone."

"Respectable female?" Beau echoed blankly before he added, "She can't stay in a gaming hell!"

"Why not?" inquired Liliane. "Your daughter did."

"You have a daughter?" Izzy asked with interest. "Will I get to meet her?"

Beau fervently hoped not. "Zoe is in Italy with her husband," he explained.

"Oh." Izzy brightened. "I have always wanted to see the inside of a gaming hell. Or I *would* have wanted to, if I had thought about it, which I hadn't because why should I? Dear uncle, do say I may stay!"

Beau experienced a vicious throbbing behind his left eye.

Chapter Three

The most respectable Miss Penelope Parrish contemplated her brother across the teapot and repressed an urge to empty the salt cellar into his cup. Mr. Philip Parrish was a surgeon, and sufficiently successful at his profession that, if he wasn't as celebrated as Sir Astley Cooper, for example, they went on well enough.

Rather, *he* went on well enough. Naturally, the family funds had gone to pay for Philip's apprenticeship and the additional training that enabled him to become not only a member of the Royal College of Surgeons but also the Society of Apothecaries, and Pen was beyond selfish to regret there'd been no provision set aside for herself. It wouldn't occur to Philip to dower her now. Even if the idea *did* occur he would immediately dismiss it, because what would be the point when, at eight-and-thirty, his sister was set so firmly on the shelf?

"*Cannabis indica,*" he informed her, "not *cannabis sativa.*" Philip was currently experimenting with the use of various substances during surgery to alleviate pain, in this specific instance the pain of having a prolapsed intestine pushed back into the patient's abdomen, before a testicle was ligated and removed.

Mr. Parrish wasn't of the opinion that female sensibilities (at least his sister's sensibilities) should be sheltered. Consequently, Miss Parrish couldn't lay claim to a single missish bone. Nonetheless, discussion of testicles over the teacups was more than she could countenance. "Cook and I came to blows over a recipe for stewed beef and celery sauce this morning," she informed him. "I stabbed her with a butcher knife and stuffed her body in the stove."

Philip regarded her suspiciously. "Are you bamming me again? I must be a dreadful trial, my head always in the clouds." The mantle clock chimed the hour and he rose hastily. "I'm late! Enjoy your afternoon, my dear." As he departed the room, he dropped a kiss on her brow.

Pen pushed away her empty teacup. Philip had no notion of how she filled her hours, and if she tried to tell him would hear only one word in ten, the rest of his attention being reserved for matters medical. She rose and went to confer with the housekeeper about the relative merits of cedar-wood, camphor, and tobacco leaves as preservatives against the ravages of moths; then descended the stair. Her brother's house was situated on the eastern side of Jermyn Street, not far from St. James's Market, with living quarters above the consulting rooms where he saw his patients, and an apothecary shop on the ground floor.

Philip had already seen patients that morning. His afternoon would consist of ward visits at St. Guy's, and lectures at nearby St. Thomas's Hospital, after which would come dissections or operations, dinner and a nap, and an evening spent seeing additional patients, preparing lectures, or writing down the results of his research.

Pen unlocked the door to the consulting rooms, and entered. Philip's current apprentice being jealous of his duties, she found not a surgical thread out of place. Before the advent of young Mr. Gordon, Pen had sometimes assisted her brother with his practice, performing minor surgical tasks, applying and changing dressings, and taking notes.

One might call her a true 'Jack of all trades, master of none,' mused Pen. She was familiar with the paradoxical benefits of poison, the medicinal properties and best applications of laudanum and paregoric and mercuric chloride; and knew as well how to restore whiteness to scorched linen, and preserve cut flowers, and make a pomade for the hair. What she *didn't* know was how it felt to be kissed by a man other than her brother. Only once had she come close.

Such stuff was for the young, and Pen was young no longer. And if sometimes she drifted off in daydreams of a handsome rogue, she would keep that weakness to herself. Romantic imaginings were most unsuited to a female of her advanced age.

Having reasoned herself into a fit of the blue devils, Pen opened her brother's black leather medical bag. Lancets and scalpels, bleeding cups and probes. Dental pelican. Multibladed phleam.

A tap sounded at the outer door. Pen looked up, surprised. The consulting rooms weren't open at this hour.

The tapping came again. Pen was tempted to ignore the summons, in hope the intruder would leave. Reflecting that Philip would hardly thank her for turning away a potential candidate for surgery performed under the influence of *cannabis indica,* she moved to the window and peered out. Red-gold hair and sapphire eyes, the figure of a sportsman, the countenance of a rake—

Pen blinked. Had she suddenly developed an ability to conjure up ghosts? Why else should this particular ghost present himself here, now? But the reason didn't matter, did it, because the mere sight of him made her pulse pound, and her belly quiver, and her fingers twitch to grasp the phleam and apply it to his all-too-tempting flesh.

She was a mature female, Pen reminded herself. Not a moon-eyed miss. Schooling her features into an expression of polite disinterest, she opened the door.

Beau Loversall was aging well, she reluctantly conceded, as he stepped across the threshold. He looked her over in turn and she saw herself as he must: a sensible-looking female with a slender figure and a practical, no-nonsense manner, hazel eyes and severely subdued — at least, she attempted to subdue it — chestnut hair.

"Why are you here?" she asked him, irritated. "So far as I know, my brother hasn't yet come up with a cure for the pox."

He glanced around the surgery; at the desk, cluttered with books, papers and bottles; the full skeleton that stood in one corner; the oak examining table and the mahogany medicine chest. "Are you still angry with me? I *did* apologize. If it would make you look upon me with more favor, I will be happy to do so again."

"Don't waste your breath. You could apologize a thousand times and still not sound sincere." Pen might be mature, but she saw no need to be polite.

His faint smile faded. "It's damned difficult to sound sincere when you're being threatened with beheading. Since Philip isn't here to do me bodily damage, I will apologize — sincerely — for attempting to steal a kiss. But in my defense, you *were* at Vauxhall and—"

"And I had so much the appearance of a ladybird?"

"It was dark and I was foxed. May we move on, please?"

Pen folded her arms across her chest. "Very well. I repeat, why are you here?"

Beau looked as if he wished he *wasn't* there. "I have a favor to ask."

Pen gaped at him. "Surely you jest!"

He frowned. "This is no joking matter. I find myself in need of a respectable female."

"Oh? Have you lost your taste for the other kind?" Pen was pleased to see him flinch. "Why would you think I'd help you? For that matter, why would you think my brother— Ah. You waited to approach me until after Philip left the house."

"I didn't want my head handed to me on a platter." Beau's gaze lingered on an especially fine amputation saw.

Pen also eyed the saw. "Or some more vital body part."

"You have no great opinion of me, do you?"

"Would you expect me to?"

"I suppose not. I was an ass. I *am* an ass. I should be grateful that you opened the door. But you *did* open it, and so here we are. Believe me, if I could think of anyone else who would suit as well, I wouldn't have approached you. Alas, I cannot. And so—" Beau awarded her a bone-melting smile.

Her knees weren't really growing weak, Pen told herself; she was much too strong-willed a woman to dissolve into a puddle at a rakeshame's feet. "That smile is far too practiced," she informed him, stiffening her spine. "And this is hardly the way to gain my assistance. No woman cares to hear that a gentleman has approached her only because he is at his last prayers."

The smile faltered, but he rallied. "Don't think of this as helping me. Think instead of assisting a young woman who is not only without protection, but devoid of common sense.'

"A Loversall, in other words."

"A niece," Beau admitted. "That I wasn't aware I had. Her father— But you won't want to hear about that."

He actually believed that no female alive could withstand his cajolery. "Not particularly," agreed Pen.

The Loversall Novellas

Beau wasn't smiling now, but scowling in a manner that suggested he'd like to give her a good shake. "I had hoped you would at least agree to meet her before you made up your mind, but it seems I was mistaken. Excuse the interruption. I'll bother you no more." He strode toward the door.

Paradoxically, now that Beau was on the verge of departure, Pen wanted him to stay. Foolish female that she was. But it was only natural — wasn't it? — that she respond to the sheer physical presence of the man after encountering his ghost so often in her dreams.

And what rousing encounters they had been. "Where is this young woman?" Pen asked.

Beau turned back, his expression hopeful. "She is currently residing at Moxley House. I thought perhaps—"

He'd left a bird-witted young woman in a gaming hell? "You *didn't* think, as usual," Pen muttered, and went off to fetch her bonnet and pelisse

Chapter Four

Liliane glanced up from the cards laid out in front of her as Beau escorted a veiled woman into the morning room. She supposed she shouldn't be surprised he had unearthed a respectable female, rakeshames apparently having an odd affinity for such. "Uncle Beau!" beamed Izzy, who looked much more respectable herself today in a cream-colored muslin dress that Liliane considered far too modest to be worn by either her employees or herself. "Liliane has been showing me how to play vingt-et-un. She says I have *flair*."

Beau frowned at Liliane. "You do realize she hasn't a ha'penny to her name?"

Liliane scooped up her cards and deftly shuffled the deck. "But of course. One must keep one's hand in. There are pigeons waiting to be plucked."

"Pigeons?" echoed Izzy. "I shan't have to eat pigeons, shall I? They are such plump and pretty birds. Not that I mean to suggest they wouldn't taste delicious! 'A sparrow in hand is worth a pheasant that flies by'."

"You don't have to eat pigeons," Beau said, a trifle desperately. "Miss Parrish, may I introduce Miss Liliane Wickersham, whose establishment this is, and Miss Iseult Kilpatrick, Izzy, my niece." Pen pushed back her veil.

Izzy rose and dropped a curtsey. "I am pleased to meet you, ma'am. I daresay you will be wondering about Miss Liliane; I did myself! But it turns out she is *not* a harlot, which is a disappointment, because I have never met a harlot in the flesh. How does one meet someone out of the flesh, I wonder? Would that person be a ghost? I do not think I would like to meet a ghost. Which is not to say that ghosts are disagreeable!" She drew in a quick breath. "Have you come to lend me your good name, Miss Parrish? I am not certain I *wish* to be respectable. I always have been, but Miss Liliane is not—" Izzy turned back to her hostess. "I mean no insult, but no one who owns a gaming hell can be considered above reproach. You are an Original!"

"*C'est vrai.*" Liliane rippled the cards from one hand to the other. "Since we are observing *les conventions*, I should invite you to sit down. You are looking a trifle overwhelmed, Miss Parrish. I should offer you refreshment, no?" Pen allowed as that would be agreeable. Liliane rang for a servant, requested tea and a posset for the troubles gathered round Beau's head.

"Miss Parrish *does* look very proper," observed Izzy. "Which is not to say that she doesn't also look very nice!"

"You need not empty the butter dish over me. I am well aware of how I look," responded Pen.

She looked the same as she had that wretched night at Vauxhall. Beau knew damned well he did not. But then, Pen Parrish hadn't spent the past several years swiving every female in sight. At least, he assumed she hadn't. Maybe he mistook the matter. He was distracted for a few pleasant moments by this thought.

The tea arrived. Pen did the honors, at Liliane's request.

"*Convenable* is as *convenable* does, Miss Parrish." Liliane was eschewing tea for a glass of stronger stuff. "A respectable female wouldn't play ducks and drakes with her reputation, is that not so? Yet here you sit. You are also an Original, I think."

"You give me too much credit," Pen retorted, in a tone that made it clear she knew she was being given no credit at all. "For one thing, I am hardly a young woman. For another, my father and his father before him were mere tradesmen. Nothing I do will fascinate the gossips. There are advantages to being a spinster."

Izzy eyed her with interest. "You haven't married, ma'am? Did you take lovers instead? I daresay it is rude of me to ask, but 'If you have not a capon, feed on an onion', and if one *doesn't* ask, how is one to know?"

Pen looked slightly startled by these dietary suggestions. "One may ask. But the person asked is not obliged to explain."

She didn't explain, to Beau's regret. He too was curious about Pen's

The Loversall Novellas

lovers. Or, more likely, her lack thereof.

"I doubt that I shall marry," confided Izzy. "Lest I turn into a Dreadful Example, like Mama says – said! – all Loversall females do. Although I haven't heard that any of *them* asked for someone's head to be lopped off, or was turned into salt. *Or* arranged for numerous murders like Jezebel, and ended up being flung by her own eunuchs from a high balcony, and was run over several times by an iron-wheeled chariot, and had her body torn apart by dogs until only her head and hands remained." She peered earnestly at Miss Parrish. "Do *you* believe in True Love, ma'am?"

"True Love is so much twaddle," Pen said faintly. "An excessively foolish fantasy that has, alas, prompted many a gullible young woman to fling her bonnet over the windmill."

Clearly, Miss Parrish had never been tempted to toss *her* headgear. Beau moved to the window and gazed down into the gardens, which had not yet recovered from being ravaged by a goat. What in blazes had possessed him, to try and kiss Pen that night at Vauxhall? More to the point, what possessed him now, because he wanted to try and kiss her still?

Beau took a swallow of his wine, spat it out. "What the *deuce?*"

"Syrup of water lily," Liliane informed him, "put into a cup of claret is an excellent remedy for an overstimulated brain."

Beau deposited the glass on a nearby table. "Mama always recommended calves' foot jelly and a restorative biscuit," offered Izzy. "But I'm sure other remedies work equally well!" Miss Parrish in her turn suggested the venerable practice of trepanning, drilling a hole in the skull.

"My brother is a surgeon," she explained to her startled companions. "I have seen an artery ligated, and a tracheotomy performed, and witnessed first hand the results of the inhalation of nitrous oxide."

"What is an artery?" asked Izzy, causing Beau to wish he might inhale some nitrous oxide himself.

In more detail, he informed Pen of the circumstances that had brought his niece to this house. "It's one thing if a Loversall female chooses to be a prime article of virtue, and heaven knows enough of them have, but to be bartered off—" He glanced at Izzy. "Well."

"What's a prime article of virtue?" Izzy asked, and received three startled stares.

Liliane recovered first. "A prime article is the sort of female who would willingly wear your crimson gown."

Izzy wrinkled her nose. "I'd never seen, let alone worn, such a garment, but Papa took my other clothes, and I didn't care to hurt his feelings. Even though I knew it wasn't quite the thing!"

"Didn't care to hurt his feelings," echoed Beau.

" 'Honor one's father and mother'," Izzy reminded him. "Though it doesn't seem quite fair to have to honor someone who is *dis*honorable. I shouldn't have said that!"

"Really," said Pen to Beau. "I don't think—"

"Of course you don't," interrupted Liliane, seeing set before her yet another *divertissement*. "But can you reconcile it with your conscience to abandon a lamb to the wolves?"

"Oh!" said Izzy. "Is there a lamb?"

"Not so you would notice," Liliane replied. "However, there are definitely wolves. Think what would happen, Miss Parrish, were this one turned loose on the Town."

"Which one?" asked Izzy, bewildered. "Are you still talking about lambs?"

"Good God," muttered Pen.

"Then you'll take her home with you?" Beau asked hopefully.

Pen scowled at him. "Can you imagine my brother's reaction were I to introduce a Loversall into his household?"

Unfortunately, Beau could.

"Mr. Loversall and my brother were friends," Pen informed Izzy and Liliane. "Until an incident at Vauxhall when Beau mistook me for a fallen female and my brother was forced to intervene. That, combined with the family's reputation, was enough to make Philip take every Loversall alive in the greatest dislike."

" 'Don't play with the bear,' " said Izzy, "if you don't want to be bit'. Or do I mean, 'Never sell the bearskin till you have killed the bear?' In any event, I'm sure it was an honest mistake. Maybe Uncle Beau needs spectacles."

"The only way a man would mistake me for an embraceable female is if his eyesight was deficient?" inquired Pen. "You're not helping your case, child."

"Oh, no!" Izzy protested. "I didn't mean—"

The Loversall Novellas

Speculatively, Liliane regarded Miss Parrish. "It's true that you don't look like a ladybird. You should stay here and lend us your respectability. We don't lack for room." Pen looked astonished. Liliane added, slyly, "It would be an excellent solution. A pity your brother the surgeon would not approve. Naturally, you would fear to make him cross."

"You think me such a coward?" Pen's eyes flashed with indignation. Her fingers tightened on the arm of her chair. "My brother wouldn't have to know. I could tell Philip I'm going to stay with a sick relative. Cousin Emily, I think. We do not have a Cousin Emily, but he won't remember that."

Things were spinning rapidly out of Beau's control. If they had ever been under his control, which he took leave to doubt. "And if your brother should recall that he doesn't have a Cousin Emily?"

Pen cast him an impatient glance. "Trust me, Philip won't. But I couldn't stay here long. Nor can you remain at Moxley's indefinitely, Miss Kilpatrick. What would you like to do?"

"Pray call me Izzy!" said that young woman. "You mean I have a choice?"

"Not much of one," Liliane pointed out. "Without a ha'penny to her name."

"One always has a choice," Pen countered. "More or less. Tell me, Izzy, if I may be frank, do you *want* to join the demimonde?"

"Just what is the demimonde, please? I will join it if you say I should." Izzy clasped her hands together, looking absurdly earnest and very, very young.

Beau might have laughed to see Pen taken aback, had he not been so appalled. "*Sacrebleu!*" said Liliane, and took it upon herself to explain the Frail but Fair.

"Would I have to, erm?" asked Izzy, doubtfully, at the conclusion of this explanation. "It doesn't sound very nice. Although I daresay I misunderstood because surely a gentleman doesn't put his, ah, apparatus *there!*"

Beau recalled the last time he had attempted to employ his apparatus. It had not gone well. "Loversalls have tumultuous passions," Liliane reminded Izzy. "No doubt you would take to it, after a time."

"But if that doesn't suit, we will put our heads together and come up with something else," Pen added.

" 'Every pot has two handles'," agreed Izzy. "Maybe I could become a milliner's assistant. I do love a pretty hat."

Beau thunked his head against the window pane.

Chapter Five

Roddy Kilpatrick was also thinking of pigeons, and lamenting that he had not managed to pluck as many feathers as he would have liked. Moreover, he thought it shockingly unsporting that his own half-brother had assaulted him, as result of which he currently sported a swollen nose and two eyes surrounded with flesh bruised a vivid purple-blue. These sentiments he was confiding to his companion, one Hector Nottingham, about whom the epithet 'more hair than wit' might have originally been coined. Mr. Nottingham was a short stout fellow whose scant dyed locks were styled in a wind-swept Brutus crop. He sported crumbs in his sidewhiskers, as well as strewn down the front of his virulently striped waistcoat. Hector was only half-listening to his friend's diatribe, being intent on washing down his mutton pie with a potent brew known as a dog's nose.

Their glasses drained, the men called for refills. Roddy had already consumed a prodigious amount of that beverage commonly called Geneva, Frog's Wine and Blue Ruin, more genteel libations not on offer in this Covent Garden tavern, The Blind Pig, named after the fine specimen standing upright on his back trotters, wearing a natty waistcoat and curly brimmed hat and holding a cane, that hung on a faded plaque that hung outside the door.

The taproom was long and low-ceilinged, the air thick with tobacco smoke. Small lamps glowed in the corners. Sawdust covered the floor.

The Blind Pig was popular with actors and managers from the nearby theaters, who were unfortunately prone to shout out quotations, and reminisce about their triumphs, and pretend their failures had never occurred.

Roddy rose to his feet, raised his glass. " 'If you prick us do we not bleed? If you tickle us do we not laugh? If you poison us do we not die? And if you wrong us shall we not revenge?' " His fellow patrons for the most part ignored him, being accustomed to such outbursts, but a couple newcomers roused to comment, and a third threw a bottle which hit Roddy's shoulder with such force that he fell back into his chair.

"It's damned unfair that one son should be plump in the pocket while the other is purse-pinched," Roddy muttered, picking up where he had left off his sulks to spout Shakespeare. "A man's daughter should fetch more than £100. Beau didn't give me half what the chit was worth."

£100, by Gad! marveled Mr. Nottingham. 'Twas a sum more than sufficient to buy a thoroughbred. Why a man would pay so much for a non-equine filly exercised Hector's alcohol-addled brain.

He was long-familiar with his friend's grudge, which had largely to do with the circumstance that Beau Loversall belonged to the privileged class, and Roddy Kilpatrick did not. It was natural, Hector supposed, that a man run off his legs would like to see the boot on the other foot.

Less natural to threaten to cut out a sibling's liver and fry it. And what had Roddy said about a daughter? Hector allowed as he was a fat-headed fiddle-faddle fellow, but he wasn't so shockingly loose in the haft as to go about siring side-slips.

Lest *he* acquire a swollen nose, Hector kept these reflections to himself. Still, comment was called for. "You left the filly at a gaming hell?" he inquired cautiously.

"At Moxley's," Roddy retorted. "And I didn't leave her there, I sold her to Beau. You'd have sold her too. Or tossed her in the Thames. Never have I known such a female for prosing on. She made my head ache. I hope she makes Beau's head ache, curse him. I'll pay him in his own coin yet."

Hector interrupted before Roddy could continue further in this vein. "You left the filly at Moxley's," he repeated, determined to get firm grip on the facts.

"Beau took her into Moxley's and she ain't come back out. I've got eyes fixed on the place." Roddy quaffed his gin, swiped the back of his hand across his mouth. "My only child — least, so far as I'm aware — wrenched so cruelly from my bosom. Unnatural, that's what it is."

His only child, far as he was aware? Hector experienced a startling vision of numerous miniature Roddys descending on the town. "Said she gave you a headache," he pointed out.

"She'd give anyone a headache," retorted Roddy. "Damned if I want to listen to the chit, but that's beside the point. The point is I *can't* listen to her. That bitch Liliane won't let me past the front door."

Roddy had a daughter. How had that come about? Hector knew how one went about the business, of course, but— "You got a whelp on a serving maid? Ran off with a dollymop and abandoned her?"

"No," Roddy retorted irritably. "I married the wench."

Hector gaped. Randy Roddy Kilpatrick, caught in parson's mousetrap? It was hard for a fellow to wrap his noodle around the notion, Roddy being an enthusiastic patron of bawdy houses and bordellos, trollops and jades and impures, and not the sort of fellow to take a lawful blanket.

He must have been in his cups. Nothing else made sense.

True, in Hector's present condition, little made sense, for he had raised his elbow more times that he could count and was, if not properly shot in the neck, more than little disguised.

Roddy scowled at his shocked expression. "The marriage wasn't legal. Of course, I didn't tell her that."

Hector was relieved to hear it. If Roddy *was* leg-shackled, some of the things they'd got up to had been degenerate indeed. Marriage never made a man a saint, but still—

"I met her at Margate," Roddy continued. "Dorothea Jordan was playing there for the first time. She received more money than the theater on each night's performance, which you may be sure was more than I did." He staggered to his feet and struck another pose. " 'But, soft! What light through yonder window breaks? It is the east, and Juliet is the sun'." A second bottle followed the first, with equal accuracy, and Roddy abruptly sat back down. "I didn't know the wench was a parson's daughter. She didn't *act* like a parson's daughter at first. But then she turned all prim and prosy and went about spouting proverbs and singing hymns until I gave her a good clout on the ear. At which point she ran off. And now I can't speak with my one and only daughter, being as I'm banned from Moxley's as result of a misunderstanding involving loaded dice."

Hector knew about loaded dice. He had several in his pocket, high fulhams for throwing five to twelve, low fulhams for one to four, so called because they were originally made at Fulham, the most notorious place for blacklegs in all England in Ben Jonson's time.

"Devil take me," muttered Roddy, "if I didn't sell the girl too cheap."

The men lapsed into silence. Roddy reflected upon the vagaries of fortune, especially as concerned the contents of his purse. Hector reflected upon the various ways of cheating, with cards and dice, by means of handkerchief or snuffbox or rubbing the eye, which brought him also, circuitously, to financial transactions that turned out to be less advantageous than anticipated. "Don't seem the thing to sell a daughter," he said. "But since you done it once, don't see why you shouldn't do it again."

Roddy might have indulged far more than was prudent in Madam Geneva, but he was not so cast-away he didn't recognize a nacky notion when he heard one, and this notion *was* nacky, in spite of its source.

He raised his glass in a salute. "And if I can't get past Moxley's front door, my lad," he said, "you can!"

Chapter Six

Izzy was enjoying her adventure. She realized now that she had previously lacked excitement in her life. Miss Parrish not proving equally enthusiastic, Izzy dosed her with laudanum and saw her safely tucked up in bed. Then she donned one of the gowns loaned her by Liliane until something more suitable could be found.

She gazed into a gilt-framed mirror, and was pleased with what she saw. Pleased, but not surprised. Even the granddaughter of a parson understood that fair-skinned blondes with sapphire eyes were flattered by certain hues; and this long-sleeved Albanian robe of Sicilian blue poplin, ornamented up the front with silver buttons, suited her to perfection, if she did say so herself, which of course she shouldn't: 'Beauty's sister is vanity, and its daughter lust.' Izzy was uncertain what lust was, precisely, but suspected from her mama's admonitions that it had to do with gentlemen's apparatuses — apparati? — and the demimonde.

Miss Liliane's explanation of the demimonde — let alone apparatuses — should have sent the gently reared granddaughter of a parson into a dead faint. However, this gently reared parson's granddaughter could claim a great-grandmother who painted her countless lovers in the nude, a great-great aunt who eloped with her own groom, and other ancestresses who had similarly misbehaved and wound up in harems, or living with gypsies, and heaven knew what else.

If only her mama, in citing these Dread Examples, had supplied more precise details. Izzy didn't want to be like the cow who didn't know what her tail was worth until after it was lost.

She gave her skirts a final twitch, and cautiously opened the door. The upper hallway was deserted. Izzy stole down the stair. She should be dressed in mourning colors, not blue but white, and should not be having an adventure, or any fun at all, and she certainly shouldn't be exploring a gaming hell; but blood told in the end, and a wild goose never laid a tame egg, and what else could be expected from a Loversall?

This hallway was wider, lined with artwork. Izzy eyed a pedestal displaying a rather unattractive bust fashioned from black basaltware and puzzled over who it was meant to be. The murmur of voices grew louder as she neared the gaming rooms, the sounds of movement, the clink of glass. She peered through the doorway into the first room, where crowded around a table marked with two red and black diamond shapes, were gentlemen in a greater variety than Izzy had ever glimpsed before: clean-shaven and whiskered and mustachioed, hair pomaded or dressed with fragrant oil; wearing evening coats of blue and brown, pantaloons or trousers, square toed shoes or Hessian boots, bulky neck cloths and waistcoats of various hues. One after another, the gentlemen turned to look at her.

Samson elbowed his way through the crowd, grasped Izzy firmly by the elbow and bustled her out into the hall. "Miss Lilianne will have both our heads for washing if she finds you here."

Izzy dug in her heels and pushed out her plump lower lip. "It doesn't *seem* so wicked. Everyone is having a good time. But you and Miss Liliane must know best."

"Aye, we do that." Samson knew a hawk from a handsaw when the wind was blowing right. If this young woman wasn't more potential trouble than a barrel filled with monkeys, he'd taken one too many clouts on the head.

Before he could shepherd Miss Mischief to safer quarters, a shot rang out belowstairs. The sound reverberated up the stairwell.

Samson shoved Izzy in the opposite direction. "Go back to your room and stay there."

Izzy considered this advice, and decided to disregard it. She trailed after Samson, but remained prudently out of reach.

At the bottom of the stairway was a door sheeted with iron and covered with green baize, in its center a small aperture through which potential punters could be scrutinized. The door stood ajar. Just outside it, gazing into a foyer with wainscoted walls and a checkered tile floor, hovered the porter, a muscular man of middle years. The current rumption, he explained to Samson, was result of young Tremaine enacting a Cheltenham tragedy on the front doorstep. Izzy edged closer so she too could peer into the room.

She saw two people in the foyer. Miss Liliane, hands fisted on her hips, was holding forth in French. Izzy lacked proficiency in the language but unless she mistook the matter, Miss Liliane was comparing her companion to the hindquarters of a horse.

This was patently absurd. The young man bore no resemblance whatsoever to a horse's hindquarters. His own hindquarters, Izzy could not help but notice, were excellently formed. As were his shoulders, thighs and calves. Izzy couldn't tell the color of his eyes, but a lock of luxurious dark hair had fallen forward on his brow. He looked most poetical, save for the pistol he held pointed at Liliane's breast.

Samson entered the foyer. "Put away that barking iron, Tremaine. You won't shoot anyone."

The young man begged to differ. "Oh yes, I will! I'll blow out my brains, and then—"

"And then you will be dead as a doornail," said Izzy, as she stepped through the doorway. "Which I don't understand why anyone would care to be because, no matter how dire the situation, 'as long as there is life, there is hope.'"

The young man swung round, and stared at Izzy. His cheeks turned pink, his mouth dropped open. His eyes, Izzy noted, were a lovely emerald green.

Collecting his wits, he bowed politely. "Allow me to introduce myself: Tremaine, at your service, ma'am. I must thank you for preventing me from doing something I would regret for the rest of my life, not that I would have a rest of my life if I had shot myself. You must think I'm the worst sort of clunch. I'm not ordinarily, but I *am* at point non plus. Under the hatches, in the basket, all aground. Pecuniary embarrassments, that is."

"'A pack of cards is the devil's prayer book'," Izzy replied sympathetically. "And 'The best cast at dice is not to play'. Did you really mean to shoot yourself? It seems to me that this business hasn't been handled well. I don't mean to criticize! Doubtless everyone was taken by surprise."

"Quite a jabberer, ain't she?" inquired the porter.

"You ain't seen the half of it," Samson replied.

" 'It is a blind goose'," Izzy said firmly, " 'that knows not a fox from a fern bush.' Mr. Tremaine looks flushed. Perhaps someone might fetch him something cold to drink." She glanced at Liliane. "If you would not object?"

"*Que diable!*" said Liliane. "While you're at it, maybe you would like to settle him in my bedroom?"

Mr. Tremaine protested that he didn't want to go near Liliane's bedchamber. Samson in his turn suggested that Mr. Tremaine give them no more of his jaw.

Several moments later, young Mr. Tremaine sat slumped on the bottom stair step, refreshing himself with a cool tankard of wine and water with lemon, sugar and borage. Izzy perched by his side. Samson blocked the stairwell. The porter had taken up a position where he could keep a sharp eye on the front door. Liliane had firm grip on the pistol, a Manton, no less.

"I admit I was foolish," Mr. Tremaine confessed, "to wager all I owned. I would happily redeem my vowels, if only I could; but I can't and now Miss Liliane will have me clapped in gaol for debt."

Izzy patted his hand. "You are making mountains out of molehills. Miss Liliane wouldn't do that."

Upon hearing this pronouncement, Samson and the porter exchanged disbelieving glances. "Wait just a bloody minute," protested Liliane.

Mr. Tremaine was gazing rapt into Izzy's face. "I only regret that I must appear so shabby in your eyes."

"Not at all!" said Izzy, and patted him again. " 'Even a good garden may have some weeds'."

Chapter Seven

Sunlight attempted unsuccessfully to penetrate the closed curtains of the morning room at Moxley House, where Pen lay on a sofa, a damp cloth draped across her forehead. "That wretched child," she muttered, "tried to poison me."

"Nonsense!" replied Beau, from his vantage point by the hearth. "I'm sure she meant to do no such thing."

"I'm not!" Pen lifted the cloth to more effectively scowl; the throbbing behind her eyes now accompanied, due to the laudanum, by a brain full of cobwebs. Pen knew the uses of antimonial powder (fever), Goulard's extract (applied to bruises and sprains; used as a lotion in cases of inflammation), Sal ammoniae (sore throat), and linseed (chest complaints). It was becoming clear to her, however, that she *didn't* know how to deal with Loversalls.

Izzy skipped into the room. "Hallo, Uncle Beau! Samson told me you were here. Poor Miss Pen, are you still feeling ill? Shall I make you a poultice of violets, or fetch some oil of the flowers of privet, or a decoction of red roses made with wine?"

"No." Pen drew the damp cloth back over her eyes. "No and no and no. I wish you would go away!"

"You don't really mean that." Izzy perched on the couch beside her. "You are merely feeling cross. Remember, 'he who would gather honey must bear the sting of the bees'."

Beau didn't know about honey, but he felt a sting in his pocketbook, or maybe it was the fluttering of moths. He knew to the ha'penny the cost of the garment Izzy was wearing: a morning gown of fine jaconet muslin bordered with needlework, beading and lace. There was a vast difference, he had discovered, between dressing a mistress and a niece. And he wouldn't, absolutely would not, permit himself to imagine what garments Pen might be wearing, or not wearing, under that long-sleeved cambric robe.

To distract himself he asked Izzy, "What in Hades were you doing in the gaming rooms last night?"

"Why shouldn't I go into the gaming rooms?" asked Izzy. "I've done nothing wrong. Even if I *did* do something wrong, it would hardly matter. My own papa sold me to a stranger. I am alone in the world."

"Hardly alone!" Pen protested. "You have me, and Liliane, and your Uncle Beau."

"But all of you would rather *not* have me," Izzy pointed out. "Therefore, you don't count."

Pen lifted the cloth and gazed pointedly at Beau. He said, feebly, "Nothing of the sort."

Izzy shook her head at him. "I may not be a paragon like Miss Pen, but I can tell when someone is telling lies. You haven't so much as invited me to visit your house."

Pen's brows drew together. "I am not a paragon."

"Oh yes, you are," Beau told her. "The ordinary sort of female doesn't go around talking about drilling holes in a chap's skull. As for taking you to my home, Izzy, I'm not eager to subject the family reputation to another round of scandal, as must happen if it becomes public that your father bartered you off."

Pen set aside her cloth and swung her feet to the floor. "Were Beau to take you to his house, Izzy, the world would deem you one of his lights o' love."

Izzy's eyes widened. "Oh! You mean his harlots? But my uncle is quite old."

"The devil I am!" snapped Beau.

"Age is in the eyes of the beholder," Pen informed him. "Perhaps you should have your niece fitted for spectacles. Loathe as I am to admit it, Izzy, your uncle has a point. Where Loversalls are concerned, perception is all."

Beau experienced a strong impulse to throttle Pen. She was hardly in her own first youth.

What had she meant about perception? Did the foolish female not realize he was London's most wicked rakehell? Maybe he should introduce her to his mistresses. Let her make what she would of Signora Giordano, Miss Fletcher, Mrs. Ormsby and Mrs. Thwaite. "Don't try and change the subject, Izzy. You don't seem to realize you could have been shot."

"*Shot?*" echoed Pen.

"Mr. Tremaine wouldn't have shot anyone!" protested Izzy. "He merely wanted to make a point. His situation sounds very dire, but once he has explained the whole to Miss Liliane she will surely tear up his vowels."

Pen asked, "What vowels?" Beau explained what had transpired while she slept the sleep of the drugged. Pen moaned.

"Does your poor head hurt?" asked Izzy. "We could try—"

"*We* will try nothing." Pen strove for a reasonable tone. "*You* are laboring under a confusion of ideas. There's little point in owning a gaming hell if one is going to write off the patrons' losses. Liliane is unlikely to forgive the young man's debts."

"The young knave, you mean," amended Beau. "This is none of your concern, Izzy. Don't be shoving in your oar."

"He is not a knave!" cried Izzy. "And if that is not an instance of the pot calling the kettle black, I don't know what it is. If you are no longer young, Uncle Beau, you are still a knave, and 'if the staff be crooked, the shadow cannot be straight'. Moreover—" Reproachfully, she regarded Pen. "'Charity begins at home'."

"Ah," Pen retorted. "But I'm not at home, am I?"

"Charity be damned!" snarled Beau. "You're not to enter the gaming rooms."

"This isn't your house," Izzy reminded him. "Miss Liliane said I may go back into the gaming rooms any time I like. She says I should grow accustomed to masculine attention if I am going to become one of the Frail but Fair."

"You're *not* going to become one of the Frail but Fair." Beau paused and counted to one hundred, lest he go off in an apoplexy, result of his advanced age.

"You aren't my father," Izzy countered, "so you may not tell me what to do. Although I'm sure you mean it for the best! Moreover, you paid £100 for me yourself."

"Don't remind me," muttered Beau.

"So much as that!" Pen marveled. "The gossips call you a pinchpenny, yet £100 would keep the demimonde in silk stockings for a year. Izzy, if you enter the gaming rooms, you will prove a grave distraction. While caught up in admiring you — and naturally the gentlemen will admire you — they will become distracted and plunge more heavily than they might otherwise and gamble away the last farthing they have in the world."

Izzy's eyes widened in horror. "Like poor Mr. Tremaine?"

Miss Parrish, decided Beau, was a woman of great good sense. Having previously had little to do with sensible females, he found himself both annoyed and intrigued.

"Exactly like Mr. Tremaine," said Pen, driving home her point. "I can't imagine you would want to be responsible for some poor fellow hurling himself into the Thames."

"Oh, no!" agreed Izzy. " 'Better be the head of a horse than the hind end of an ass'." She trailed from the room.

Pen stared after her. "Did she just call me an ass?"

Beau didn't care to think of asses, or bosoms or arses, in the present company.

And so, of course, he did.

Moxley's was becoming a refuge for wayward females. First Zoe, who had run away from her husband. Then Kate, who had given up her virginity in the distant past to the previously most wicked of London's rakehells. And now Izzy and Pen, the least wayward of them all.

At least, he assumed she wasn't wayward. Thus far, he'd seen no sign. If she *was* wayward, he'd like to shake the hand of the man who had divested her of her innocence, and then wring his bloody neck.

Where the deuce had *that* come from? Perhaps he was running mad. Beau hoped he might not end up like a certain 17th century Loversall who had spent his declining years in a lunatic asylum, drooling and compiling his memoirs, which were (fortunately, in light of his long association with the 2nd Earl of Rochester) written in a cipher no one else could understand.

He wondered if Kate could be persuaded to visit him in Bedlam. "You're not going to hedge off, are you?" Beau asked her. "Cousin Emily isn't going to have a miraculous recovery?"

Pen lay back on the sofa, groped for the damp cloth, and plopped it on her brow. "Cousin Emily is in the grip of an influenza. I doubt she will survive."

Chapter Eight

The various establishments that lined the Haymarket were doing a brisk business this night: hotels and cafes and taverns; the King's Theater for Italian Opera; the Theater Royal. Carriages drew up in front of Moxley House, at the wide thoroughfare's northern end; disgorged their passengers, and rattled off again. Punters entered through the front door and exited the same way, the former full of high spirits, the latter generally less ebullient, save for those too drunk to grasp how deeply they'd gone down.

One carriage, a shabby specimen, didn't approach the front door but halted a short distance down the street. The door opened and two passengers climbed down. One was a plump fellow with carefully dyed locks, clad in a suit of ditto: coat, waistcoat and breeches all a tasteful tobacco brown. The other wore a many-caped coachman's greatcoat around his shoulders and a curly brimmed beaver hat on his red-gold curls. Roddy's nose was still swollen, the flesh around his eyes now green.

"But how am I supposed to get her out of the place?" Hector whined.

Roddy glanced at the driver, an evil-looking individual who'd been paid a pretty penny to keep his eyes blinkered and his mouth clamped shut. One couldn't be too cautious when dealing with villains of his ilk. Roddy gripped Hector's arm and urged him forward, until they stood by the horse's head. Hector eyed the sorry nag and hoped they wouldn't need to make a quick escape.

"There's a seldom used side entrance," Roddy said, in lowered tones. "I happen to have a key." He reached into his greatcoat and drew out the key and a sheet of foolscap, which he unfolded to reveal a floor plan. "Don't try and cry craven now. This was your idea."

Was it? Hector couldn't recall. If it *had* been his idea to snatch up a young lady — if a daughter of Randy Roddy's could be fairly called a 'lady'– he was much more sober now. "Not crying craven," he protested. "Just don't see why you're so set on making off with her tonight."

"Because I've found another buyer," Roddy retorted. "Old Babcock will pay £200 if she's still untouched. And she had better be untouched or I'll know the reason why."

Hector didn't want to know the reason why Lord Babcock, who was rich as Croesus and no younger than Methuselah, was willing to pay such a sum. He suspected it may have had to do with the old reprobate being poxed. "You don't say," he said.

"I do say," hissed Roddy. "What are you waiting for?" The horse disliked his tone. It arched its neck and bared its teeth.

Impressively large teeth they were, what remained of them, yellow and stained. The men moved a safe distance away. "Be off with you," Roddy demanded. Hector straightened his jacket, brushed flecks of some unknown substance from his breeches — the interior of the job carriage had been as begrimed as its exterior — and set out.

"And be quick about it!" Roddy called after him.

Obediently, Hector shuffled up the street. He longed to duck into a tavern and boost up his courage with a glass or two. But Roddy was his friend, and Hector couldn't leave him in the lurch. Or he *could* have, but a generous stipend was involved. He had already been paid a portion, which rendered his pockets plumper than they had been in weeks.

Lights blazed from the large, widely spaced windows of Moxley House. Hector paused to admire the structure, which was fashioned of dull red brick. He had never visited here before, Moxley's being an establishment that adhered to strict rules of fair play.

He had no difficulty passing the porter's sharp-eyed inspection. Hector's amiably vacuous expression raised no alarms concerning either Captain Sharps or representatives of the law.

He started up the stair. Much as he might dislike this business, and Hector did dislike this business, he would oblige Roddy all the same. Still, a man had to draw the line somewhere. If he must make off with the girl, which clearly he must, he would treat her with respect. At least he would try to, respect not being something Hector generally accorded the fair sex.

The Loversall Novellas

As he approached the gaming rooms, familiar sounds fell on his ear: hushed voices, the click of dice, the whir of a revolving wheel. Hector felt himself quiver like a cat sighting its prey. Not a cat, he amended as he entered the first room, but a bloodhound on the scent. There were two kinds of people in the world: sharps, ready to cozen a man on any occasion; flats, ready to be duped.

Crystal chandeliers and thick carpets, stands to hold the punters' glasses, deep leather chairs met with his approval, as did the display of alcoholic beverages set out on a table against the far wall. Gaming hells always offered liquid refreshment, men bleeding most freely when under the influence of strong drink.

He wasn't meant to get fuddled, Hector reminded himself, as he strolled past the rouge et noir table. Female croupiers, by gad!

In the second room, hazard reigned supreme. Here, the croupiers held hooked sticks instead of the usual rakes. They, too, were female. Moxley's, Hector marveled, might as well be a whorehouse for all the women it employed.

The third room was devoted to faro and E.O. His fingers itched. If not a Greek, blackleg or ivory tuner, Hector was an experienced nurse of the dice.

He joined the men gathered round the E.O. table, which was being set in motion by a russet-haired young woman with a friendly smile. Hector fingered the rolls of soft in his pocket. Sweat broke out on his brow as he struggled with the urge to wager recklessly on the spin on the ball.

Next came the crowded faro table, which was rectangular in form and covered with green felt, and presided over by a statuesque brunette. Hector knew the various ways of cheating. There wasn't a cheater in the house.

Nor was there anyone resembling a Loversall in the gaming rooms. Including Beau, to Hector's relief.

Maybe Roddy had the wrong sow by the ear. Maybe his filly wasn't here.

Roddy said he'd set spies on the place. Could she have snuck out that little-used side door? Hector was tempted to follow suit. But if Hector snuck out the side door, Roddy would find out about it and track him down. Hector wasn't of a mind to get his own nose broke.

Too, he needed Roddy. Debauchery wasn't half so satisfying when embarked upon without company.

Hector returned to the hall, which was at the moment empty of both servants and clientele; unfolded and scanned his map. In one direction lay the stairway that led to the front door and the street outside. In the other— He craned his neck.

Candles burned in sconces along the narrow corridor. Artwork adorned the walls. At the far end, on a pedestal, rested a bust fashioned from black basaltware. Hector rubbed his eyes, feeling for a moment as if he *had* indulged in champagne or hock or porter. Drifting down the hallway was a vision wearing a long-sleeved white satin dress trimmed with lace, azure satin slippers with silver clips, and matching gloves. Her hair was confined atop her head with a fancy comb. All she needed was a harp and she might have been an angel floating down from a cloud.

This was no angelic vision. If an angel wafted down from the heavens, it would hardly seek him out. Now that his initial shock was passing, Hector noticed the resemblance that he should have seen at once. The vision's hair might be a lighter shade than Roddy's, her eyes a paler blue, but she was without doubt a Loversall.

His Loversall, Hector reminded himself, and he must intercept her before she entered the public area.

"Good evening!" she said politely, as he approached her. "Are you looking for the gaming rooms? I hope you're not going to play beyond your means, because 'It is not only butter that comes from the cow.' Not that it is my place to tell you so!"

Hector was uncertain what cows had to do with anything. He had no doubt, however, that the young woman chattering at him was the young woman he'd been sent to fetch.

She was trying to read the paper in his hand. "Is that a map of the house? How came you by it, sir?"

Hastily, Hector tucked the map away. "Nothing of the sort! It's, ah— The British Museum."

She clapped her hands together. "I have always wanted to visit the British Museum! Well, not always, because I hadn't heard of it before I came to London, but ever since I *did* hear of it, I have yearned to inspect the stuffed giraffes."

The Loversall Novellas

Here was a tempting armful. Old Babcock had bought himself a lively piece. Had Hector possessed £200, he might have been tempted to purchase her himself.

Might have been tempted, were she not such a babblebox. Hector interrupted her observations on the art of taxidermy, elephants and polar bears. "Your da would like a word with you. He's waiting outside." He grasped her arm and tried to hustle her down the hall.

"But I do not wish to speak with him." She tried to pull away. "What's more, Miss Liliane has already scolded me for going off with Beau, and he is my uncle. Ouch! You're hurting me. If you don't release me at once, I am going t scream." Her pretty lips parted. She drew in a deep breath.

So much for behaving in a respectful manner. Hector drew back his arm and punched her in the jaw. She crumpled and he caught her, meaning to fling her over his shoulder and beat a quick retreat.

She sagged in his arms. Amazing that so small a female could weigh so much. Hector had little experience with manipulating unconscious bodies, Roddy being the one who generally dealt with matters of that sort.

As he struggled to hoist the girl over his shoulder, Hector heard a shriek. He spun around to see a plainly dressed, dark-haired Fury bearing down on him, the basaltware bust raised high above her head.

Chapter Nine

Lamplight cast flickering shadows on the bedroom wall. The small chamber was comfortably furnished with wardrobe and chest, dressing table and marble-topped washstand, two mattresses atop a mahogany four-post bed. On that bed lay Pen, a cloth again draped across her brow.

She heard the door open. Footsteps crossed the wooden floor, the rug. Footsteps too heavy to be Izzy's, which was a good thing. Toward that young woman, Pen wasn't feeling charitably inclined.

The mattress dipped as her visitor sat down on the edge of the bed. Pen immediately knew who it was. She didn't need to see him, or smell him — impossible to smell anything beyond the oil of roses and juice of sicklewort with which Izzy had liberally anointed her temples and brow — to be aware when Beau Loversall entered a room.

She tossed aside the cloth; squirmed into a sitting position; recalled that she was wearing next to nothing, and pulled the bedclothes up to her chin. "Have you spoken with your niece?"

"I have," Beau said. "I gave her a stern scold. She earnestly assured me that she'll cause no more trouble for anyone."

Pen snorted. "I threatened to dose her with Daffy's Elixir. Izzy suggested that I might like some lettuce water to cool my brain. At least she didn't blithely go off with a stranger. Even if he did tell her that her father is anxious to speak with her."

"Why was that?" Beau wondered. "How did they come by a diagram of the house? That must be what he had, and not, as Izzy insists, a floor plan of the British Museum. I hear you assaulted the intruder." Faint amusement glimmered in his eyes.

"None too successfully, I fear." Pen touched her head, and winced.

Beau leaned closer. His fingers moved gently through her hair. Pen was suddenly aware that, while she wore only a chemise made of cotton so finely woven it was almost sheer, he was fully clothed. Hessian boots and stockings; form-fitting inexpressibles; waistcoat and coat; fine linen shirt and elegantly tied neck cloth; knee-length cotton drawers, with an opening in the front. She imagined herself peeling off his layers, one by one.

Pen had spent no little time perusing her brother's anatomical texts.

Beau touched her cheek. "You're flushed."

"Um." He was so close she could feel the heat of his body. Prickles of awareness danced down her spine.

Firmly, Pen redirected her attention. "One doesn't water a camel with a spoon. Or so your niece informs me. Maybe you can tell me what she meant."

"She believes you should have been better prepared when you went to her rescue, the ungrateful little wretch." Beau lowered his hand. "Are you sure you're all right?"

She would be better if he put his hands back on her. Pen marveled at the far-reaching effects of a blow to the brain. "I'm not a faint-hearted sort of female. Surgeon's sisters seldom remain squeamish long. I did refuse to tend to the colony of leeches that live in a covered, water-filled glass bowl, so evidently some delicate sensibilities remain."

Beau settled more comfortably against a bedpost. "I couldn't make any sense of Izzy. Tell me what took place."

He was perfectly at ease, sitting on her bed. And why, considering the man's vast acquaintance with ladies' bedchambers, should he not be?

Pen strove for equal nonchalance, no easy thing when she was so vividly aware of being alone (and barely dressed) in her bedchamber with a notorious Lothario. "I suspected your niece was up to mischief. Primarily because she had been trying so very hard to convince me she was not. When I went to check on her, I discovered she wasn't in her room. Maybe you might try tying her to her bed."

Maybe Beau might tie *her* to the bed. Pen felt her cheeks flame.

Hastily, she added, "I set out for the gaming rooms, and came upon that man dragging her down the hall. Izzy had refused to go with him. He knocked her unconscious—"

"—and you rushed to the rescue, brandishing the bust of Voltaire."

"Is that who it's meant to be? I bashed him with the bust, and then he bashed me with it." Pen grimaced. "He was stronger than he looked."

"How *did* he look?" asked Beau.

"Ordinary. Short and stout and balding, his remaining hair dyed black. I'm sure I've not set eyes on him before."

Idly, Beau smoothed his fingers over the counterpane. "That sounds like half the gentlemen of my acquaintance. How did he escape?"

"I doubt most 'gentlemen' go about hitting people over the head with basaltware busts," Pen responded wryly. "We caused such a commotion that people rushed into the hall. While everyone was fussing over me and Izzy, mostly Izzy, our villain escaped through a side door." She pushed herself further up among her pillows. "I hadn't previously realized how uneventful a life I've lived. In the past few days I have run away from home, and been dosed with laudanum, and assaulted. I only regret that I failed to witness Izzy's encounter with Mr. Tremaine."

"As did I," admitted Beau.

"You were off being knavish," Pen consoled him. "I'm sure it was more fun."

"I wasn't being knavish," Beau said, ruefully. "You may find this difficult to believe, but I haven't been knavish for some time."

He was right; Pen didn't believe it. The man was devastating at a distance, let alone in such close proximity. He could, had he wished to, have charmed her right out of her chemise.

Were she not a paragon. Dull as ditchwater, in other words.

But he had once mistook her for a bit o' muslin. An embraceable female. Due to a deficiency of eyesight, according to his niece.

It occurred to Pen that the bedchamber was dimly lit.

She took a deep breath. "About that night at Vauxhall— I have changed my mind."

He eyed her, warily. "You have?"

"I have." Pen let go of the bedclothes she'd been clutching to her chest. "You may kiss me now."

This could hardly be the first time Beau had been thus addressed by a nearly-naked lady. Nonetheless, he seemed stunned. "Consider it in the nature of an experiment," Pen added. "How am I to understand you Loversalls if I have never been kissed?"

He was staring at her as if she spoke some unknown language. Pen moistened her lips. His eyes lingered on her mouth.

Was he wondering what it would be like to kiss her? Pen prayed he was. Her heart was hammering in her ears, and her skin felt clammy, and she had the oddest conviction that if Beau refused to kiss her, she would never be kissed at all.

His expression altered. Pen realized, to her horror, that she'd said this last aloud.

Pen had never been kissed? Beau was shocked to his boot soles. *He* had envisioned kissing her more than once, most recently mere moments ago, because her cheeks were rosy, her hair tousled, her eyes bright; and he was a man alone with a woman in her bedchamber, after all.

Pen crossed her arms and scowled at him. "You want me to understand your niece, do you not?" she asked.

Beau, in that moment, could have cared less about Izzy. *Mad,* he berated himself; *mad as a March hare.* But he had glimpsed the swell of one sweet breast when she dropped her coverlet, which had much the same effect as waving a red flag at a turkey cock, and so—

He reached out, threaded a hand in Pen's hair, tilted her head back; brushed his lips against her soft, thick lashes; followed the curve of her cheek to the corner of her mouth; touched his lips to hers in a featherlight caress. And then, having delivered the chastest kiss of his entire life, he drew back.

Rather, he attempted to draw back. Pen moved with him. He found himself leaning back against the bedpost with an armful of fragrant female lying across his chest.

If he had been disinterested in such things of late, he was definitely interested now.

She wriggled closer. Her mouth was warm and sweet against his. Abandoning his good intentions, he coaxed her lips apart. Her fingernails dug into his skin. Beau's hand slid down her side to the curve of her hip and back up again. His fingers hesitated on the ribbon at the gathered neckline of her chemise, grasped it and tugged. The fine fabric parted. His fingers rested against soft flesh.

Pen gasped and sat abruptly upright, clutching the garment to her bos-

The Loversall Novellas

om. She wore a dazed expression. Beau was feeling rather dazed himself. He leapt up from the bed as if he had been spider-bit, and fled.

Chapter Ten

Sunlight stole into the private garden behind Moxley House, tiptoed along high leafy branches and lower branches that bore no leaves at all, the trees having been stripped of vegetation to the height of a man's head. Wisteria drooped forlornly over tall stone walls. The skeleton of an orange tree protruded from a neoclassical urn.

Young Mr. Tremaine's boot soles crunched in the gravel as he paced in an agitated manner around the shell-shaped bench where Izzy perched. "Someone tried to remove you from Moxley's? Unconscionable! Is that how you came to the bruise on your cheek?"

Izzy nodded. "And not only that." She pushed out her lower lip so he might see how it had been cut.

Mr. Tremaine gaze lingered on her mouth a little longer than it should have. "Unconscionable," he said again. "Your family must be mad, permitting you to reside in a gaming hell. Forgive me for speaking so bluntly. I have no right to do so. If only I were in a position— But, alas, I am not."

Izzy peered at her surroundings. She didn't want this conversation to be overheard. Difficult for an eavesdropper to hide behind a naked honeysuckle bush, however. Or amid the ruins of morning glory and camellias and various shrubs; the patch of bare earth where herbs had once grown.

Spleenwort was good for melancholy people; as were peony, and fumitory, and feverfew.

And if one tied sow thistle around a cat's neck, the cat would become a better mouser. Sow thistle also cured the Black Plague.

What ailed Mr. Tremaine was not so easily remedied, alas.

"I came as soon as I received your summons, Miss Kilpatrick. Tell me how I may be of service to you." He ran a restless hand through his wavy hair.

Izzy had some notions along those lines. Mr. Tremaine made a splendid figure in his buckskin breeches, Hessian boots, and dark green double breasted coat. She admired the intricate manner in which he'd tied his cravat. His hair was dark as a raven's wing, one lock flopped forward on his brow in a most poetical manner; his eyes as green as— Emeralds? Izzy had never seen an emerald, and so discarded that comparison. His eyes were as green, she decided, as springtime grass. Izzy had often stolen peeks at the young men in her grandpapa's congregation, some of whom had dared in turn to cast shy glances in her way; but they could no more compare with this Adonis than pigeons with a peacock.

He was waiting for her answer. "It's not what you can do for me, but for yourself! I have been teasing myself with thoughts of how you may be extricated from your predicament. It has me quite in a puzzle, I confess. I did think that once you explained the whole to Miss Liliane she would forgive the debt, but I'm told that is not likely to be the case."

Mr. Tremaine resumed his pacing. He paused by the ancient climbing roses which had fared better than the other vegetation, being liberally festooned with huge thorns. "I doubt that anything I do will cause Miss Liliane to look more kindly upon my debts. It should surprise no one that I'm fit to stick my spoon in the wall."

"I suppose not," admitted Izzy, "but suiciding oneself is a cowardly act. Moreover, suicides cannot be buried in hallowed ground, or so my grandpapa said when Mr. Pennyfeather jumped from the top of the clock tower after Mrs. Pennyfeather ran off with the blacksmith and took all the money they'd saved up." She caught the young man's wrist as he passed by her and tugged him down beside her on the bench. "You must not lose heart. 'A bare foot is better than none', you know. And 'Every herring must hang by its own gills'. It is shockingly forward of me to ask, but— Are you married, sir?"

"Who would marry me," he muttered, "the pickle that I'm in?"

Mr. Tremaine was looking more morose with every passing moment. Izzy must elevate his spirits. A pity she wasn't wearing another of Miss Liliane's garments instead of this demure dress of spotted cambric with its high waist, puffed sleeves and prim flounced skirt, gentlemen being susceptible to the teeniest hint of bosom, or so she had been told. Perhaps a glimpse of ankle would suffice?

Surreptitiously, Izzy rearranged her skirts. "I doubt that I shall marry," she confided. "Being as I have tainted blood."

Was he peeking at her ankle? At any rate, his head jerked up. "Miss Kilpatrick! You must not speak so of yourself."

"But it's true!" insisted Izzy. "Mama said I must try prodigious hard to be good. I don't *feel* wicked, but that may mean she was right. All the family craves excitement, and I have lately discovered an appetite for adventure in myself. I understand your urge to gamble. To stake all on one more fling of the dice."

Mr. Tremaine clutched her hands as if he expected her to momentarily hop up off the bench and set off down the pathway to perdition. "Promise me you will do no such thing."

"Of course I won't!" Izzy assured him. "I only meant that I understand how someone *could*. Now we must determine how you are to pay your debts."

"I don't know why you should care what becomes of me," the young man sighed. "I have been the worst kind of fool."

"Why shouldn't I care?" Izzy asked him. " 'Every path has a puddle'. Perhaps you could work off your debts?"

"Doing what?" Mr. Tremaine relapsed into gloom.

" 'Ill goes the boat without oars'," Izzy told him, sternly. "I have heard of people making fortunes on something called the 'Change."

He looked even more dejected. "One must have funds to invest. And wait for the investment to pay off. If it pays off. In short, one needs money to make money, and I have none."

Izzy disliked to see him so disheartened. In search of a solution, she surveyed her surroundings. "Could you be a gardener? Miss Liliane needs one."

Mr. Tremaine slumped lower on the bench. "I can't tell duckweed from dandelions. What happened to this place?"

"A previous owner of Moxley's used to accept pledges of good faith. One such pledge was a goat." Pensively, Izzy nibbled at her lower lip. "*You might give Miss Liliane some item in lieu of monies owed. And then, when you have the money, you could buy it back.*"

"If ever I had the money," Mr. Tremaine said glumly. "At the moment, I own naught but this." He pulled off one glove to reveal a heavy gold ring. "It was on a string tied round my neck when I was left on the orphanage's front step."

"Oh! You are an orphan! How very sad."

"Is it? I can't say. I don't know who my parents are, or were. I only vaguely remember my mother, and my father not at all."

Izzy's tender heart was touched. "It may be for the best. "No sooner did I meet my own papa than he sold me to my Uncle Beau." Mr. Tremaine was no less handsome, she noted, when his eyes were starting from his head. "That man who tried to snatch me said my papa wished to speak with me. It was when I said I didn't wish to speak with my papa that he tried to drag me outside." She gestured at the bruise on her pretty chin.

Mr. Tremaine might not have heard the latter part of her explanation. "Your own uncle? That blackguard!"

Recalling Miss Liliane's explanations, Izzy realized she'd omitted a few details from her account. "I didn't mean that Uncle Beau— Because he didn't, and he wouldn't, at least I don't *think* he would with me— That is, you mustn't think I'm that sort of female."

"Nothing of the sort," stammered Mr. Tremaine. "I'm shocked that you would think *I'd* think — because I'd never — Your uncle is a curst rum touch."

"Because he bought me, you mean?" asked Izzy. "But if he hadn't, someone else would have and so Uncle Beau saved me from a fate worse than death — although what might be worse than death, I cannot conceive! Maybe Papa means to sell me again. It's difficult to say, because if he's been drinking, and Papa is always drinking, he might try anything." Mr. Tremaine possessed a truly splendid profile. "How pretty you are."

He turned quickly toward her, a becoming flush staining his cheeks. "Never say so, Miss Kilpatrick. I'm not half as pretty as you are."

"Oh, do call me Izzy. And I shall call you—"

He blushed all the harder. "Tristan."

"Tristan — Tristen — and I am Iseult! I believe this must be fate. We shall be buried side by side and have trees planted above our heads." Mr. Tremaine was looking fairly horror-struck and Izzy quickly added, "But not for a long time yet. I have an idea."

The Loversall Novellas

Before Mr. Tremaine could inquire as to the nature of that notion, footsteps sounded on the gravel path. Into view came Miss Liliane, accompanied by Samson and the footman Figg, who was wearing a queer costume of white cotton drawstring trousers and matching jacket, a black belt tied tight around his waist. Izzy adopted an innocent expression. Mr. Tremaine rose quickly to his feet.

"*Zut alors!*" muttered Liliane. If ever two people looked as if they had been caught doing something they should not. She wondered how Beau would react to the intelligence that his niece had excited the admiration of a young wastrel who lacked even a pot in which to piss.

To Mr. Tremaine she said, "You, go and find my money." When the young man proved reluctant, Samson took firm hold of his arm and led him away. Mr. Tremaine cast a wistful glance over his shoulder at Izzy, who gazed with equal wistfulness after him.

Liliane reached out and pinched Izzy. "Listen to me, miss. I have changed the locks and put the staff on guard. But in case that doesn't serve—" She beckoned to the footman. "Figg is going to introduce you to the Art of Yielding and Pliability, otherwise known as Japanese jujutsu."

Chapter Eleven

Randy Roddy Kilpatrick scowled at his companion. "You cobbled it, you bottle-head. You had her and you let her go."

"Couldn't help but let her go!" protested Hector. "The she-devil attacked me with a basalt bust."

"Corkbrain." Before Roddy could comment further on his companion's mental capabilities, or lack thereof, the crowd around them roared as one of the boxers came into view. Roddy elbowed his way closer to the roped-off ring eight feet square where Tom Trotter and the Blacksmith would each attempt to give the other his bastings. He had wagered all his blunt on the outcome of this prize fight.

The day was fine and sunny. Not a dark cloud marred the sky. More than a thousand people, along with their gigs and curricles and carts, were packed in a circle around the ring. Pickpockets and straw-heeled damsels and petty criminals worked their way through the throng. Vendors of various substances shouted to make themselves heard above the din. All ranks of society rubbed shoulders at ringside, from the noble patrons who arranged the prizefights to the thugs who fixed matches and occasionally broke uncooperative bones.

Bare-knuckle boxing was illegal. Bouts often took place well away from Town. A few days prior to a match, the word went out from the London boxing clubs. This being a prudent time to be absent from London, Roddy and Hector had immediately set out for Bath.

Odds favored the Blacksmith, a giant of a man who had never lost a fight. So convinced was the Blacksmith of his superiority that he had placed an advertisement in the public papers daring any boxer to meet him for a five hundred guinea purse. His challenger, Tom Trotter, was a man of science who bewildered his opponents by bobbing about and throwing unexpected blows, his preferred target the face.

Bare-knuckle blows could cause horrific facial injuries. A misplaced punch could fracture the fist that dealt it, with crippling results.

Still smarting from having been called a spoil-all — what had Roddy expected him to do, shoot the she-devil? — Hector followed his friend through the crowd. He was as fond as any man of a good bout: pugilists, stripped to the waist, chopping at each other, dislodging teeth, flattening noses, tearing eyes from their sockets, while blood poured on the grass.

Fond as any man, or woman. A young whore caught Hector's eye. She was a trifle chicken-breasted, and definitely wide in the bough, but Hector wasn't a particular sort of fellow. He winked and earned a saucy glance. Maybe after Roddy's man had won — Roddy had assured Hector it was a Sure Thing; Tom Trotter had no more chance of besting the Blacksmith than a cat of surviving in hell without claws — and they had received their winnings, he would invite the saucy strumpet to dance the feather-bed jig.

Hector joined Roddy at ringside. Excitement hung heavy in the air. Heads turned as the Blacksmith strutted forward. Would he be able to make good his boast that he could beat any fighter in the land?

The Blacksmith swaggered into the ring, sucking on an orange. He spat seeds on the ground. The crowd boo'd and cheered and stamped their feet as the pugilists shook hands.

Tom Trotter was five feet eight inches and a half, weight about sixteen stone. The Blacksmith stood six feet two inches and weighed in at seventeen stone.

The bell rang. The fighters left their corners. Broughton's rules applied. Hitting below the waist was not allowed, nor was hitting an opponent who was down. Wrestling holds were permitted only above the waist. A pair of umpires decided how to deal with questionable practices such as holding a man's hair to render him immobile while being hit. In case the umpires disagreed, a referee had the final word. Despite all that, ears were often bit clear through, and eyes gouged, and bodies assaulted below the waist while the referees looked the other way and the onlookers cheered. Spectators might fairly expect to see a great deal of sweat and shouting, splashing of blood and crunching of bone, for a round ended only with a knockdown or a fall and the bout went on until one of the bruisers was so badly beaten or exhausted that he couldn't come up to the scratch in the half-minute allowed between rounds.

This match got off to a slow start, much caution being shown on both sides. Four minutes elapsed before either fighter attempted a blow, which gave the spectators ample time to express their dissatisfaction and offer their advice.

Circling his opponent, Trotter got in the first strike. The Blacksmith's head snapped back. The next three rounds ended also in Trotter's favor, to the crowd's dismay. But then, after taking a few sharp hits, the Blacksmith caught Trotter in a clinch and delivered a good kidney pummel. The spectators roared approval. Roddy shouted, "Break his bread!"

The Blacksmith jabbed Trotter in the stomach, delivered a round blow to his left ear, severely cut his lip. "Smite his costard!" Hector howled.

Trotter landed a powerful straight punch to the Blacksmith's forehead. The Blacksmith landed a wallop that closed one of Trotter's eyes. "That's it! Crack his napper!" Roddy shouted, but Trotter danced away. The Blacksmith swung and missed. Trotter parried a cross-buttock blow and broke open the Blacksmith's nose; followed this immediately with a clout to the face with the back of his hand.

Grunts of effort. Taunts and curses. The thud of fist against flesh, and bone. Head butts, elbow throws, biceps strikes and hammer fists— And drowning out all else, the excited uproar of the crowd. The Blacksmith became so befuddled by Trotter's rapid movements and unexpected assaults, his constant changes in direction, that the odds, which were once with him, turned against him ten to one.

Round after round, the fight wore on. The Blacksmith fought low, and chopped at Trotter's face, tapping his opponent's claret, but to no avail. It was, someone would remark later, like watching a giant trying to swat at a gnat, the giant lumbering about while the gnat swooped in and took a bite of flesh and then darted off again. The Blacksmith was weakened by his frustrated efforts to grab hold of Trotter and pound him into the ground. With each of the Blacksmith's failed attempts, Trotter seemed to grow stronger, darting about, bobbing and weaving, hurling taunts as well as blows. At last Trotter gathered himself and landed a tremendous strike on the Blacksmith's jaw and knocked him out. The crowd went wild.

Maggie MacKeever

The Blacksmith, despite all his fine boasts, had had his jacket laced handsomely. Forty rounds, the battle lasted. Thousands of pounds were lost on the outcome.

A fair number of those pounds had belonged to Roddy. "Hell and the devil confound it!" he said.

Hector had, as usual, followed his friend's lead, and consequently had gone down heavily as well. Unlike Roddy, he'd had the foresight to tuck a twenty-five pound note into his boot, which if not enough to buy a thoroughbred, still left him enough to purchase a nice mare.

He had no desire to purchase a mare, but it was good to know that if he did decide he wanted to, he could.

Roddy pulled out his pocket flask, which had been filled with Blue Ruin at the bout's beginning, and was almost empty now. "Can't see why Izzy wouldn't go with you," he muttered. "You must not have handled the business right. Damned if she ain't as disobliging as her mother. 'How sharper than a serpent's tooth it is to have a thankless child'."

Hector didn't know about 'disobliging'. He wouldn't have gone with himself either, had he been the girl. This reflection, he kept private. Roddy was already in a bad skin.

Diffidently, he reminded Roddy that this was hardly the first wager he had lost.

Roddy unscrewed the stopper from his flask. "Babcock won't wait for delivery forever. I ain't lucky enough than the old man will stick his spoon in the wall before he decides he wants his money back."

Hector blinked. "Babcock handed over the ready rhino *before* you gave him the filly?"

" 'Age from folly could not give me freedom'." Roddy raised his flask and drank.

Hector ruminated for a moment. Roddy had Babcock's coin. Babcock wanted Roddy's girl. "So give the money back."

"Can't," retorted Roddy. "Beau's money's already spent. I lost Babcock's blunt on the outcome of this match."

Now Hector understood why Roddy was so out of curl. He'd wagered on the Blacksmith, but Tom Trotter had dressed the Blacksmith's hide neatly, and thereby run Roddy all aground.

"I need to get my hands on Izzy," Roddy added. "And I've a notion

The Loversall Novellas

how."

"Can't go back to Moxley's!" Hector protested. "They wouldn't let me in. They might even turn me over to the Watch, and I don't want to go to gaol. Stands to reason: already been in gaol and it's not what I can like. How's a fellow supposed to get out of debt when he has to pay for his keep? Fees for food and lodging. Fees for turning keys or taking irons off. Dungeons." He shuddered. "Rats."

Roddy offered no assurances. In search of solace, Hector scanned the crowd for the saucy whore. She was no longer in sight.

There were gentlemen aplenty present but no ladies. A lady would never be seen at a prize fight. Nor were they generally to be found at gaming hells, but Hector would bet his favorite yellow-and-green checked waistcoat that it had been a lady who attacked him with that bust.

Why a lady would be frequenting a gaming house, he couldn't say. She might have had a gambling habit or a taste for low life. Or maybe she had an attic filled with bats, because if anyone was to learn a lady had been at Moxley's, it would be as much as her good name was worth.

Roddy had been only half-listening to these remarks, finding Hector as annoying as a buzzing gnat. At mention of good names, however, both his ears perked up.

Easy enough to discover the identity of Hector's 'lady.' If she *was* a lady, Hector having scant experience with such.

"You needn't go into Moxley's," Roddy told his friend.

Hector was relieved to hear it. His relief was, alas, short-lived. Roddy tucked away his flask and said, "You'll lure Izzy outside instead."

Chapter Twelve

Having never been kissed by any gentleman other than her brother, Pen was uncertain how gentlemen were wont to respond to an embrace, but doubted that they customarily fled as if the hounds of hell were in pursuit. Had Beau found her unattractive? He hadn't kissed her as if he found her unattractive, and if she was hardly a diamond of the first water, surely she wasn't so homely as to make a man take to his heels.

Was she? Pen studied her reflection in the looking glass. Face, oval; eyes, hazel; nose, straight. Hair, chestnut, currently escaping from its prim coil at the nape of her neck. Figure, adequate if on the slender side, and hardly set off to advantage in this practical dark blue dress.

Pen sighed. She did look like a paragon. Prior to kissing her, she doubted Beau Loversall had kissed a paragon in all his rakish life.

Pen could still feel his hands on her body, his fingers on her flesh.

She'd reacted like a startled virgin. She *was* a startled virgin. Who wanted very much to kiss Beau Loversall again.

Now that he had kissed her — or she'd kissed him — Beau would try to avoid her. Such was the perverse nature of the male sex.

Beau mustn't be permitted to avoid her. Pen set out in search of Liliane.

The hallways were deserted. Moxley's was quiet this early in the day. Liliane's employees had not yet arrived to take up their duties, and the servants were preparing the public area for the evening to come.

Pen found her hostess in the morning room, poring over a ledger that lay open on the corner desk. On one green-and-striped wall hung an oil painting portraying Bacchanalian children playing with apples and grapes, fruit and flowers and some drunken-looking bees. Pen marveled that Liliane possessed such a conventional room.

Conventional, that was, save for the stained carpet, the walls, the faint lingering odor of wet goat.

Bent over the ledger, wearing a muslin morning dress, Liliane looked little older than Izzy. Pen wondered about the nature of Liliane's relationship with Beau. She had seen no evidence of affection between them, but Beau trusted Liliane enough to bring his niece to her house.

Were Beau to kiss Liliane, Pen reflected gloomily, his kiss would not be chaste.

Liliane closed her ledger, pushed back her chair and stood. "How are you feeling? I've taken precautions. That bugger will not again enter this house."

He would not? For a horrid moment, Pen thought Liliane referred to Beau. Realizing her error, she sank down into a chair.

Liliane frowned. "Does your head still hurt?"

"My— Oh!" Pen touched her abused brow. "No. Not at all. But if that, er, individual doesn't return, some other might."

Unlike Miss Parrish, Liliane's head *did* pain her, sums not coming easily to one who could barely read and write. When interrupted, she had been trying to decide if she should expand Moxley's menu to include asparagus pudding and fried cow heel.

If a punter was prone to plunging heavily, it might as well be at Moxley's as not.

A pity Beau wouldn't agree to Izzy putting in regular appearances in the gaming rooms. Liliane could have advertised her as the angel of the hell.

Izzy was no angel. Neither was her duenna, judging from the wistful way Pen watched Beau when she thought herself unobserved. "In the mops, are you?" Liliane asked her. "Tell me what's amiss."

Pen gave herself a mental shake. "Izzy's father was eager enough to be rid of her, from all accounts. I wonder why he's changed his mind."

"He means to turn a better profit." Liliane sat down in a chair facing her guest. "It is the way of the world."

Not Pen's world. She thought of her brother. Was Philip aware she wasn't in his house? Surely he must be. Had he failed to notice her absence, the servants would have told him she was gone.

She'd left him a note. Whether Philip read it remained to be seen.

Guilt smote her. Where the gossips might have little interest in the misbehavior of an ordinary spinster, they would have a great deal of interest in the circumstance that the spinster's brother was surgeon to the *ton*.

She was playing ducks and drakes not only with her reputation, but his. Still, had she refused Beau's request, it was unlikely that their paths would have again crossed.

Pen could not have borne it had their paths never again crossed.

And she really must stop dwelling on the last time their paths had crossed, lest her hostess deemed her daft.

Liliane was explaining how the footman Figg had tried to teach Izzy the art of self defense, a pointless endeavor since Izzy couldn't bear to damage anyone. "Or so she told us. In case you didn't know it, 'One cannot hide an eel in a sack'."

Pen was growing heartily tired of Miss Izzy. "I need your help."

"*Hein?*"

"I want to look like a ladybird."

"Have you been at the port?"

One always had a choice, Pen reminded herself. Except when one had none at all. She drew in a deep breath. "Please try and understand. In the ordinary way of things, the most excitement I can hope for is that my brother will permit me to hold the basin while he lances a boil. Don't think me ungrateful. I realize that far too many people haven't food enough to eat, or a roof over their heads."

"In other words," Liliane said shrewdly, "you would like to know what it is like *not* to be respectable before you return home. But you make yourself disreputable by simply being here at Moxley's, no?"

"Not disreputable enough, it seems," Pen muttered. "I need to look like a different sort of female. The sort of female who would frequent a gaming hell. I wouldn't wish to be recognizable, of course. Or maybe just a little bit. Not recognizable to a casual acquaintance, but recognizable to someone who knows me well. Or if not well, more than casually. Oh, devil take it! I want to look as I must have looked that night at Vauxhall."

Liliane was reminded of hares in mating season, hoping and jumping about and behaving in general like loonies. Maybe there was something in the air.

"Beau isn't tupping me," she said bluntly. "Or any of the women who work here. In case you were wondering. It's long been a rule of the house."

Cheeks flaming, Pen fixed her gaze on the long case clock. "Oh, no! I didn't mean— That is, even if he were — er — it would be none of my concern. You can't think this is about Mr. Loversall."

Liliane knew bloody well this was about Beau Loversall. "It is important to you, this becoming disreputable?"

"Just for a little while," Pen reminded her. "It is. And I realize I can't do it without your help. I know I'm asking a great deal, but please say you will."

Liliane had been feeling a little bored before the arrival of a proverb-quoting skitter-wit on her doorstep, semi-respectability proving not altogether to her taste. At least, she reflected, no one would ever ask *her* to hold a basin while a boil was being lanced. "I could pay you," Pen added. "I have money of my own."

"*Vraiment?*" Well, then. Contemplating her companion, Liliane tapped her fingers against her chin. Any number of scandalous gowns were tucked away in closets, Moxley's employees not being permitted to take them home. The French gown of lavender crepe? The raspberry silk robe?

No, Liliane decided; the dress of raw silk gold. Add a little rouge, a touch of kohl, lower the bodice and tousle the hair— Presto! A tart.

It might prove an amusing entertainment. Liliane made a mental list of gamesters who might care to place a wager on the outcome.

And if Pen's deception was discovered—

C'est la vie.

Chapter Thirteen

Mad as a March hare, Beau told himself. Why in blazes had he kissed Pen? Or allowed her to kiss him? True, he had wanted to kiss Pen for a long time, but that was beside the point. Ladies like Pen Parrish should have nothing to do with gazetted rakehells.

Let alone go around kissing them.

But what a kiss it had been.

He'd felt her shiver with excitement.

Had experienced an insane desire to continue kissing her until she abandoned all common sense.

A man of the world, Beau knew when a woman was ripe for seduction.

Seducing Pen would be very much the act of a Loversall.

He could not. Or if he could, he must not. And because his will power was not great, Pen must change her mind.

Startling, the realization that he didn't want her to change her mind.

Dissolute, he reminded himself. *Debauched. Depraved.* Tonight Pen would realize how great a profligate he was. She would bid him to the devil, and the business would be done.

Marveling that it felt so wrong to do what he knew was right, Beau passed through the front door of Moxley's, on one arm the fair Mrs. Ormsby, and on the other the dark Mrs. Thwaite. His inamoratas had temporarily set aside their mutual antagonism to band together against the threat of Signorina Giordano. Who, Beau might have told them, was actually no threat at all, having exchanged his lukewarm attentions for those of a Royal Duke.

Mrs. Thwaite was dramatic in a crimson satin slip worn underneath a three-quarter length frock made of silver-striped gauze. Disposed about her person were a large quantity of pearls, including a headdress *á la Chinoise*. Mrs. Ormsby languished in an evening gown of light pink satin trimmed around the bottom with a deep lace flounce. Her hair was caught up in a flower-encrusted cluster on the crown of her head.

Moxley's was doing a brisk business. Patrons lined up on either side of the rouge et noir table, gathered in one of the private alcoves to play whist for ruinous stakes, crowded several deep around the faro table set up in the next room.

Tall statuesque Adele presided over faro, her lush assets admirably set off by a blue velvet Albanian robe. As she announced the result of the last play, she winked at Beau.

"Brazen!" breathed Mrs. Ormsby.

"'Pon rep!" said Mrs. Thwaite.

Beau snatched a glass of brandy from a passing servant. He wasn't in the habit of losing himself in strong spirits, but this seemed a good day to start.

His companions wished to wager. Beau escorted them to the circular E.O. table, where player's chances of winning were nineteen in thirty-nine.

Russet-haired Rosamond, who presided over the table, caught his eye and smiled. She was luscious in a French gown of lavender crepe.

"Another female elbow-shaker, as I live," huffed Mrs. Ormsby.

"She seems to know *him* well enough," added Mrs. Thwaite.

Beau ground his teeth together and spent the next half hour banking the ladies as they punted on the gyrations of the little ball, at the end of which endeavor he'd gone down to the tune of one hundred guineas.

One glass of brandy, he decided, wouldn't be enough.

"It is better to have a hen tomorrow than an egg today," he told his companions, as he steered them toward the supper room. When the ladies expressed bewilderment he added, "Half an egg is better than an empty shell." This unfortunately reminded them that, due to recent lukewarm displays of interest, each feared he favored the other; and they immediately began vying to discover if that was indeed the case.

Liliane stepped into their pathway. Tonight she wore all black. "*Pardon, mesdames,* I must borrow your *preux chevalier*. I'll return him to you unsullied, *je t'assure.*" She tucked her arm through Beau's and drew him aside.

"Impudence!" sniffed Mrs. Ormsby.

Observed Mrs. Thwaite, "It would appear that Beau is playing a deep game."

Yes, and he wasn't the only one. Beau asked Liliane, "What are you about?"

She gestured toward the doorway. "*Regardez!*"

Beau looked, as he'd been bidden. He choked on his brandy. Liliane thumped him on the back.

"What the *deuce?*" inquired Beau, when he had caught his breath.

Liliane gave him one last thwack. "She wants to be unrespectable. Just for a little while."

Pen looked more than unrespectable. She wore a dress of raw gold silk that clung to every curve. Draped around her shoulders was a scarf of cream-colored sheer muslin embroidered with drawn work and gold metal thread. Her hair had been parted in the center, confined in the Grecian style, and threaded with golden cords.

She shimmered — there was no other word for it — like an exorbitantly expensive *fille de joie*. Beau wanted to throw his coat around her shoulders and shelter her from public view. Or, alternately, peel off that so-suggestive gown and discover precisely what, if anything, she wore beneath.

But this was Pen, the previously irreproachable Miss Parrish, and he truly was a profligate for imagining such things.

Mrs. Ormsby and Mrs. Thwaite were also intent on the new arrival. Said the first, "*Another* female? He is taking shameful advantage of our obliging natures." Agreed the second, "He is a humbug. A vile seducer, a capricious weathercock."

Seducer he might be, but Beau took exception to 'vile.' "Since between the two of you, you share not a single moral," he growled, over his shoulder, "that is doing it rather too brown."

"This passes human bearing!" pronounced Mrs. Thwaite.

Mrs. Ormsby groped for her vinaigrette.

Murmured Liliane, "What a kick-up. You're not smiling. You used to have a sense of humor, Beau."

So he had. Before Izzy — and Pen — had interrupted the easy tenor of his life.

Pen was making her way toward them. Damn, but she looked fine. Beau wasn't the only one to notice. Numerous punters glanced up from their cards and dice to stare. Only Samson's forbidding presence at Pen's side kept the predators at bay.

Beau would have liked to pop the gawkers' corks. It was a novel sensation. Usually, he was the one inspiring outrage.

Definitely, he was becoming a candidate for Bedlam.

As was Pen. Beau wanted to turn her over his knee. At thought of what he might do once he had her in that position, he almost groaned aloud.

She was looking straight at him. Here was an excellent opportunity to demonstrate that he was the most wicked rakehell in London and thereby give her a disgust. Beau would say, in his most rakish manner— What? 'You look like a tart,' while true, was hardly dastardly enough.

Pen drew nearer. Mrs. Thwaite and Mrs. Ormsby glared.

Pen *did* look like a tart. Beau was fond of tarts. He reminded himself that this was one pastry he could not consume.

Before Beau could make any off-putting pronouncement, Pen forestalled him. "Has anyone seen Izzy?" she asked.

Liliane frowned. "Izzy wasn't feeling well. She said she was going to dose herself with dwarf elder and lie down in her room."

"She isn't in her room," said Pen. "I just left there."

"Hell's teeth!" muttered Beau.

Chapter Fourteen

They had retired to the morning room, Pen and Liliane and Beau, along with Mrs. Ormsby and Mrs. Thwaite, who were clinging to him like— Limpets? Barnacles?

Leeches, Pen decided, and wished she could stick them in a jar. Both ladies were lovely. A connoisseur like Beau would settle for no less.

Pen knew she wasn't lovely. And not by so much as an eyelid's quiver would she betray her desire to cling to Beau herself.

If only she hadn't kissed him. Or he hadn't kissed her. Ignorance, in this instance, had definitely been bliss. One could hardly miss what one had never had.

Had Beau been kissing Mrs. Ormsby and Mrs. Thwaite? If so, had they liked it as much as she?

Silly goose. Of course he had. Of course they did.

The ladies were surreptitiously inspecting their surroundings. Mrs. Ormsby's attention had been caught by the stained carpet. Mrs. Thwaite tsk'd at the ink stain on the wall. "Blame it on Beau's daughter," Liliane told them. "She shot her husband, or so it's said. I didn't witness the incident myself."

"Shot!?" echoed Mrs. Ormsby. Mrs. Thwaite uncorked the vinaigrette and waved it under her nose. Beau picked up the decanter that was sitting on the desk and poured some brandy into a glass, offering it not to the ladies but drinking it himself.

A tap came at the door. Samson entered, informed his mistress that there was no sign of Izzy in the house. Liliane dispatched him to keep watch on the gaming rooms.

Mrs. Thwaite had been avidly eavesdropping. "Who is this Izzy?" she asked.

"No one who needs concern you," retorted Beau.

"But everything that concerns you must concern us," protested Mrs. Ormsby. " ' A trouble shared is a trouble halved'."

" Don't the pair of *you* go spouting proverbs at me!" warned Beau.

"Unfair!" cried Mrs. Thwaite. " 'Twas you that was talking about hens and eggs."

Beau bared his teeth at her. "And he who endeavors to play with a cat should be prepared to bear its scratches. Shall I continue, ma'am?"

Pen was getting a very odd notion of Beau's relationship with his paramours. "This is all fair and far off. Izzy has gone missing. Shouldn't we *do* something?" she asked.

Beau scowled. "Like what?"

"Call in Bow Street? Or the watch?"

"*Absolument pas!*" interjected Liliane. "I lay out a goodly amount of coin to keep the constabulary *off* the premises, thank you very much."

Beau ignored the interruption. "Consider what you're saying, Pen. Would you announce your presence to the world?"

Pen bit her lip. "Surely no one need discover I am here?"

Mrs. Ormsby and Mrs. Thwaite exchanged glances. They had taken Miss Parrish in mutual dislike, result of each lady wishing she was the one wearing that shocking gown. Inquired Mrs. Thwaite, sweetly, "And why shouldn't you be here, my dear?"

Added Mrs. Ormsby, "I don't believe I caught your name?"

Mrs. Thwaite continued, "And just who is missing, pray?"

Beau turned on them. "What business is that of yours? For that matter, why are the two of you still here?"

Mrs. Thwaite tittered. "You brought us here, remember? A gentleman would hardly leave a lady to find her own way home."

"Find her own way home?" echoed Mrs. Ormsby. "I feel a spasm coming on!"

"I shouldn't marvel at it, after this remarkable display of rudeness." Mrs. Thwaite gazed reproachfully at Beau. "But we will forgive him. He is clearly overset."

"I am *not* overset. And if you forgive me, I will be forced to insult you even worse." Beau crossed the room and flung open the door. "Figg! Have someone see these 'ladies' home. There. You can't say I didn't behave like a gentleman. Now go away."

"I disremember when I have been so insulted!" gasped Mrs. Ormsby.

"You'll regret this!" promised Mrs. Thwaite.

The Loversall Novellas

The door closed smartly behind them. Beau moved to the brandy decanter and refilled his glass. His gaze fell on Pen. "What the devil were you thinking? You look like a ladybird."

Pen drew the scarf more closely around her shoulders. So much for gaining Beau's attention. What, really, had she expected he would do?

"*Imbécile*," remarked Liliane, but didn't explain to which one of them she referred.

Beau shrugged out of his coat, which was a lovely shade of blue, and made of superfine. He tossed it at Pen. "Cover yourself."

Pen tried not to gawk at him. She'd seen her brother in his shirtsleeves. But Philip hadn't filled out his shirt half so well.

She snuggled into Beau's coat, savoring his lingering warmth. "I thought you liked ladybirds."

"I liked *you*," he retorted. "Before you became a featherhead."

"You didn't act like you liked me."

"Of course I didn't act like I liked you. You're a respectable female. I'm a bloody rakehell."

Liliane interrupted. "Izzy is still missing. Do we wish to get her back?"

Beau didn't answer. Pen said, hastily, "How did Izzy manage to leave the house?"

Liliane replied, "You may be sure I'll find out."

Another tap sounded at the door. Figg the footman entered and presented Beau with a note. "Under the circumstances," Pen suggested, "perhaps Moxley's should have remained closed."

"If I had closed Moxley's," Liliane reminded her, "you wouldn't have had the opportunity to wear that dress."

"It is a lovely dress." Pen fingered the fabric. "What there is of it."

"It's a damnably indecent dress." Beau gestured with the letter he'd been reading. "And *this* is a ransom note. We may have Izzy back for the sum of £500."

Pen gasped.

"We are to await further instructions." Beau crumpled the letter in his hand.

"*Putain de merde*," muttered Liliane.

Wait they did, Liliane seated at the desk and Pen on the sofa, Beau standing in front of the fireplace with the brandy decanter close at hand.

"I hope nothing dreadful happens to Izzy," Pen said into the silence.

"Or that it has not already happened," added Liliane.

All came to attention when at last the door opened. Figg brought not further instructions, however, but a visitor whose coat collar he held in a firm grasp. He propelled the man forward. "Mr. Kilpatrick. As was caught skulking outside."

"*Parfait!*" Liliane said grimly. "You may leave him to us."

Roddy straightened his coat. The bruising around his eyes had faded to a bilious yellow. "This is no way to treat a fretting father. What have you done with my girl?"

"I haven't done a damned thing with her. As you bloody well know. Or are you going to claim you know nothing of this?" Beau handed him the crumpled ransom note.

Roddy peered at the paper. "£500? That's more than double what I asked for her, by God. Begging your pardon, ladies. You can't think that I— Well, I didn't! Though I'll admit I might have, had I thought of it. What were you thinking, letting Izzy get snatched right out from under your nose? Don't bother pointing out I tried to snatch her myself; it's the principle of the thing. If she *did* get snatched, and you're not keeping her for yourself."

Beau refilled his brandy glass. "Why shouldn't I keep her? You sold her to me, if you will recall."

"That was a mistake," Roddy admitted handsomely. "Tell you what, I'll take Izzy off your hands."

"You can't take her since I don't have her. But if I have her, you'd offer to return the sum I paid?"

"Well, no. I can't say I'd do that. You shouldn't have bought her in the first place." Roddy looked sly. "What if word was to get out?"

"Don't try and blackmail me!" snapped Beau. "You're the one that sold her. What if word of that out?"

Roddy glowered. "*You* could come down with the darbies, if you wanted to."

"But I don't want to," said Beau.

"If that ain't the outside of enough. 'Ingratitude, thou marble-hearted fiend!'"

Beau snorted. "What the deuce do I have to be grateful to you for?"

"Sold Izzy to you, didn't I? Could have as easily sold her to someone else. And now you've let somebody filch her. Damned if I don't feel like putting out your daylights."

Beau said, "Be my guest."

The Loversall Novellas

Roddy took off his coat.

Beau was a member of the Pugilistic Club. Roddy didn't play by Broughton's rules.

He jabbed. Beau ducked and circled. Roddy swung a roundhouse right and missed. Beau got in a good body blow. Roddy cuffed Beau smartly on the ear. Beau feinted with his left and planted Roddy a facer with his right.

"Blast you, not my nose!" swore Roddy.

"Hit him again!" cried Pen.

Liliane snatched up the inkwell as Beau swept Roddy's legs out from under him, and the men went rolling around the floor. "Would you care to place a small wager on the outcome?"

A chair crashed over on its side, followed by a table. Pen retreated to the fireplace.

Beau wrapped his hands around Roddy's neck. Roddy drew a knife from his boot. Pen grabbed the brandy decanter from the mantle and brought it down on Roddy's head.

The heavy crystal didn't break. The same couldn't be said of Roddy's head.

He sprawled senseless on the carpet. Liliane gingerly skirted the blood and brandy seeping into her carpet, bent over Roddy's body and relieved him of his knife.

Beau rose unsteadily to his feet. "Pen, I am in your debt."

Murmured Miss Parrish, "We ladybirds aim to please."

"Merciful heaven!" cried a voice from the doorway. "What has happened here?"

All eyes fixed on Izzy. By her side stood young Mr. Tremaine.

Chapter Fifteen

"Why are the gentlemen half-dressed?" inquired Izzy, who was seated on the sofa with young Mr. Tremaine at her side. "Have we interrupted a *tête-à-tête*? Or do I mean a *ménage á trois*? I am not precisely sure what a *ménage á trois* entails."

Mr. Tremaine could not drag his gaze away from the body bleeding on the carpet. "You should not say such things."

"Whyever not?" Izzy demanded. "Uncle Beau is a notorious philanderer. Miss Liliane runs a gaming hell. True, I wouldn't have thought Miss Pen— A virtuous woman is worth more than rubies. And 'a prostitute can be had for a loaf of bread'."

"Who are you calling a prostitute?" inquired Pen.

Izzy blinked at her. "Why are you wearing Beau's coat?"

"Your uncle didn't approve of my gown."

"He didn't? How odd in him. You look like a harlot. I thought he liked harlots very well."

"I don't—" Beau's voice trailed off. While it was true he nourished no fondness for harlots at the moment, not so long ago he had liked them well enough.

Roddy stirred, drawing Izzy's attention. "Oh! Papa isn't dead. I know I shouldn't say so, but things might be much simpler if he was."

"Simpler for you, maybe," Pen set the empty brandy decanter on the mantle. "You're not the one who would stand her trial for murder."

Izzy eyed the decanter, which was smeared with blood. "Was it you that hit him? I don't mean to be critical, but do you think it's a good idea to go around bashing gentlemen?"

"You might want to keep a civil tongue in your head," Liliane advised. "Lest she bash you next."

Slowly, Roddy sat up. The smell of spilled brandy hung heavy in the room. He hoped there was more brandy at hand, and so he said. This request was somewhat garbled, owing to the circumstance that Roddy's mouth was swollen, his nose and scalp were bleeding, and he was missing an additional front tooth.

Liliane curled her lip. "Not for you, *cochon*."

Roddy wiped his nose on his sleeve. "Was it you who cracked my napper, then?"

"No, it was Miss Parrish. If you don't behave, we'll let her do it again."

Roddy eyed Pen in a manner that prompted her to burrow more deeply into her borrowed coat. Leering, he lisped, "Thocking company you keep, Miss Parrith. Doubt it would help your reputation if it got out that you wath thpending time here."

"No one cares about my reputation," Pen informed him. "You must have mistaken me for someone else."

"'Go to the ant, you sluggard'," advised Izzy; "'consider its ways and be wise.' But I thought—"

"Don't!" Beau warned her. While he'd lost none of his teeth in the scuffle, one eye was swollen shut.

"Thave your breath to cool your porridge," said Roddy. "I know what I know. Nothing perthonal, mind you, but I've had a thpot of ill luck lately and thertain people who could lend a helping hand if they wath withful, *won't*. If you don't want the world to learn you've been tying your garter in public, Mith Parrith, you'll thee your way clear to making me a thmall loan."

Beau started forward. Liliane stepped in front of him. "*Non*. There is already blood enough on my rug."

"Have the two of you been fighting?" Izzy's tone was disapproving. "'A soft answer turneth away wrath'."

Reminded of her presence, Beau and Roddy swung round in unison. "Where the *devil* have you been?"

"I've been trying to tell you, haven't I? You've been too busy quarrelling to pay me any heed."

"Tell uth now," snarled Roddy.

The Loversall Novellas

"We're listening," spat Beau.

Liliane joined Pen at the fireplace. "How are you enjoying being not-respectable?" she asked.

Pen rolled her eyes.

Izzy folded her hands in her lap. "We were going to hold me to ransom. But then I realized I couldn't accept a ransom from Uncle Beau. He has been so kind, finding me a place to stay and bringing Miss Pen here to lend me countenance. Although now I've seen her in that dress, I wonder just how much countenance she has! In any event, you must not scold Tristan, because he didn't approve of my plan. But 'if you dance you must pay the fiddler', and I couldn't come up with any other way for him to pay off his debt."

Liliane protested, "Tremaine hardly owes me £500."

"No," Izzy said reasonably. "But since we were asking, it seemed a good round sum."

"A nice round sum, indeed," said Roddy. "Beau may pay it to me."

Beau righted the overturned chair and sat down it. "Has it occurred to no one that I might not *want* her back?"

"You have taken me in dislike!" lamented Izzy. "It makes me very sad. Though I will admit I perfectly understand why you might."

"Damned if I know how I thired thuch a thilly widgeon." remarked Roddy. "If you can't hold yourthelf to ranthom, mithy, *I* thurely can."

"No, you can't!" Izzy fired up. "You can't hold me to ransom *or* sell me again — I credit it was you who sent that dreadful little man to steal me — because you already sold me to Uncle Beau."

"Where are your mannerth?" Roddy demanded. "Honor thy father, girl."

"Why should I?" retorted Izzy. "My father doesn't honor me. He has behaved consistently in a manner that can only be considered *dis*honourable. Just look at yourself."

"I could have put you up for auction at a bagnio, you ungrateful twit. Yeth, and I thtill can. You needn't look to Beau. I have parental righth. He don't."

"I have right of ownership." Beau flexed his fists. "Moreover, I'm not paying a bloody ransom. You may go to blazes. Izzy remains here."

Mr. Tremaine cleared his throat. "As to that—"

"I have tried so hard to withstand temptation," lamented Izzy. "But it is *very* difficult."

"That's because you are a Loversall," Pen told her. "And prone to tumultuous passions as a result."

Izzy's lips trembled. "You mean I am a goosecap."

Mr. Tremaine clasped Izzy's hands in his. "You are nothing of the sort! And even if you were, you would be the prettiest goosecap that ever lived."

"Truly?" Izzy asked him, tear forgotten.

"Truly!" said Mr. Tremaine.

Watching them, Beau muttered, "It needed only that."

"It was a *coup de foudre*," Liliane informed him. "We see before us a man struck by Cupid's dart."

Roddy disliked this development. "I thay! Unhand my girl!"

Mr. Tremaine was impressed by neither Izzy's papa nor her uncle, both of whom looked like they had been brawling in some alleyway. "Moderate your manner. You are speaking of my wife."

Roddy's mouth dropped open. "Your what?"

" 'There shall a man leave his father and his mother, and shall cleave unto his wife; and they shall be one flesh'." Mr. Tremaine turned anxiously to Izzy. "Did I say that right?"

Izzy beamed at him. "You did."

Roddy wanted to hear no further talk of cleaving. "You can't be married. Even if you managed to get a thpecial license, Ithy ith underage."

"Not to mention that each participant must be of sound mind," Pen murmured to Liliane.

"I didn't mean to marry," Izzy confessed. "Lest I turn into a Dread Example, like Mama said all Loversall women do. But Mr. Tremaine pointed out that I am a Kilpatrick, *not* a Loversall. 'Marriage is honourable in all, and the bed undefiled. But whoremongers and adulterers God will judge.' "

"Did she just call me a whoremonger?" Roddy asked.

"Aren't you?" inquired Beau.

Roddy said, with dignity, "All the worldth a thtage. One man in his time playth many parth." Delicately, he inquired as to whether his daughter had enjoyed a wedding night.

Izzy admitted that she and Mr. Tremaine had spent a night together in

The Loversall Novellas

a private chamber at a coaching inn.

"Curtheth!" roared Roddy. "Only a pig-widgeon will pay £200 for soiled goods."

Pen wrinkled her brow. "£200? Beau said it was 5."

"That was the amount of the ransom demand," Beau told her. "Apparently Roddy asked for less."

"Soiled goods?" echoed Izzy. "I'm no such thing. You've no right to speak to me that way." Mr. Tremaine made to rise, and she clutched his arm. "No, you mustn't fight with Papa! He would probably try and cheat,"

Roddy had no intention of engaging in further fisticuffs this evening, or for a good long time. Still, the suggestion that he might behave in an underhanded manner rankled, being as it came from his own flesh and blood. "Mind your mannerth, mith. Theeing as I'm the one as was cheated, you've no cause to be thtiff-rumped."

" 'It is no sin to cheat the devil'," Izzy told him. "And I am not stiff-rumped!"

"Of course you are not, angel." Before Mr. Tremaine could assure his bride, and the assorted spectators, that her posterior was faultless, a tap came at the door.

Figg entered the room, bearing a silver tray. Resting on the tray was a pasteboard card.

Chapter Sixteen

Ebenezer Dunbobbin, Lord Babcock, was slender as a reed and pale as a wraith, with eyes as black and beady as a weasel's, his hair the color and texture of dandelion seeds.

In other words, he was ugly as sin. Since he was also one of the warmest men in England, this circumstance seldom got in his way. This evening he was rigged out in a prune-colored coat and swanskin waistcoat, kerseymere breeches and white stockings, shoes with large gold buckles; and additionally adorned with pocket watch and fob, gold framed quizzing glass suspended from a golden chain, enameled snuffbox, and tall ebony walking stick.

He raised the quizzing glass to his right eye and inspected the occupants of the morning room, all of whom were regarding him with expressions of astonishment. Roddy Kilpatrick was the first to speak. "Lord Babcock! Thurprised to thee you here."

And so he should be. Lord Babcock had never visited Moxley's before, preferring establishments of lower repute. In his prime he'd desported himself with like-minded companions such as the Barry Brothers, Hellgate, Newgate and Cripplegate, true paragons of perversity.

The Barrymores were long dead. Even Old Q, the Duke of Queensbury, was gone these past four years.

Lord Babcock lowered his quizzing glass. "How d'ye do?" he said politely. "Is there some reason I shouldn't be here? Ye're a sight to curdle cream, Kilpatrick. Wasn't trying to avoid me, was ye, knave?"

Of course Roddy had been. "Of courth I wathn't," he protested, as perspiration trickled down his bloody brow. "Thing ith, there'th been a change of plan."

Lord Babcock wondered when Kilpatrick had taken to talking with a lisp. He'd been engaging in some curiously cockish capers, from the looks of his bloodied person and Loversall's black eye, the disordered condition of the room and the stink of brandy in the air. However, the man's sexual proclivities were no skin off *his* nose. This reflection reminded Lord Babcock of his own sexual proclivities, which had resulted in the recent purchase of a Grand Anti-Syphlicon from Mr. Eglington's in the Strand at six shillings a pot; Dr. Boerhaave's Infallible Red Pills, advertised for the cure of A Certain Insidious Disease; and Mr. Hoffmann's Botanical Pills, all to no avail.

"*I* ain't had a change of plan." Lord Babcock limped forward and without waiting for an invitation, seated himself in a chair. "I'm prepared to go a-wooing. Produce me the female. 'Tis a matter of some urgency. I ain't anxious for me pizzle to fall off."

Pen bit back a shocked giggle.

"What's a pizzle?" Izzy asked.

Liliane swung accusingly on Roddy. "Are your brains in your ballocks? Look at him. The man is poxed!"

All eyes fixed on Lord Babcock. " 'Tis a waspish tongue, egad," he informed them, irritably. "Live long enough and ye'll be poxed and in search of a virgin too."

"*Non, jamais,*" said Liliane. "There are things one simply doesn't do."

"Is that so?" inquired his lordship. "I ain't found one yet."

Izzy looked bewildered. "What's poxed?"

Beau said, "Never mind."

Liliane might like a profit as well as any man, or woman, but she also — to her surprise — felt a certain responsibility for her houseguest. "No one is taking Izzy anywhere. You should all go away."

Lord Babcock thumped his cane on the floor. "God's life! What's an Izzy? Are ye all queer in the cockloft? I ain't going anywhere without either my money or the gel."

"The gel's name *is* Izzy," Beau informed him. "Roddy can't sell her to you because he's already sold her to me."

Lord Babcock raised his quizzing glass and inspected Roddy through the lens. "Double-dealing, are ye? Burn it, man, have ye taken a maggot in

The Loversall Novellas

yer brain?"

"Here, now," muttered Roddy. "No need to cut up thiff."

"Cut the cackle, beef wit," responded his lordship.

Lord Babcock would have his money or he'd have a virgin. He surveyed the room. The brass-haired hussy dressed in black was a tasty bit, but he knew a trollop when he saw one and he was looking at one now. The chestnut-haired female briefly held his notice — if a little long in the tooth, she was neither corny-faced or freckled — but no virgin would get herself up like a bawd.

Why was the bawd wearing a man's coat around her shoulders? Why were both men in their shirt sleeves? Numerous intriguing scenarios sprang to mind. Lord Babcock had been a regular out-and-outer in his day.

Hence, his malady. And his presence here.

The yellow-haired chit was gaping at him. She looked virginal enough, save for the bruise on her chin. "How now, miss! Be *ye* untouched or no?"

Izzy's forehead wrinkled. "Untouched? How could I be untouched? Any number of people have touched me. Mr. Tremaine is touching me right now. Indeed, he is clutching me so tightly that it is quite painful, and I wish he would not — though I'm sure he means it for the best and I am not one to complain."

"Faith, 'tis a pea-goose," observed Lord Babcock. "Have ye ever danced the blanket hornpipe, miss?"

Young Mr. Tremaine had, he considered, thus far comported himself with perfect propriety under very trying circumstances. However, this last remark strained forbearance too far. He leapt up, hands clenched. "I demand satisfaction! How *dare* you speak in such a manner to my wife?"

Lord Babcock turned the quizzing glass on him. "Here's a fine how-de-do. You say the gel's bespoke?"

" 'What ho, Brabantio! Look to your houth, your daughter and your bagth!' " Roddy refrained from adding further poetic references to old black rams tupping white ewes, and Barbary horses, and the devil's grandsire. "The marriage ain't legal, at any rate."

"Legal or not," said Mr. Tremaine pugnaciously, "we've had our wedding night. You may look for your virgin elsewhere."

"Oh!" said Izzy. "Is that what this is all about? Why does the old gentleman require a virgin? Isn't it dangerous for someone to exert himself so mightily at his age?" Unlike the other occupants of the morning room, she had not heard of Lord Babcock, having led a much more sheltered life.

Beau refused to contemplate Izzy's mighty matrimonial exertions. He retreated to the fireplace, where Pen still stood.

She whispered, "Admit it. This is almost better than a play."

"I demand satisfaction!" young Mr. Tremaine repeated. "Name your seconds, my lord."

"Devilish ticklish, ain't ye?" Lord Babcock inspected the fist that was being brandished so close to his face. "God's bones. How came ye by that ring?"

Mr. Tremaine looked confused by this turn of conversation. "It was left at the orphanage. On a string tied round my neck. I was very young, and can tell you no more than that."

"I'll see it, if I may." Lord Babcock held out one frail, imperious hand.

Such was his lordship's manner that Mr. Tremaine removed the ring and dropped in on his palm. Lord Babcock inspected the ring closely. "What do ye call yerself?"

"The orphanage gave me the surname Tremaine because it's etched inside the ring. My Christian name, Tristan, was embroidered on my shirt."

"Tristan, is it?" Lord Babcock rose, clutching the ring, with the assistance of his walking stick. "Romantic falderol. But your mother was that sort."

"My mother?" echoed Mr. Tremaine.

"Behold me aquiver with remorse," Lord Babcock said impatiently. "I didn't know she was increasing, did I, when I gave her her ticket of leave? And even if I *had* known, I'd have suspected there was a cuckoo in the nest. Easy enough to prove. D'ye have the birthmark?"

Mr. Tremaine echoed, "Birthmark?"

"He does have a birthmark!" cried Izzy. "It's shaped like a duck. On his—" Blushing, she broke off.

For some reason, while Pen was paying rapt attention to the unfolding drama, her hand had crept into Beau's. "I feel like I've stepped into the pages of a melodrama," she confided. "Now Babcock will make young Tremaine his heir."

"All the males of the family have that accursed birthmark," explained

The Loversall Novellas

Lord Babcock. "Ye were born on the wrong side of the blanket, so ye can't inherit the title, but—" He clapped Mr. Tremaine on the shoulders. "Welcome to the family, boy."

Pen groaned.

Liliane beamed. *"Très bien, papa!* You may pay his gambling debts."

"Just what sort of lordship are you?" inquired Izzy. "If Tristan is your heir, Papa can have no objection when I marry him again."

This remark reminded Lord Babcock that his absence of other heirs wasn't due to lack of trying, which was how he'd caught the pox. "Thought ye *was* married," he said suspiciously.

Roddy experienced a surge of renewed optimism. "The marriage ain't legal," he repeated.

'A broken sack will hold no corn'," Izzy pointed out. "But it is true that I am underage."

"My wife," Mr. Tremaine reminded Lord Babcock, "has already enjoyed her wedding night."

"I *did* enjoy it!" agreed Izzy. "Although from what Miss Liliane told me, I thought I would not."

"I'd give ye joy but I'm still peppered," said Lord Babcock. "Don't suppose there are any virgins among the gels downstairs?"

Pen cleared her throat. "Deflowering a maiden, my lord, is no cure for the pox. The only effective treatment is with mercury."

Lord Babcock fixed his cold eyes on her. "And how do ye know this, pray?"

"My brother is a surgeon." Recalling that said brother wasn't meant to know her whereabouts, Pen added, "There are various methods of application. Fumigation, in which the sufferer is placed in a tent in an overheated room and cinnabar burnt on a stove for him to breathe in until he can take no more; inunction or rubbing into the skin of mercury or a mercurial compound; ingestion of the metal in pill or liquid form; and injection by syringe into the, ah, male appendage."

Looking a little green, Lord Babcock sank back down into his chair.

"And *that* for you!" added Pen, under her breath.

"You are a force to be reckoned with, Miss Parrish," said Beau.

Pen glanced at him. "Is that why you ran away from me? Because I am a force to be reckoned with?"

"I ran away before I could do something we would both regret," Beau told her. "I had already embarrassed myself as far as you're concerned."

"Oh?" inquired Pen.

The door banged open. Panting on the threshold was a short stout fellow with side-whiskers and dyed hair fixed in a Brutus crop. He wore a suit of ditto and an exceedingly vulgar waistcoat. And he held a pistol in one hand.

That hand was trembling. He was none too steady on his feet. "I've come to fetch the filly!" he told his startled audience. "Give her to me."

"That is the man who tried to steal me," Izzy announced. "Miss Pen should have bit him harder. Not that I mean to complain."

Roddy glowered at the late arrival. "Damnation, Hector. Put down that barking-iron."

Hector had spent the past several hours imbibing innumerable glasses of Geneva while he brooded over how badly he had let down his good friend Roddy, having failed to come up with a ploy to lure Roddy's girl out of Moxley House. Now he found Roddy *in* Moxley House. Where he'd previously been denied entrance. How could that be?

Had Roddy also come to steal the filly? In that case, a fellow should have been warned before he snuck in through side doors and skulked through hallways until he reached the family rooms, peering through one doorway and another until the voices led him here.

Roddy looked like he'd engaged in fisticuffs with Tom Trotter, and lost. His nose resembled an overripe plum. His expression suggested a lack of appreciation for the effort Hector had undertaken on his behalf.

Maybe Hector was mistaken? This wouldn't be the first time his eyesight had suffered as result of overindulgence in the grape. Not that gin was made from grapes. At least, Hector didn't think it was. He even fancied he saw Lord Babcock, which was most unlikely, his lordship known to frequent only the lowest hells.

The room was bright. Hector squinted. "Kilpatrick? You here?"

"Of course I'm here!" Roddy replied. "Get your head out of your arse."

"Don't have my head up my arse!" retorted Hector. "And you've no cause to say I do."

Izzy parted her lips to speak. Mr. Tremaine shook his head.

"Give me the pistol, there's a good fellow," sighed Beau. "You don't want to go to gaol."

Gaol. Fees, dungeons, and rats. "I won't go back! You can't make me!" Hector looked frantically around the room, half-expecting a gaoler to pop out of the woodwork.

He backed toward the doorway. "*Pour l'amour de Dieu!*" muttered Liliane, and put herself in his pathway.

Hector spun round, found the proprietress of the establishment standing much too close. "Keep your distance!" he warned her. "I have a gun."

"So I see." Liliane twisted her body, raising her front knee to hip level; snapped her leg and kicked him in the ribs.

Hector howled and toppled sideways. The gun discharged as he fell.

Chapter Seventeen

"Leave off fussing," Beau protested. "The bullet passed cleanly through my arm."

"Yes," retorted Liliane, "and embedded itself in my wall. Which was already splattered with ink because of *your* daughter. Not to mention my poor carpet. One can hardly see the pattern for the stains."

"I'll pay to have the damned wall fixed. *And* the room repapered and the rug replaced, if you'll leave me alone."

"The chair also. You are bleeding on it," Liliane reminded him.

"I'll replace all the bloody furniture if you'll cease plaguing me!" Beau snapped.

Pen placed a cool hand on his forehead. "It is as I feared: a delirium of the brain. Calm yourself or I will have to apply leeches to draw off the overheated blood."

"Are there leeches on the premises?" Izzy asked, wide-eyed.

"Only the human sort," Liliane replied.

Beau reached for the decanter resting on the table at his elbow, alongside a bowl of bloody water and strips of torn cloth. With the hand Pen hadn't rendered immobile, he poured brandy into a glass and drank. Izzy meanwhile took it upon herself to educate Lord Babcock and Mr. Tremaine about the relative merits of feverfew and willow tree bark, stinging nettles and witch hazel and rosemary. Liliane interjected an occasional '*Mais non*' and '*D'accord.*' Roddy and Hector were no longer present, having been forcibly escorted from the premises by Figg and Samson, who took the opportunity to discover who among the staff had been responsible for Roddy's possession of a certain map and key. When Roddy proved unforthcoming, Figg subjected him to a demonstration of the Art of Yielding and Pliability, at the end of which Roddy supplied not only the requested information but admitted to a great many other sins.

"You are fortunate," Pen told Beau, "that the bullet didn't hit the bone." She went on to describe in what he considered an unnecessarily graphic manner how amputations were performed and the various implements involved, dwelling at great length upon the tenaculum, a small hook used during surgery to seize the end of a vein or artery, pull it out and hold it while it was being sutured.

"Stab me," said Lord Babcock. "I've a mind to take the air. Ye'll come with me, my fine young April gentleman."

Mr. Tremaine was not enamored of his newly-discovered sire's suggestion. In point of fact, he didn't care much for his newly-discovered sire. However, he had a bride to provide for and gambling debts to be paid.

Over his shoulder, he cast Izzy an apologetic glance. She raised one hand and gave him an approving finger wave.

Pen had left off describing a seventeenth century Bullet Extractor that her brother had in his collection, not to be confused with a Goat's Foot Elevator used in the removal of teeth, to observe this interaction. As the door closed behind the departing gentlemen, she murmured, "Had I foreseen, when you showed up on my brother's doorstep—"

Beau turned his head so that he might see her face. "Yes?"

She grinned. "I would have come anyway."

The door no sooner closed than it reopened. Apologetically, Figg informed his mistress that a stranger insisted on speaking with the owner of the establishment. The gentleman refused to give his name.

Liliane sighed and left the room.

" 'Three things drive a man out of his home: smoke, rain and a scolding wife'," said Izzy to her uncle. "Papa tells me I am not legally Tremaine's wife, but the principle remains the same."

"You'll marry Tremaine right enough, and soon," Beau retorted. "Or he'll answer to me."

Replied Izzy, cryptically, " 'Muzzle not the oxen's mouth'."

Had she called him an ox? Beau splashed more brandy into his glass. Pen finished up her handiwork with a neat little bow.

"What a nicely arranged bandage," applauded Izzy. "How *handy* you are, Miss Pen. Just think we might not have met, in the ordinary course of events. Which goes to show that if one lets them, things work out for the best, because Papa sold me to Uncle Beau, and Uncle Beau brought you to Moxley's because of me, and now here we are."

So they were. Life, reflected Pen, was going to seem prodigiously dull after the excitement of the past few days. Without Izzy and Liliane. And Beau. Once she left Moxley's, she could never return.

Beau had been watching her face. "What is it, Pen?"

The morning room door opened. Liliane had returned. Accompanying her was a familiar figure. Pen moved quickly to block her brother's view of Beau.

Philip goggled at her. "Good God, Pen, have you gone mad? What are you doing here? Scant wonder Loversall took you for a lightskirt if you were dressed like that at Vauxhall."

"I wasn't dressed like this at Vauxhall!" Pen protested. If only she hadn't taken off Beau's jacket, the better to tend his wound. "Stop gawking at me. You look like a fish."

"I didn't take her for a lightskirt," put in Beau.

Philip recognized that voice. He grasped his sister by the shoulders and set her aside.

One of Beau's eyes was swollen shut. A fresh injury, judging from its color. He wore neither coat, waistcoat, nor cravat. His shirt was bloodstained, one sleeve slashed. Pen had done a good job with the bandage. Philip recognized the bow.

He recalled to whom the bandage was attached. "You! *Again*? By God, I'll black your other eye."

"No, you will not!" interjected Liliane. "It is understandable that you might desire to damage Beau, *monsieur*, but he has already been shot. I'll have no more blood spilled on my carpet, so you must restrain yourself."

"Was it you who shot him?" Philip asked her. "If so, I'd like to shake your hand."

"Are you Miss Pen's brother?" inquired Izzy. " 'Physician, heal thyself!' In case you do not know it, chamomile is good for an agitated brain. I'm not surprised that you have grown over-excited: 'Much learning makes men mad.' And women also, I should think, because it was Miss Pen's decision to wear that shocking dress and she knows a great deal more than a female should. I don't mean to criticize, of course. I am Izzy, sir, Beau's niece. My father sold me to him, you see."

Philip narrowed his eyes at Beau. "Indeed I do."

"No," interrupted Pen, "you don't! So pray try and keep a civil tongue in your head."

Unaccustomed to opposition from this source, Philip stared at her in surprise.

"It was Papa's friend who shot Uncle Beau," continued Izzy. "He also tried to steal me, but Miss Pen bashed him over the head, which was very brave of her. I doubt he meant to shoot Uncle Beau, but 'as you sow so shall you reap'."

"'Bashed him over the head'?" Philip repeated. "What has got into you, Pen? Pray explain to me why you are here, and wearing that damned dress. Where is Cousin Emily? Have you left the poor woman to fend for herself?"

"There is no Cousin Emily," Pen retorted crossly. "As you would know if you paid attention to anything other than your cadavers and your *cannabis*."

Philip flinched. "Dash it, Pen. That's unfair."

Maybe it was, but Pen felt the better for saying it. "How did you discover I was here?"

"Wetherwax stopped by Moxley's to try his luck at the faro table, saw you in the gaming rooms, and immediately came to tell me so. That no one else recognized you, we can only hope!" Philip's voice had risen as he spoke. By the time he finished speaking, he was fair frothing at the mouth.

"Have some brandy, do." Liliane shoved a glass into his hand.

"Pray don't scold," begged Izzy. "This is all my fault. Uncle Beau needed someone to lend me respectability and while Miss Pen may not look respectable at the moment, I assure you she is."

Philip wasn't certain how he came to be clutching a glass of brandy, but since he *was* clutching it, he raised the glass and drank. Excellent brandy, it was. Doubtless smuggled in from France.

How in Hades was his sister supposed to provide respectability whilst sojourning in a gaming hell?

The young woman — Izzy? — was waiting for his answer. Philip finished off his brandy in order to clear the cobwebs from his brain. "No one need tell me my sister is respectable. It's the rest of the world who will think that she is not." He scowled at Beau. "I'll have your head, you cur."

Beau glowered back at him. "That's what you said the last time. On a platter, was it not? It's a poor sort of surgeon that can't come up with a more original threat."

Philip started forward. Liliane caught his arm. "*Mais non!*"

" 'A good name is better that riches'," Izzy informed them. "Do you want to plunge your sister deeper into the scandal-broth, sir? Because a gentleman doesn't go around carving up his brother-in-law."

"My *what?*" demanded Philip.

"His *what?*" echoed Beau.

Pen picked up the brandy decanter and poured herself a glass.

Liliane was put in mind of certain wagers that had yet to be resolved. "*Corbleu!* It is the perfect way to salvage her reputation. She must marry him."

"No, she mustn't!" Beau protested.

" 'Forbidden fruit is sweet'," Izzy informed him. " 'When the pear is ripe, it falls'."

"There was no fallen fruit," said Beau. "I may have drunk a fair amount of brandy lately, but I'm sure I would remember *that*."

"Enough!" broke in Pen, pink-cheeked. "Go away, the lot of you. I must speak privately with Beau."

Philip was reluctant to leave the room. It wasn't proper, he told his sister, for an unmarried female to be closeted alone with a male. Pen informed him that his concern was touching but rather beside the point since he had left her to fend for herself these past many years.

Philip had the grace to look embarrassed. "That may be, but I cannot in good conscience leave you and this scoundrel unchaperoned."

"But of course you can," said Liliane, and slipped her arm through his.

Philip glanced down at the little hand resting on his arm. Then he looked more closely at the rest of Liliane. "It is an *affaire de coeur*," she told him, with a provocative eyelash flutter. "You do comprehend matters of the heart?"

Philip did. Rather, he had, before matters of medicine began to occupy his every waking thought. Perhaps it was time to refresh his understanding. Abandoning his sister once again to her own devices, Philip allowed

Liliane to draw him out into the hall.

Izzy paused in the doorway. "I'm going to my room now. Thank you for lending me countenance, Miss Pen. Such as it was." She made a pretty curtsey. "I am glad to have made your acquaintance, Uncle Beau. 'There's many a good tune played on an old fiddle,' in case you didn't know."

The door closed behind her. Pen moved swiftly across the room, wrestled a table in front of it, retrieved her brandy glass, and drank. "You didn't take me for a lightskirt at Vauxhall?" she added, after she had ceased coughing and caught her breath.

Beau eyed the barricaded doorway. "I did not."

"But you tried to kiss me!" She was walking toward him, a determined expression on her face.

"I had wanted to kiss you for some time. That particular night I consumed a great deal of arrack punch. You can't seriously consider marrying me, Pen."

She shrugged, which had an interesting effect on the bodice of her gown. "Mayhap I have run mad. As I have heard sometimes happens to females of a certain age."

"You are little more than a girl."

"And you are in need of spectacles, as your niece pointed out." With careful consideration for his wounded arm, Pen settled on his lap. "I don't want Philip to damage you. Or vice versa. We might try a trial betrothal. If you decide you don't care to be married, I can cry off."

Care to be married? Of course Beau did not. He was the wickedest rakehell in London, after all.

Was he not?

"I'm a poor risk," Beau told her, as he slipped his uninjured arm around her waist.

"True. But beggars can't be choosers and I *am* on the shelf. Too, I am appallingly uninformed about amorous matters." Pen touched his cheek. "Whereas you are a Loversall."

So she was. So *he* was. "I haven't had much to do with maidens," Beau admitted, as he smoothed his hand over her back.

"You have had a great deal to do with the other sort of female. I have decided I would like to be that sort of female." Pen traced the contours of his mouth.

The Loversall Novellas

Her fingers were feather-light and incredibly erotic. Where might she touch him next? And what the deuce had she just said?

Pen's hand trailed from his mouth to his throat. "Would you mind so very much?"

Mind what? Beau struggled to retain, or regain, his common sense. "You'd marry me, despite my reputation? I may not be as heartless as I am portrayed, but I *am* a rakehell, Pen." Was it wishful thinking or could he see dusky nipples through the flimsy fabric of that damnable gown?

She drew back, frowning at him, then picked up the knife that lay on the table by the chair. For one startled moment, Beau thought she meant to slit his throat.

"Tsk!" she said, and raised the blade. "Look at the shocking condition of that shirt." Fabric tore. Buttons popped off. In the twinkling of an eye, Beau found himself naked to the waist.

The air was cool, but he was warm. Beau had been undressed countless times by women. None of those previous ladies had displayed such a fascinating lack of finesse.

If Beau had been uninterested in enjoying melting moments with his inamoratas, he was very interested in enjoying an infinite number of melting moments with Pen.

He waited with no little anticipation to discover what she'd do next.

Pen considered him, one finger to her lips, head tilted to one side. Then she dropped the knife on the table and glanced at her blood-spattered skirts. "Oh! My poor gown. I can't bear that anyone should see me in such a sorry state." A shrug of her shoulders, a twist of her wrist, and the scandalous gold gown puddled at her feet. One thin petticoat followed, and then she was unlacing her shockingly unsubstantial stays.

Beau had wondered what she was wearing under that damned dress. Very little, as it turned out. She kicked off her shoes and stood before him in only her stockings and a gossamer-thin chemise.

Pen's cheeks were pink. Her lips trembled. She couldn't meet his gaze.

Lord, she was beautiful. "Come here," Beau said, in a voice he barely recognized.

She obeyed, looking defiant and apprehensive and as if at any moment she might run from the room. Beau caught her wrist and pulled her back down on his lap.

His injured arm protested. He ignored it. "I don't know if I have it in me to be faithful, Pen."

"I think you do," she told him. "And if you prove me wrong, I shall ask Philip for the loan of a surgical saw."

Beau didn't doubt her. Bluntly, he asked, "Why?"

"Why what?" Pen looked confused.

Beau ran his hand up one stocking-clad leg. "We needn't go so far as marriage to hush up this night's business."

"I don't give a fig for marriage, but I *will* have this," she told him, as she slid her arms around his neck. "I can't say when it happened, but I have fallen in love with you, Beau."

She couldn't love him. Could she? "You said that True Love was so much twaddle."

Pen had moved so close — or had he drawn her to him? — that her soft breath brushed Beau's lips. She whispered, "I was wrong."

There was nothing for it, then. "I'm going to kiss you now," Beau murmured.

"Pray do." Pen buried her fingers in his hair.

Kiss her he did, and she kissed him back: soft kisses, drugging kisses, slow sweet kisses that made hearts race and toes curl; and at length a kiss so deep, so carnal, they both forgot to breathe.

Reluctantly, Beau drew back from the embrace. Pen looked dazed, disheveled, and determined. He was feeling more than a little dazed himself. Pen's slight weight on his lap, her warmth stealing through the thin chemise—

Nothing in his life had ever felt so right.

"I swear I won't betray you," he said, surprising himself, meaning every word.

Pen let out a relieved breath. Her gamble had paid off. "I was afraid you'd laugh at me," she murmured. "Liliane bet me you would not."

"Liliane has won her wager. Had the house caught on fire, I couldn't have moved from that chair."

Pen felt the chemise slipping off her shoulders. A skilled seducer, it appeared, could divest a female of her clothing with only one hand.

Life with a Loversall, she thought, would never be dull.

And then Beau's mouth was on her breasts, and Pen thought nothing at all.

Epilogue

Izzy did marry young Mr. Tremaine, with her father's blessing, after Lord Babcock paid out the handsome sum of £300. Following the ceremony, Roddy Kilpatrick and his good friend Hector Nottingham set out on a round of debauchery that lasted several weeks and resulted in the both of them being thrown into the Fleet. Available virgins proving no more plentiful than hen's teeth, Lord Babcock eventually gave himself over into the care of a certain eminent surgeon. A large needle was involved. If Lord Babcock was never again seen at Moxley's, Mr. Parrish often was, though never in the public area: Liliane, upon receiving word of his arrival, would greet him in her own room, having realized the advantages of having a medical man in her pocket, so to speak. Word did get around, assisted by the efforts of Mrs. Ormsby and Mrs. Thwaite, that Mr. Parrish's sister had been seen at Moxley's, got up like a Bird of Paradise; but that on-dit was overshadowed by the far more shocking circumstance that the most faithless of flirts disbanded his stable of sweethearts and retired from the lists. Past Loversall misadventures were remembered, indiscretions involving convents and Red Indians, grooms and gypsies, shepherds and strolling musicians; suicides committed by leaps from battlements, and drinking poison, and being eaten by a bear — though there was some question whether the latter Loversall had visited the Tower with that intent.

There was much speculation as to why, with such adventurous blood running in his veins, Beau Loversall had chosen to do something so very conventional as to tie the knot; and speculation, when time passed and he showed no inclination to return to his wicked ways, that maybe his mother had paid his father false.

Maggie MacKeever

To this nonsense, Beau and his bride paid no heed.

They were too busy exploring their tumultuous passions.

And, lest the reader harbor lingering reservations, during the rest of their long life together, no surgical implements were required.

Made in the USA
Columbia, SC
20 June 2025